DEATH BY CAFÉ MOCHA

"I'm not getting involved," I said, wondering how true that statement really was. I might not want to be a part of them, but somehow, murder investigations had a way of finding me.

Which made me wonder . . .

Penny had said Charles was lying in a pool of his coffee. Thomas had been hurrying down the hall not too long ago, fresh coffee stains on his shirt. Had he been telling the truth, and it was his own coffee, spilled in a cleanup accident? Or was it Charles's café mocha that had sent him rushing for his room to change?

And what about Tara? She'd stormed off to find Charles ten to fifteen minutes before he was found dead. Had she found him? Did they argue? And if they *had* argued, could it have led to a spur-of-the-moment murder?

No, Krissy, no. I couldn't start thinking about the case, or else I wouldn't stop. I would *not* get involved; not this time.

Books by Alex Erickson

Published by Kensington Publishing Corporation

DEATH BY CAFÉ MOCHA

Alex Erickson

KENSINGTON BOOKS
www.kensingtonbooks.com

KENSINGTON BOOKS are published by

Kensington Publishing Corp.
119 West 40th Street
New York, NY 10018

All Kensington titles, imprints, and distributed lines are available at special quantity discounts for bulk purchases for sales promotion, premiums, fund-raising, educational, or institutional use.

Special book excerpts or customized printings can also be created to fit specific needs. For details, write or phone the office of the Kensington Sales Manager: Attn.: Sales Department, Kensington Publishing Corp., 119 West 40th Street, New York, NY 10018. Phone: 1-800-221-2647.

Kensington and the K logo Reg. U.S. Pat. & TM Off.

First Printing: September 2019
ISBN-13: 978-1-4967-2111-2
ISBN-10: 1-4967-2111-X

ISBN-13: 978-1-4967-2112-9 (ebook)
ISBN-10: 1-4967-2112-8 (ebook)

10 9 8 7 6 5 4 3 2 1

Printed in the United States of America

Chapter 1

My luggage felt as if someone had loaded bricks into it by the time I reached the front of the line. Huffing and puffing, I dragged it the last few feet and leaned it against the counter, where a smiling clerk waited.

"Hi," I said, rubbing at my aching shoulder. "I have a reservation. It should be under Krissy Hancock."

"One moment." The clerk behind the counter typed my name into the computer with an energetic click-clack. He was humming a tune under his breath and genuinely looked as if he enjoyed his job. He also looked to only be about twenty years old, so it was likely that would change in time.

While he looked me up, I glanced around at the hotel lobby. It was packed with guests, many just arriving, as I was.

"I'm sorry, ma'am, but we do not have a reservation under that name."

"Oh." Mild worry welled in my gut. "Try Vicki Patt—err, Lawyer." I shook my head, trying to dislodge my best friend's maiden name from my mind. It had been almost a year since she'd gotten married, and yet I still kept forgetting. "Vicki Lawyer. She made the reservations and might have put them under her name." Though she had told me she'd made them under my name, as I'd requested. The hotel was my treat. She'd paid for the convention badges for all three of us, so it only seemed right.

And yes, I did mean three.

"Oh, Lordy Lou! Would you look at that!"

I glanced back to find Rita Jablonksi looking up at the hotel elevator. Even though she was short and stocky, her presence practically filled the room, as did her voice.

"There's fifteen floors to this place!"

Fifteen floors *were* a lot, but not so many I thought they deserved such a loud and boisterous exclamation. But that was Rita for you. Everything was loud and boisterous, and often exaggerated to the point of disbelief.

"I'm sorry, I still can't find it," the clerk said.

"I'm sure it has to be there." The worry tried to bubble up into a full-on storm of panic. I mentally stomped it flat. "We made the reservations over two months ago. We're going to JavaCon."

"I'm sorry." The clerk didn't look sorry at all. He looked annoyed. So much for his chipper mood.

"But I . . ." My mind raced. JavaCon was in its first year, yet it had sold out within a month of registration going live, likely thanks to all the social media advertising they had done. People really liked their coffee, and they obviously preferred staying in the hotel connected to the convention center, much like I did. The hotel was booked solid, and another con was happening downtown, meaning if our registration had somehow gotten lost, we'd have nowhere to stay.

"Is there something wrong with the reservation?"

I breathed a sigh of relief as Vicki joined me. Even after our long drive, she looked perfect. Not a single hair was out of place. The clerk's eyes widened briefly and he stood up straighter. If he didn't close his mouth soon, he'd end up drooling all over himself.

"He can't find it," I said. "I tried both our names, but he says it's not there."

"If you have the confirmation email, it would help," the clerk said, never taking his eyes off Vicki.

"Sure." Vicki whipped out her phone and brought up her email app. "I've got this, Krissy, if you want to keep an eye on Rita." She shot a look at the woman in question, who was now running her hand along the back of a lobby couch, oohing and aahing, much to the annoyance of the people sitting on said couch.

"Thanks," I said as I grabbed my suitcase. I don't typically do well around a lot of people, and with an impatient line behind me and only three clerks working behind the desk, I was feeling especially out of my depth.

My things in hand, I backed away from the desk to give Vicki room.

"Oof!" A heavy thump and a clatter accompanied the sound as I collided into the person who'd been standing behind me.

"Oh my gosh!" I said, spinning. Already, a red ring of embarrassment was working its way up my neck to color my face. "I'm so sorry!"

The man staggered back a step and nearly bumped into the woman behind him. He was tall, with dark hair combed back from a rather attractive face. I fully expected him to yell at me, but instead, he broke into a wide, chagrined smile.

"I'm sure it was my fault," he said, voice tinged with a hint of an accent I couldn't place. "Had my nose in my phone and was probably standing too close."

There wasn't a phone in his hand. After a quick glance around, I found it lying on the floor at my feet.

He bent down and picked it up before I could do so myself. He glanced at the screen briefly before shoving the phone into his pocket.

"Did I break it?" I asked as he righted his luggage, which had been the source of the thump that had accompanied his phone's clatter on the hard tile.

"Not a scratch," he said, patting his pocket. "Are you okay? You seem flustered."

Flustered? Me? I brushed my hand through my hair and tried on a smile. I didn't even want to know what I looked like after spending the last five hours in a car. "Just a little trouble with our reservations," I said. "My friend is working it out."

He glanced past me to Vicki before nodding. "Are you here for JavaCon?"

For some reason, my heart gave a little leap at the question. "We are."

"Me too." He reached out a hand. "Thomas Cole."

I shook. His handshake was firm, yet surprisingly soft at the same time. "Krissy Hancock."

"May I help who's next?"

Thomas gathered his luggage. "That's me," he said. "I hope to see you around, Krissy."

"You too, Thomas."

I watched as he sauntered up to the counter to check in. I had to admit, it wasn't an entirely unpleasant sight, considering the tight jeans he was wearing.

Not that I was looking, mind you.

Okay, maybe I was a little, but it wasn't like I was in the market for a new boyfriend. I hadn't been single for *that* long, all things considered. I needed a mental break from all the distractions relationships caused. This trip was supposed to be all business, and darn it, I was going to make sure it stayed that way.

"You could bounce a Ping-Pong ball off those cheeks," Rita said into my ear.

I nearly leapt from my shoes as I spun on her. "Don't do that!" I said. "And keep your voice down. He might hear."

She was grinning, a mischievous gleam to her eye. "So what if he does? It's not like you're seeing anyone. Honestly, dear, it might be good for you to loosen up a bit. The way I hear it, you've been so tense lately, people are starting to talk."

"Talk about what?" I asked.

The look on Rita's face told me everything I needed to know. Honestly, I wasn't sure how my sex life—or lack thereof—was anyone's business.

Genuinely flustered, and a whole lot embarrassed, I fumbled for my phone. "Stay here and watch my bag," I said. "I need to make a call."

Rita nodded and turned back to admire Thomas's backside some more.

She can have him, I thought as I walked across the room to the far corner, where it was quieter. As I said, I wasn't in the market, and it wasn't like there could be anything between us even if I was. As far as I knew, he lived halfway across the country from Pine Hills, the small town in Ohio where I lived. There was no way I was going to entertain thoughts of a long-distance relationship.

I dialed and put the phone to my ear. A woman with a gray beehive hairdo entered dragging five suitcases behind her as if they weighed nothing. Her fingernails were bright red, as was her lipstick. She wore large sunglasses that covered half of her face, which looked slightly swollen, as if she'd recently been stung or had gotten an injection of some kind. Her nose turned up at the tip, and deep lines framed her mouth, despite the puffiness of her face. She was even wearing a faux fur coat that went all the way to her red heels. All that was missing was a small dog tucked under her arm.

"Death by Coffee, this is Lena speaking."

"Hi, Lena, it's Krissy. I'm just calling to let you know we've made it all right. How are things back home?"

"Great," she said. "We've been giving Mason a hard time, but it's all in fun."

Vicki's husband, Mason, had offered to help out around Death by Coffee, our bookstore café, while we were gone. Our three other employees, Lena, Jeff, and Beth, could all handle themselves to varying degrees, so it wasn't like he *needed* to help out, yet he'd insisted.

I hoped he knew what he was in for.

"There've been no issues since we left?"

"It's been one whole day," Lena said. "We're fine."

"I know, but . . ."

"We've got this, Ms. Hancock. Trust us."

I took a deep breath and let it out slowly. "I do," I said. And I did. But this was the first time neither Vicki nor I would be in town in case something happened. "I needed to call for my peace of mind."

"Totally get it. But you'll only be gone for a couple of days. I promise we won't burn the place down in your absence."

"Ugh, don't even joke about that. I'll have nightmares."

Lena laughed. "Go. Have fun. You deserve a break."

"Yeah, I guess I do."

"And find us some awesome-tasting coffee while you're at it."

"I'll try. Let me know if anything comes up."

"Will do."

I hung up, feeling only marginally better. I knew Lena and the others would be fine, yet I kept imagining the place caving in or flooding while both Vicki and I were gone.

But it wasn't like we were off on a sunny beach vacation—though one of those did sound nice. Our trip to JavaCon was with the intent of discovering new coffees we could add to the menu at Death by Coffee. As soon as I saw it would have tastings, as well as a competition for the best brew, I knew I had to come.

Rita, on the other hand, was here to take in the sights. When she'd learned Vicki and I were coming, she'd practically begged to be included. I had no problem with it, and neither did Vicki, so here we all were.

I was about to head back to Rita when I caught a glimpse of a pair of new arrivals. The two men were walking with their heads nearly touching as they talked in hushed voices. One man appeared to be in his late thirties, early forties. The other was well into his fifties. As soon as they entered, the older man shook his head, frowned, and then nodded, which caused his companion to smile.

"I know what you're doing!" The woman with the big hair I'd noted earlier strode over, waggling a finger at the two of them. "It's not going to work, Charles."

"It's good to see you too, Winnie," the younger man—Charles, I assumed—said.

"Don't give me that." Her hands found her hips and pressed into the tight red dress she was wearing under her now-unbuttoned coat. "You can't buy your way into everything."

"Now, Winnie . . ."

She spun on the older man. "I thought you had better morals than this, Carmine!"

"Morals are for people who *lose*," Charles said. "If you'll excuse me, I need to check in." He nodded once to Carmine, winked at Winnie, and then headed for the line.

Carmine opened his mouth as if he was going to try to explain himself, but Winnie huffed and spun away without letting him get a word in. His shoulders slumped as he dragged his bags to the check-in line.

Drama already, I thought, wondering if they were there for the con or if they were here for the pediatrics convention happening downtown.

Then again, looking at Winnie, I seriously doubted she'd be able to handle kids, let alone the rigors of practicing medicine.

Putting the three out of my mind, I glanced toward the counter and noted that both Thomas and Vicki were no longer there. It took only a moment to spot Vicki, who was heading my way with Rita in tow.

"It's all taken care of," Vicki said when they joined me. "Took him a few tries, but he eventually found it."

"So the registration *was* there?" I asked, taking my suitcase from Rita with a murmured "Thanks."

"It was. He apologized at least five times for the delay and even offered to give us free Wi-Fi instead of making us pay for it."

"Sounds good to me," I said. I was glad we could nix that charge from my card. The hotel charged fifteen dollars a day for Wi-Fi, which, considering the cost of a room, along with the cost of parking, seemed awfully expensive. Before long, hotels were going to start charging for towels as a way to nickel-and-dime their guests to death.

"We're on the fifteenth floor," Vicki said, handing me my keycard.

"The top floor!" Rita said, eyes glowing as if the prospect of riding an elevator all the way to the top was the most exciting thing she could imagine.

All I could think about was the long walk up and down the stairs if the elevators were to stop working.

If that were to happen, I'd probably just crash in the lobby, because there was no way I was going to survive a hike like that.

"Let's drop our stuff off in the room and then have a look around," Vicki said. Her smile was mile-wide. "Isn't this exciting."

"It is," I said, pushing all my worries aside. Death by Coffee would be there when we got back. So would my house. I was still worried about how my neighbors Jules and Lance, and their dog, Maestro, were faring with my cat, Misfit. He probably had them trapped in a corner, claws and fangs bared in warning.

No, that's not right. He likely had them waiting on him hand and foot while he basked in the sunlight coming in through Jules's kitchen window.

"I wonder what they have to eat in the hotel restaurant?" Rita said as we all gathered our things and made for the elevator. "I'm absolutely ravenous."

Next to me, a woman scolded a sullen teenager. At the counter, an older man was yelling at one of the clerks, who bore it with a stiff smile.

The elevator doors slid open. I got on with Vicki and Rita, dragging my suitcase behind me. It was old, with a loose wheel, so it clattered on the hard floor loud enough to earn me a glare from a couple of other people.

Relax, I told myself, letting out a pent-up breath. I was in a strange place, surrounded by strange people, but this was supposed to be fun.

As the doors closed, I forced the tension out of my shoulders and allowed myself a smile.

Chapter 2

I was in seventh heaven.

The entire convention center smelled of coffee. It was strong enough I felt as if I could just stand there breathing it in and get a caffeine high.

The convention didn't officially start until tomorrow morning, but unofficially, it had already started. People milled about checking out the various stations set up along the hallways and in some of the rooms. None of the actual events had started, but small companies were already handing out samples and talking about their coffee to anyone who would stop to listen. There were even pastries being offered, including a small kiosk selling row upon row of delicious-smelling doughnuts. If I wasn't careful, I'd end up gaining ten pounds after the first day.

"Oh my," Rita said as we started walking through the chaos. "There's so much!"

"Yeah," I said. I was feeling overwhelmed, yet fascinated at the same time. To some, coffee is coffee.

They brew it, pour it into a mug, and that's that. It doesn't matter where it came from, what brand or blend it might be. As long as it gets the job done, that's all they care about.

But here at JavaCon, the people knew there was far more to coffee than the jolt it could give you in the morning. There were so many brands with roasts that I'd never even heard of before, it boggled my mind. I imagined that if I were to go from station to station, tasting every sample offered, I'd find each and every one to have completely different flavors, and, quite possibly, even textures. Some would be bitter, others smooth. Some would be nutty, others would taste of vanilla or cinnamon.

I also had a feeling I'd love every second of it.

"Tomorrow is going to be crazy," Vicki said. "Even after looking at all the events in preregistration, I didn't realize how big it was going to be."

"Me neither." JavaCon was chock-full of stuff to do. If the event planner was anything to go by, all three of us could hit up different events every single hour and still not do everything. There were actual panels, how-to instructional classes, professionals talking about the quality of beans, and so on and so forth. While I didn't plan on growing my own coffee beans or creating my own brand, there was still a lot I could learn. I planned to sit in on as many of the events as I could in the hope of learning something that would help make Death by Coffee even better.

"Where do we start?" Rita asked.

"I say we just roam," Vicki said. "Check out what's here and then go from there tomorrow when the thing officially kicks off."

"We're just browsing today," I said. "Taking it all in."

We passed by a room filled with people. Peeking in, I noticed signs in front of small stations, each manned by two or three people. Small cups sat on counters. As I watched, browsers would stop by and take a cup or two before wandering off again.

"What is it?" I asked, checking the digital sign on the door. Nothing had been added to it yet, other than a welcome message to all con goers.

"I think it's a tasting room." Vicki leaned her head in and breathed in the scents wafting out the door. "I wonder if it's all small companies, or if some of the bigger ones are represented. There are quite a few brands I've been wanting to try but never had the chance."

"Can you buy anything here?" I asked, checking for a checkout line near the door.

"Looks like they're selling their own stuff." Vicki nodded toward one of the stations, where a couple had just finished trying one of the coffees. After a brief conversation, they snatched up a bag that was sitting on the counter next to the samples. They added it to a quickly growing stack they were carrying.

"Why aren't you here with your coffee?" Rita asked. "I bet it would bring in more business if you were to advertise outside Pine Hills more."

I glanced at Vicki. "Could we?"

She shrugged. "I'm not sure. I think everyone here has their own brand. We don't yet."

"Maybe we could look into it," I said, warming to the idea. "We could come up with something that people can't get anywhere else. I don't mean just a brand, but maybe a specialty coffee you can only get at Death by Coffee."

"Like our own blend?" Vicki asked.

"Kind of." I thought about it some more. I had to admit, the idea had some appeal. Perhaps, if it became popular enough, people would travel to Pine Hills just to try it. It would take a lot of work, and a whole lot of word of mouth, but even if it was something that became popular only in Pine Hills and the surrounding area, it would be worth the effort.

"We'd have to come up with something that really stands out," Vicki said.

"What about the coffee you made for Cameron Little when he was in town?" I asked. The literary agent had loved it. "The really caffeinated stuff."

Vicki nodded slowly. "It could work. We'd need to come up with a catchy name for it, though. It'd have to be something original, something that would make it stand out."

"It could be a souped-up coffee for late-night workers or early risers." I smiled. "Something that keeps the world moving."

"It's actually a really good idea," Vicki said. "But how would we go about doing any of that?"

I spread my arms wide. "We're in the perfect place to find out. We could try some different coffees, see what others are doing, and use them as a guide for us." And if we could find someone who could teach us what kind of beans to use, or at least what brands would work best for what we wanted to do, then all the better.

Someone inside the room yelped. The man leapt back from the counter, dumping a small cup of coffee onto the floor. He fanned at his mouth, tongue hanging out, as if he hadn't realized the coffee he was about to drink might be hot. Two older women rushed to his aid and helped clean up the mess.

"I think I'm going to head in there and talk to some people," Vicki said. "Maybe I can pick some brains and see how we can get started on getting our own stuff out there."

"I'll come with you," Rita said, fanning herself off. Sweat beaded her brow. "I think I see someone with some iced drinks in there. It's awfully warm out here, isn't it?"

It *was* warm, but I didn't think it was too bad yet. With the press of people and the steam coming from some of the espresso machines, I could see the heat getting uncomfortable before long.

"What about you, Krissy?"

"You go ahead. I think I'm going to wander a bit."

"You sure?" Vicki asked.

"I'm sure." I was hoping to get a good look around before the convention started in full so I wouldn't get lost later. While most everything was being held in the main couple of ballrooms, there were a few events taking place down some of the other halls. "I'll catch up with you in a little while."

Vicki and Rita waved as they headed into the room with all the samples, leaving me to explore at my own pace. Anxious to take it all in, I got started.

Large windows looked out over the little slice of Maryland where JavaCon was being held. The sun had gone down some time ago, which meant the entire block was lit up by lights from the hotels and office buildings in the area. It was quite pretty, and I imagined it would be even prettier from above. It made me want to go up to my hotel room to check, but I could do that later.

I drifted down the hallway, past booths with people setting up for tomorrow. In a place filled with coffee, it was strange to see many of them yawning, exhausted looks on their faces. I supposed it was probably a good idea for them not to load up on caffeine tonight so they could get a good night's sleep before the big event tomorrow, but I still found it odd. Many looked like they still had hours of work ahead of them.

I turned the corner and was about to head to a door marked LOUNGE when I noticed someone I recognized standing just inside the hallway leading to the bathrooms. He was talking with another man, this one somebody I didn't know.

Charles. I couldn't remember if anyone had said his last name earlier or not. He was leaning in close as he talked to this man—a white-haired man whose face made him look younger than his hair indicated.

Charles spoke in a whisper that didn't carry. His hand was resting on the other man's back, and from where I stood, it appeared as if he was gently rubbing it in circles.

The other man shook his head at something Charles said, then frowned when Charles spoke again.

Out of habit, I took a step toward them before catching myself. It was none of my business as to what they were talking about. I didn't know these people. I had no reason to pry.

Still, I was curious. After that small scene in the lobby earlier, I couldn't help it. I was drawn to drama.

I forced myself to turn away, determined to be good, and walked directly into Thomas Cole.

"Oh!" I said, jerking back a step. "I didn't see you there."

Thomas was balancing a pair of small cups in his hands. He deftly avoided spilling any on me, or himself. "It's my fault," he said. "I was sneaking up on you again."

"Again?" I asked, and then abruptly cleared my throat, realizing how dumb that sounded, considering how we'd met.

"Earlier, in line," Thomas said, as if I could forget. "I saw you standing over here and thought I'd come over and say hi."

"Oh, well, hi." I smiled. "I see you made it okay."

"It wasn't far," he said, gesturing with his elbow back toward the hotel lobby.

My face flushed immediately. I was sounding like a total dope. "I know. I meant no one else tried to trample you on your way across the room."

"Ah." He smiled. Admittedly, he had a really nice smile. "So far, you're the only one who's dared."

"I'll try not to make it a habit."

His gaze drifted past me and his smile faltered. I glanced back to see Charles hurrying away from the white-haired man, who was staring after him, an unreadable expression on his face.

"Know them?" I asked.

"Not well," he said. "Charles Maddox is the man walking away. He has . . . ." He seemed to fumble for the right word before settling on, ". . . a reputation."

"Oh?" Curious, I glanced back, but Charles was gone.

"He makes a nuisance of himself at these sorts of things. Thinks he's a bigger deal than he really is."

"And the other man?"

"That's Clint Sherman. He's one of the organizers of JavaCon. He's been to a lot of these things, but I've never met him face-to-face. If his picture wasn't in the program next to his name, I wouldn't know what he looked like."

I hadn't paid attention to the faces, but I thought I might have seen him when browsing the JavaCon program. The name did sound vaguely familiar.

"I saw Charles talking with another man earlier," I said. "Someone named Carmine? They were approached by a woman named Winnie, who gave the both of them a real dressing-down."

Thomas smiled. "Wynona Kepler. I've had the pleasure. We rode the elevator together on the way up to my room. It's not an experience I wish to repeat."

"She seemed pretty intense."

"That she is." He looked down at his two cups. "I should probably get these to Tara."

My heart did a little hitch at the woman's name. *Stop that,* I scolded myself. I was *not* interested in Thomas Cole, no matter how friendly or good-looking he might be.

Even *I* almost eye-rolled at that.

"Is Tara your girlfriend?" I asked after making a quick peek at his finger to make sure he wasn't wearing a ring.

Thomas snorted a laugh, very nearly spilling his coffee when he did. "No," he said. "Tara and I are setting up next to one another for tomorrow. I offered to grab us each something to drink. I was on my way back when I saw you."

"Setting up?" I asked. "You're presenting?"

"Not presenting, but I am taking part in the tasting competition tomorrow morning. The winning coffee will be advertised heavily by JavaCon, and it should earn the winner a little bit of airtime on local stations. Good press, you know?"

"You make coffee!" I said, realizing how silly it sounded only after it was out of my mouth.

"I do," he said, unable to suppress his smile. "You should stop by my booth tomorrow. It would be great to see you. The judges will determine who wins, but anyone who shows up gets to taste the coffees. I'd love to see what you think."

I'd already planned on making the tasting a priority, yet now I had an even better reason to attend. "I'll be there," I said.

"Good." Thomas glanced down at his coffees and grinned. "I'd better go before these get cold. I like iced coffee, but there's something about room-temperature coffee that I can't stomach."

"Then you'd better hurry," I said with a gentle nudge to his arm. "I'll see you tomorrow then, Thomas."

He winked. "You too, Krissy." And then, with a one-cup salute, he hurried away.

"Who was that?" Vicki asked, causing me to jump. She was watching Thomas walk away, an intrigued look on her face.

"Just some guy I met," I said as casually as I could manage. "He asked if I'd check him out at the tasting tomorrow."

"Oh really?" From the amused gleam in her eye, I could tell she'd taken that entirely the wrong way.

"I don't mean it like that!" I said, wishing I could just sink into the floor. Why did everyone think I wanted to throw myself at the first good-looking guy who talked to me? "He makes his own coffee. He's going to be in the competition tomorrow morning."

"And we're going, right?"

"We are," I said, not liking how she'd said that. "I was thinking we could see about stocking the winning coffee in our store. It would help promote the winner, and hopefully draw more interest in us from outside of town."

"I'm sure that's all it is." She was grinning so fiercely, it made me want to hide my face. I could feel the flush deepening.

"Vicki, I . . ." My mouth opened and closed a few times before I could formulate an argument to her implications. "I'm not interested."

"Uh-huh." When I groaned, she laughed. "I think you should let loose for a little while. I'm not saying you should date the guy, but he obviously likes talking to you."

"I'm not looking to date anyone."

"Exactly. Just talk. Have fun. This is your chance to get away and put everything else behind you. This might not be Vegas, but the same rules can apply, if you know what I mean."

"I do," I said. And honestly, it wasn't that bad of an idea. We were here to have fun. It wasn't like I was going to jump into bed with the guy or make out with him in a corner somewhere. I could see forty sneaking up on me even though my twenties weren't that far behind me. I was well past the age when those sorts of thoughts should be going through my head.

Yeah, keep telling yourself that, I thought, taking Vicki by the arm.

"Come on, let's go explore," I said.

And together, we did just that.

Chapter 3

I was up bright and early the next morning. I was determined to make the tasting competition on time, yet I still struggled to drag myself out of bed. Vicki was already showered by the time I'd rubbed the sleep from my eyes, though Rita was still snoring softly on the couch. She claimed it was more comfortable than the hotel beds. After sleeping on one of the hard mattresses, I wasn't so sure I disagreed.

I tiptoed to the bathroom and slipped inside. I quickly showered and hurried through my morning routine. By the time I was done, Rita was up and stalking around the hotel room like an angry bear. She glared at me on her way to the bathroom and grunted something completely inarticulate. Apparently, she wasn't a morning person.

"I'll meet you guys downstairs," I said.

Vicki flashed me a smile and waved before she returned to her makeup. I checked to make sure I had the correct badge around my neck and left her to it.

The door across the hall opened almost the instant I was out of the room. Charles Maddox exited, coming to an abrupt stop when he saw me. His eyes were a little wide as he pulled the door quickly closed, like he thought I might try to peek inside.

"Good morning," I said, refusing to let his suspicion mar my morning.

"If you say so." He gave me a hard, calculated look before he hurried down the hall toward the elevator.

Thomas had said Charles had a bad reputation, and my brief meeting with him only solidified the idea in my mind that he wasn't the pleasantest of people.

Then again, he, like Rita, might not care for early mornings.

I didn't want to share an elevator with Charles, not if he was going to glare and grouch at me for breathing his same air as him, so I took my time meandering down the hall. I could smell fresh paint, telling me they'd done some renovations to the hotel recently. Everything looked bright and new, which helped keep my mood high, despite Charles's short tone.

By the time I reached the elevator doors, Charles was long gone.

While I waited for the next car, I browsed the conference schedule, mentally taking note of the locations of the seminars and workshops I wanted to attend. Since most everything was in the main ballrooms, I didn't think it would be too hard to find my way around. Still, a part of me was terrified I'd somehow get lost along the way. I rarely left my house, let alone Pine Hills, when I wasn't working. This was an entirely different state, full of people I didn't know. I was well outside my comfort zone here.

The elevator doors opened and I stepped inside. Just before they closed, someone called out, "Hold the car!" I managed to stick my foot in the doorway just before it slid closed.

"Thanks," the man said. It was the white-haired man I'd seen with Charles yesterday: Clint. He looked a bit disheveled, and a whole lot worried. He was adjusting his suit jacket like he'd just pulled it on, and a strand of his hair was sticking up at the back of his head.

"No problem," I said before sticking out a hand. "Krissy Hancock. I'm here for the con."

"Clint Sherman," he said, shaking. When he withdrew his hand, he reached into his pocket to remove a small travel-sized hand sanitizer. He spritzed some onto his hand before offering it to me. "You can never be too careful at these things," he said. "Germs are everywhere, and I'd rather avoid the crud if I can help it."

I let him spritz my hands and then rubbed them together. "I saw in the program you're a judge in the competition this morning." I'd looked him up last night. His picture was right beside Carmine Wright's.

He nodded with a slight frown. "I suppose I am."

"You didn't want to do it?"

Clint caught a glimpse of his hair in the silver metal door and grimaced. He worked at smoothing it down as he spoke. "I didn't have much of a choice. I helped organize the con, and well, there wasn't anyone else to do it, so all five of us appointed ourselves judges." He lifted his hand, and when the strand of hair remained down, he dropped it to his side. "It's a lot of work. The competitors spend so much time groveling, hoping to earn extra points with the judges, I get frustrated. I'll be happy when it's over."

"Is that what Charles Maddox was doing last night?" When Clint's eyes widened, I added, "I saw you talking yesterday. He seemed angry."

"Oh." He cleared his throat and shrugged. "He's one of them. Wynona Kepler's just as bad."

"I met her briefly." Well, I at least saw her, which counted, I guess. "She's got a pretty big personality."

Clint made a pained look, like merely thinking of Charles and Wynona was enough to give him a headache. "Between the two of them, I'm not sure there's much room for anyone else—personality-wise, that is."

We made several stops on the way down. By the sixth floor, all conversation had ceased, and the car was packed full. Clint pressed himself into the corner, doing his best not to touch anyone, but it wasn't easy. The big guy who'd gotten on last filled much of the space himself, pressing the rest of us together.

Thankfully, it was only a few seconds more before we reached the hotel lobby. I followed the big man off and stepped into chaos.

The lobby was full of people talking at full volume, many in large groups. There were a few kids running circles around the couch in the center of the room. A harried-looking older man was trying to get them to settle down, to no avail.

Clint hurried past me without saying goodbye, which was fine by me. He seemed pretty rattled this morning, and considering the pressure he was under,

I didn't blame him. A lot of people were counting on him. I hoped he came out of it okay.

Checking my watch, I pressed through the masses, wanting to get to the tasting early. It was due to start in fifteen minutes, and I hoped to get there with enough time so I could spend a few minutes with Thomas before it began. I wasn't sure I wanted to do anything more than talk to him, but Vicki was right; I needed to let loose and have a little fun.

If it smelled blissfully of coffee last night, it was downright heavenly today. My mouth watered as I made my way down the hall to grand ballroom A, where the tasting was to take place. I'd eschewed the coffee the hotel offered in the room—if you counted those little packets they provided as coffee—figuring I'd have more than enough to choose from at the tasting.

The doors to the ballroom were closed. I considered going in anyway, but after a quick look around, I decided against it. No one else was making a move toward the doors, and a short line had formed to one side, though a majority of the people were standing randomly around the hall. There was no sense making a nuisance of myself by poking my nose where it didn't belong, so instead, I moved to stand by the floor-to-ceiling windows to wait.

A sense of excitement zipped through me as I watched the people milling about. The tasting was the first big main event of the con, and everything else was going to build off of it. I was anxious to see how it all played out—and if Thomas won, all the better.

A woman in jeans and a red and black plaid shirt slipped through the doors and inside. She had dark hair, and darker eyeliner, which went well with her porcelain-pale skin. As she entered, her badge spun, giving me a glimpse of her name: TARA MADISON. I wondered if she was the Tara Thomas had mentioned, then scrubbed the thought from my mind. If it was, so be it. It didn't matter to me.

But she *was* pretty.

The hallway started to fill up so that it was impossible to move without bumping into someone. The con was expected to hold a couple hundred people, and it felt like most of them were here now. It only added to my excitement, despite the discomfort.

Wynona poked her head out the doors, looked around briefly, and then vanished inside again. A moment later, the doors opened all the way, and the crowd surged forward.

I hung back, hoping to catch a glimpse of one of my friends before taking the plunge. If they were in the crowd somewhere, however, I wasn't seeing them. I waited until nearly everyone was inside before heading in myself.

Stations had been set up around the ballroom. There were ten in all, each manned by what I assumed were the competitors. The program had said there were five judges. Clint Sherman and the man I'd seen yesterday, Carmine Wright, were two of them. I had yet to see or meet the other three, though I'd memorized their names: Dallas Edmonds, Pierre Longview, and Evaline Cobb. I figured if anyone knew something about coffee, it would be the people who organized a convention all about coffee. I hoped to make their acquaintances at some point.

I worked my way slowly around the room, starting nearest the door. I caught a glimpse of Thomas, whose station was between the dark-haired Tara and Charles Maddox. Two stations down from Charles was Wynona Kepler. She was glaring daggers at him, even as people came up to sample her coffee.

As I moved from station to station, I took the offered samples, but paid little mind to the competitors themselves. I found my gaze was drawn to Thomas—and how whenever he got a moment, he'd say something to Tara, who was clearly smitten with him. Every time she looked at him, her eyes lit up and she smiled.

It's none of your business, I reminded myself.

I reached Wynona's station and took the small cup and sipped. So far, the coffees I'd tried were okay, but none of them were anything special. When I took a drink from hers, my eyes widened.

"This is really good," I said.

Wynona's smile was a little condescending when she said, "I know. It's my own personal blend."

I finished off the small cup, wishing I had more, but it felt wrong to grab another sample. There was a nuttiness to the flavor, and a hint of something else I couldn't place. I made a mental note to find out later, when it wasn't so busy. Maybe I could order it for Death by Coffee.

I moved on, impressed. Thomas's coffee was going to have to be really good to beat out Wynona's.

When I reached Charles's station, his smile faltered before firming. He obviously remembered me from our brief interaction outside our hotel rooms. Apparently, I hadn't left him with a good impression, despite having tried to be pleasant. "Please, try some," he said, before adding, almost sarcastically, "neighbor."

Unsure what I'd done to earn his disdain, I almost passed, but decided to at least try it. I was here looking for new coffees for Death by Coffee, not to make friends. If it was good, I didn't need to like the person who made it.

I took a sip from the cup and was surprised to find the coffee to be full of flavor. Somehow, I had thought that a nasty man like Charles couldn't possibly make a good cup of coffee, but it appeared I was wrong.

"It's a variant of a café mocha," he said, watching me. He looked pleased by my initial reaction. "I'm sure you can taste the chocolate, how it accentuates the flavor, but doesn't overpower it. I don't use just any chocolate, mind you. I was very particular about what I used."

"It's good," I said. It appeared as if Thomas had some serious competition. "Good luck."

Charles sniffed and glanced at Thomas with a superior smirk. It made me want to take back my compliment.

I held my tongue, however, and moved over to Thomas's station, truly hoping his coffee would blow the rest of them out of the water. It would serve Charles right to be humbled after acting so standoffish.

"Krissy," Thomas said. His radiant grin lit up his entire face. "I'm glad you came."

"I'm glad I came too."

He laughed before motioning toward his offering. "Please, try some."

"Don't mind if I do." I picked up a cup, held my breath, and said a little prayer before taking a sip.

I just about melted into the floor.

"This is amazing," I said. It tasted of a blend of vanilla and chocolate. It could have been awful—I'd tried mixing the two before to unappetizing results—but it wasn't. "And I'm not just saying that."

Thomas beamed. "I'm glad you like it."

"Excuse me." A big woman elbowed me out of the way before I could respond. "You're holding up the line."

I stepped aside, rubbing at my arm where she'd bumped me. She had pointy elbows. "I'll talk to you after it's over," I told Thomas before moving on to Tara.

She eyed me as I picked up my cup. She had pale blue eyes, which stood in stark contrast to her dark makeup. It was striking. I couldn't fault Thomas for being interested—if, indeed, he was.

Stop it! I mentally reprimanded myself as I took a sip.

"It's good," I told her, and it was. It wasn't as good as Thomas's—nor Charles's nor Wynona's—coffee, but it was good nonetheless.

"Thank you." She returned my smile before turning her attention to the next person in line.

Dismissed, I moved on around the room, tasting each and every coffee. Some were great, a few were duds, but in general, I enjoyed most of them. The headache I'd felt coming on was long gone too, which only added to my enjoyment of the experience.

"Krissy!" Vicki called, waving me over as I finished up the last sample, which tasted more like pecans than hazelnut, despite what the woman serving it had told me. I joined both Vicki and Rita by the door. "Did you try them all?"

I nodded. "I really liked Thomas's and Wynona's." And then, grudgingly, "And Charles's was good too, I suppose."

Vicki gave me a questioning look, and I realized she hadn't been given introductions like I had.

"The man over there, and the woman in red." I pointed out Charles, then Wynona. "And that's Thomas."

"Ah." She was trying hard not to smile as she eyed Thomas. "I liked all of them too."

"One of them should win," I said, and I wasn't just saying that because I recognized their faces. Theirs were genuinely the best coffees in the room.

"Maybe we should see if any of them distribute to coffee shops," Vicki said. "Even if they don't win, I think our customers would like them."

"I imagine they will." I did have some worries about how some of our staunchest customers would react to new coffee choices, even though we weren't going to replace their favorites, only add to them. Some people simply didn't like change, and I knew a few of them around Pine Hills.

The noise in the room made it hard to hold much of a conversation, so we watched and waited as the judges made their rounds. They mingled with the regular guests, so it wasn't easy to pick them out from the rest of the crowd. I recognized Clint and Carmine, of course, but I didn't see the other three until they made their way to the front of the room, where microphones had been set up.

The judges huddled together to confer among themselves. I noted how they kept shooting glances at the competitors. It might have been my imagination, but I was pretty sure they were keeping an eye on Charles more than anyone else.

Chatter died down as all eyes followed the judges. You could feel the anticipation in the room. This was a room full of coffee lovers, and I was sure everyone had their favorites. It was a brief, tense conversation, with two of the judges—Dallas and Pierre, if I remembered them from their photos correctly—looking especially put out by whatever was decided.

Carmine was the one to step up to the mic.

"Welcome, everyone, to JavaCon," he said. His voice was nasally, and he sniffed after each sentence, as if he had a cold. "I am Carmine Wright. We are honored to be here today to judge these amazing coffees."

The room erupted in applause that seemed to catch Carmine by surprise. He removed a handkerchief from his pocket and wiped his nose before stuffing it away. Behind him, Clint removed his hand sanitizer and spritzed it onto his own hands.

"It isn't easy picking the best coffee from such a wonderful bunch." His gaze flickered to Charles. "But we had to pick just one winner." Another round of applause. "We judged not just on flavor, but on consistency and aroma. The winner will not only be heavily featured at this year's con, but will be featured as a guest of honor next year as well."

The applause this time was deafening.

Carmine's smile was strained as he waited it out. He didn't look like he enjoyed being the center of attention, and the longer it dragged out, the worse he seemed to feel. "If the contestants would please join us," he said as the noise faded away. He motioned to his left.

The ten contestants left their stations and moved to stand where indicated. They arranged themselves in nearly the same order in which they'd been stationed during the tasting, with Tara and Charles standing on either side of Thomas.

As I watched, Charles leaned in and whispered something to Thomas, whose smile faded. Tara must have overhead what was said, because she leaned past Thomas to whisper a harsh word of her own to Charles, who merely laughed.

"Something's going on up there," Vicki noted.

"They're probably fighting over the woman," Rita said. "Men always do."

Once everyone was settled, Carmine returned to the mic. "The winner of this year's JavaCon Taster's Choice award is . . ."

There was no drumroll, but he paused for effect as if there was.

". . . Charles Maddox!"

Charles stepped forward as the room erupted in

applause. My heart sank, but I joined in just the
same.

"This is a travesty!" Wynona shouted over the
cheers. "Charles cheated!"

"Please, Wynona—"

"Carmine, if you tell me to calm down, I am going
to make you regret it."

Carmine quickly backed away from the mic.

"You bought your way to a win, admit it!" she
shouted, pointing a painted nail at Charles. "It's not
even your blend!"

Charles didn't appear fazed at all by her outburst.
"There's no truth to that, I can assure you." He leaned
forward and spoke directly into the microphone so
everyone could hear. "Thank you so much for this
award. You don't know how much it means to me."

Wynona's face turned an alarming shade of red.
"You will regret this, Charles. You won't get away with
this!" she shouted before spinning on her heel and
storming out a side door.

A stunned silence followed. It was broken by
Charles leaning into the mic and chuckling, "Somebody's a sore loser." The comment drew a smattering
of laughs.

As Charles went on with his acceptance speech, I
found myself wondering if what Wynona had said
was true, and then decided it didn't really matter.
What was done was done, and I was supposed to be
enjoying myself, not worrying over whether or not
one of the competitors had cheated.

Besides, I had more important things to worry
about. I caught Thomas's eye and gave him a thumbs-

up and a mock frown. He smiled, then shrugged in an
"I tried my best" kind of way, but I could tell some-
thing was bothering him. When he looked back to
Charles, his smile faded away to nothing.

Was it merely because he'd lost the tasting? Or was
it because what Wynona Kepler had said held some
kernel of truth?

Chapter 4

I spent the next hour in a seminar about the process of choosing the perfect coffee bean. It had sounded interesting when I'd scheduled it, but after about twenty minutes, I was bored to tears. The woman standing at the podium spoke in a monotone that put half the people in attendance to sleep, while the other half shifted uncomfortably. At least five people walked out mid-lecture.

The presenter didn't seem to notice.

Rita had smartly opted out before the event started, and Vicki had gone to a different seminar on her own. I hoped they were having more fun than me.

By the time I left the room, my head felt fuzzy and I was ready for a nap. I checked the time and realized I was due to meet Vicki and Rita for another seminar—this one on different brewing techniques—in ten minutes. I doubted I'd survive another seminar after the last, so I shot Vicki a quick text, letting her know I'd meet up with her later. I felt a little bad about skipping out, but hey, it was better than snoring through someone else's presentation. She'd understand.

The main hallway was mostly empty by now, since most everyone was in some event or another. I sank down into one of the chairs in the corner and watched what few people were wandering the halls. There was coffee being offered in a room nearby, but I wasn't so sure that's what I wanted. Despite how sleepy the seminar had made me, I was afraid of overdoing it on the caffeine. What I needed was water.

I rose and found a vendor selling bottled water. Four dollars later, I was back in my chair, the water already halfway gone. I'd have grumbled about the price, but it tasted so good, I forgave the price gouging, though I doubted I'd be buying any more for the rest of the con.

Capping my water, I went back to people-watching. Charles Maddox was talking to a red-haired woman in a white dress by one of the ballroom doors. She said something to him and ran a hand up and down his arm. He laughed and shook his head, which caused the woman to frown, but she didn't relent. She said something more and tried to snuggle in close, but Charles was having none of it. He stepped back, said something else, and pointed.

Both the redhead and I looked. Clint Sherman was standing by the bathrooms. When he saw Charles pointing, his eyes widened, and his mouth fell open. He stared at them for a long moment before he turned and hurried away.

Charles laughed loud enough for everyone to hear, including the retreating Clint. He said something more to the woman, and then he turned and vanished into the ballroom. The redhead paused to stare after where Clint had gone, then she followed him into the room.

The curious part of me wondered what that was all about. The realist in me realized I didn't really care. I found I didn't like Charles all that much, though I knew a part of it had to do with how he'd spoken to Thomas. There was something slimy about the man. It made me wonder if Wynona was right and he'd cheated his way to his award.

Closing my eyes, I leaned my head back and listened to the sounds around me. The murmur of voices, the faint sound of applause in a ballroom somewhere. It was oddly soothing. I felt myself relax, the tension bleeding from me.

I must have dozed off, because when I opened my eyes again, twenty minutes had passed and a man in a bright orange sweater was eating a salami sandwich in the chair next to me.

"I feel ya," he said through a mouthful of his lunch, before he let loose a yawn that spilled crumbs onto his sweater.

I gave the man a quick smile and rose. The nap had done me some good and I felt refreshed. I was ready for that coffee now.

I made it all of a couple of steps before I saw Thomas Cole hurrying down the hall in my direction. His hair was rumpled, like he'd been running his fingers through it repeatedly, and his shirt had come untucked. I imagined the whole affair, both with the tasting and with Charles winning, had to have been stressful on him. He looked like a man who wanted to get away for a quiet few minutes.

I considered letting him escape, but decided to at least say hi.

"Thomas!" I called, catching him before he could pass. "I really enjoyed your coffee. I'm sorry you didn't win."

He came to an abrupt halt, eyes going wide for an instant before he gave an easy smile. He seemed to realize how unkempt he looked and tucked his shirt in. It was then I noted the big coffee stain on it.

"It's all right," he said. "Only one person can win, right? I had quite a few people come up to me afterward, complimenting the coffee, which was good to hear. I think it's all going to work out."

"That's great." I then pointed to the stain. "Looks like you had a harrowing experience."

"Hmm?" He looked down. "Oh! Had an accident while cleaning up. They're planning a little party later tonight in honor of the winner." He took a frustrated breath. He might claim he was okay with Charles winning, but I could tell it bothered him. "The rest of us had to get our things out of there so they could set up for it. It should be fun."

"I doubt Wynona's having much fun," I said. "She didn't seem very happy Charles won."

"You noticed." Thomas laughed, eyes drifting from me to a pair of men who walked past us arguing in hushed voices. It took me a moment to realize it was two of the judges, Pierre Longview and Carmine Wright.

"Do you think any of it is true?" I asked.

"What's that?" Thomas asked, turning back to me.

"What Wynona said about Charles. Do you think it's true?"

He shrugged. "Doesn't really matter one way or the other. He won. If he cheated, it sucks, but I'll get over it."

I glanced over his shoulder when I saw a flash of black and red coming toward us. Tara's face was pulled in a tight grimace as she approached. I had a feeling she was thinking about Charles too.

"Hi, Tara," I said when she joined us. "We haven't officially met. I'm Krissy. Thomas mentioned you when I talked to him yesterday. I really did like your coffee."

"Thank you," she said. There was uncertainty in her voice, but she covered it quickly. "I still can't believe that weasel won."

"You don't like him?" I asked, not all that surprised. It seemed not many people liked Charles all that much.

"I've been to a few events with him before," Tara said. "It always seems like he's up to something."

"I think he usually is," Thomas said. I noted he took a step away from both Tara and me, as if standing there with the both of us made him uncomfortable.

Could he be interested in one of us? I wondered, and then squashed the thought. I didn't need to be thinking about Thomas in that way, even if, just maybe, he was thinking similar thoughts about me.

"Has he won a tasting before?" I asked.

"I don't think so," Tara said. "I always thought his

stuff tasted off, like he used cheap beans or something."

"I don't think he knows what he's doing, honestly," Thomas said. "This is the first time I think he's come anywhere close to winning anything."

It made me wonder about what Wynona had said. If Charles was winging it, using bad beans or putting unsavory stuff into his coffee, then how had he suddenly come up with something that was good enough to win him an award?

Sure, he could have improved in his craft, found better beans, or discovered just the right combination of flavors. People got better at their passions all the time, so why not Charles?

"You know what?" Tara said, pushing the sleeves of her shirt up to her elbows. "I think I'm going to find Charles and give him a piece of my mind."

"Are you sure that's a good idea?" Thomas asked. "You know what he can be like."

"I know, but I can't just let it slide." Tara took a deep breath and then stormed off to find Charles before either Thomas or I could stop her.

Thomas watched her go. Was it a longing stare? Or was he concerned for her well-being? Who knew how Charles would react when confronted?

As soon as she vanished around the corner, Thomas turned back to me, seemingly more at ease now that she was gone.

"It'll blow over," he said. "Tara will have her say, and Wynona will rant some more, but I think we'll all forget about it by the time JavaCon is over."

"So you aren't mad?" I asked. "If he cheated . . ."

"It doesn't matter. This is supposed to be fun, right? I think I'd much rather focus on something enjoyable, rather than what Charles Maddox may or may not have done. Making a big deal out of it won't help anyone."

Hearing it put like that, I wholeheartedly agreed.

"So . . ." I started, not quite sure where to go from there. I didn't want to talk about Charles anymore. I didn't want to talk about Tara either. But what else was there to talk about that wouldn't lead back to them? It wasn't like I knew anything about Thomas or his interests—outside of coffee, of course.

"So." Thomas appeared to be at as much of a loss for words as I was. He looked around a moment before he wiped at the stain on his shirt. "I should probably get changed."

"I think it adds character," I said, resisting the urge to playfully poke the stain. "It shows that you worked hard."

"Or that I'm clumsy."

"I know what that's like," I said. "Rarely does a day go by when I'm not tripping over something or hurting myself."

"Don't remind me," he said with a grin.

My face flushed briefly. I'd almost forgotten that we'd met because I'd tripped over *him*.

A woman stormed by. She nearly ran into Thomas as she hurried past. She muttered something that might have been an apology, or a curse, before she swerved and rushed down a hall. Her badge swung wildly around her neck.

"I think all the coffee is rattling everyone," Thomas said. "We're all going to be jittering around the place by the end of the night."

"We're at a con," I said. "Who needs sleep anyway? We can keep each other up all night if that's what it takes."

Thomas eyed me with an amused grin. It took me a moment to realize why, and when I did, I very nearly died.

Before I could sputter out a course correction, however, he asked, "What are your plans this evening?"

"Plans?" I squeaked. "I'm, uh, I'm not sure."

"Well, I'm going to be sitting in on a workshop until five. After that, I'm free."

My mind blanked. Vicki and I had planned on doing quite a few events together, both today and tomorrow, but I had no clue what those plans were anymore.

"After the stresses of today, I could use some company for dinner," Thomas added.

"Yeah. I mean, sure. Everyone has to eat."

He laughed. "That they do."

"If you want to invite Tara, that's okay too." At least now it didn't sound so much like a date.

He gave me a surprised look. "Tara? I could if you want me to, but I could use a little time away from everything coffee related."

"It was just an idea." I mentally smacked myself in the back of the head. *What is wrong with me?*

Thomas checked his watch. "I'd better get changed. I'll meet you in the lobby at, let's say, seven?"

"Sounds good."

"Great." His smile was radiant. "See you then."

I watched as Thomas hurried toward the elevators, catching them just before the doors closed. What in the world was I getting myself into?

It's just dinner. Maybe if I kept reminding myself of that, I'd eventually believe it.

Unsure what to do, or where to go, I hovered, hoping that either Rita or Vicki would show. I needed to talk to one of them about Thomas before I burst. I wasn't sure if I was thrilled or terrified by the prospect of dinner with him. I supposed it was a little of both.

Ten minutes passed without sight of either of my friends. I was about to go in search of them when a scream echoed from down the hall, drawing my attention. The handful of guests who were milling about all stopped what they were doing and turned toward the sound.

Thanks to where I was standing, I was the only one who had a good look at the screamer. The woman was running down the hall, eyes bugging nearly out of her head. She reached the main hallway and looked wildly around, as if she didn't know where to go, or who to run to.

"Are you okay?" I stepped forward, into her line of sight.

The woman was older, and frightfully thin. Her eyes locked onto me like I was the only one who could save her. She rushed at me and grabbed hold of my arm, nails digging small crescents into my skin as she clutched at me. She was breathing fast and hard. I was afraid she might be having a heart attack.

"He's dead," she said between pants. "I found him, and he's dead."

"Who?" I asked. The woman was wearing a ring, and I wondered if it was her husband who had passed.

She took a shuddering breath before answering. "Charles Maddox," she said. "The man who won the competition. I found him back there." She pointed back the way she'd come. "And I think . . . I think he's been murdered!"

Chapter 5

The crowd milled around outside Ballroom A. Police officers stood at each entry, blocking anyone from entering. The doors were closed, so no one could see inside, yet people were watching anyway, myself included.

The older woman—Penny, she told me when she'd calmed—was sitting in a quiet corner with a paramedic. She'd grown faint, and I was worried she might have a heart attack or stroke or something. Her husband, if he was in attendance, had yet to appear. She was calmer now, talking and occasionally smiling at whatever the paramedic was saying, so it looked like she was going to get through the experience without much more than a bad memory.

The same couldn't be said about Charles Maddox.

"Who do you think did it?" Rita asked. Both she and Vicki had found me loitering near the main doors to the ballroom soon after the discovery of Charles's body.

"We're not sure he was actually murdered," I said, though the heavy police presence told me otherwise. They were watching everyone with a suspicion that could only mean foul play.

"Do you think they'll cancel the rest of the con?" Vicki asked. "This is a pretty big deal. I'm not sure how they can go on after this."

"I don't know." Canceling it would be the right thing to do, but with how little Charles was liked, I wouldn't be surprised if they continued on. "I'm not sure they'll have much of a choice. The police might shut us down."

"It'd be a shame, but totally understandable," Vicki said.

Penny hadn't said enough for me to determine exactly what had happened. She said she'd wandered into Ballroom A, looking for something to do since her workshop had let out early, and found Charles lying on the floor. She'd been too panicked to pay much attention to *how* he'd died, only noticing that he was lying in a pool of his specialty café mocha— she could smell it—and that there was glass every-where.

"Maybe we should go in there," Rita said.

I glanced at her out of the corner of my eye. "Why would we do that?"

"To help, dear. Why else?"

I shook my head. "No way. I'm not getting in-volved in this." Sure, that old familiar itch was dig-ging at me, the need to *do* something, but I was determined to ignore it.

"Why not?" Rita planted both her hands on her hips and gave me a perplexed look. "You're practically a professional. Why, I bet you have more experience solving murders than any of the policemen here. *You* should be teaching *them* how it's done!"

"I doubt that," I said. I might have helped out back home a few times, but that didn't make me an expert. In fact, I found myself in dangerous situations far more often than anyone in their right mind should. Maybe I was bad luck. Over the last few years, it seemed like no matter where I went, someone died, and it was rarely of natural causes.

I was afraid that, eventually, that someone might be me.

A gleam came into Rita's eye then. "Well, there's only one way to find out, isn't there?"

Before anyone could stop her, Rita marched straight for Ballroom A, acting like she had all the right in the world to be barging in on the murder scene.

The cop at the door looked startled by her approach, but quickly recovered. He moved to bar her way. "Ma'am, please step back."

"My friends and I need to get inside," she said. "We have experience with these sorts of things and can be of assistance."

The cop glanced behind her, but since neither Vicki nor I had followed her, there was no one for him to look at but a crowd of people doing their best to look innocent.

"Please step back, ma'am," he said. "No one is allowed inside."

Rita huffed and looked back at me. "Can you believe him? I swear, no one has respect for their elders these days."

I hurried forward and took Rita by the arm. "I'm sorry," I said, forcing a smile. "My grandmother sometimes forgets where she is."

"Your grandmother?" Rita's tone was incredulous, but at least she allowed me to drag her away. "I look nothing like a grandmother, and especially not *yours*. Your mother maybe . . ."

Vicki was trying to suppress a laugh as I maneuvered Rita away from the police officer and to the back of the crowd, where she could cause less trouble.

"I'm sorry," Vicki said. "I know I shouldn't laugh, but the look on his face when you turned away . . ."

"I don't see why you're resisting," Rita said, smoothing down her dress as if I'd tackled her and then manhandled her forcibly into the corner, rather than just having guided her away. "We could solve the case in minutes."

"No," I said. "We couldn't."

"But—"

"No buts. I don't know these cops." I shot a glance toward the one at the door. He was watching us, though I couldn't tell if he was suspicious of us or worried *about* us. "Paul lets me get away with more than he should." In fact, most of the police force back home tended to give me a lot more freedom than I deserved, even if grudgingly. "If we try poking around at a murder scene, we're going to get arrested."

"Not if we solve the case." Rita crossed her arms over her chest. All that was missing from a full-on pout was a jutting lower lip.

"I'm not getting involved," I said, wondering how

true that statement really was. I might not want to be a part of them, but somehow, murder investigations had a way of finding me.

Which made me wonder . . .

Penny had said Charles was lying in a pool of his coffee. Thomas had been hurrying down the hall not too long ago, fresh coffee stains on his shirt. Had he been telling the truth, and it was his own coffee, spilled in a cleanup accident? Or was it Charles's café mocha that had sent him rushing for his room to change?

And what about Tara? She'd stormed off to find Charles ten to fifteen minutes before he was found dead. Had she found him? Did they argue? And if they *had* argued, could it have led to a spur-of-the-moment murder?

No, Krissy, no. I couldn't start thinking about the case, or else I wouldn't stop. I would *not* get involved; not this time.

"What should we do?" Vicki asked. "I feel bad for him, yet I don't want to go home. Do you really think the police will shut the con down?"

"They might," I said. "Or the organizers might. This is going to put a stain on the con's reputation, that's for sure."

Stain. Like the one on Thomas's shirt. I gritted my teeth against the urge to go find him and ask him about it.

A man was dead, possibly murdered. They couldn't continue JavaCon after that, could they? And if they did, it was unlikely people would fall back into the rhythm of things like nothing had happened. There'd be panic, worry. It would be chaos.

Or so I thought. Next to me, a trio of women were discussing a panel they planned on sitting in on later. Across the room, other small groups were breaking off, looking at programs. There were still a lot of people staring at the ballroom, waiting to see what would happen next, but I had a feeling that if the police didn't shut the con down, it *would* go on.

Eventually, paramedics came out of the room, wheeling Charles's covered body away. The crowd parted to let them through. A handful of police officers was making the rounds, talking to the onlookers, taking statements, and hoping to find someone who could tell them exactly what happened.

I scanned the crowd, not sure what I was looking for. A guilty face, perhaps? Thomas?

I didn't see Thomas or his stained shirt, but I did spot someone else I knew. Her red and black shirt stood out, as did the frightened, worried look on her face.

"Be right back," I told Rita and Vicki. "There's someone over there I know."

Rita made a sound of protest, but Vicki shushed her as I crossed the packed hall over to where Tara stood by the bathrooms, nearly in the same spot where I'd seen Clint earlier.

Tara saw me coming, but she didn't make a move to run, which was a good sign. Her eyes, which were slightly wider than they should be, with an almost vacant look in them, weren't. She looked like she was in shock.

"Tara," I said as I came to a stop in front of her. "Are you all right?"

She nodded in a jerky manner that told me that no, she was most definitely not all right.

"I suppose you heard what happened."

"He's dead," she said. Her voice was airy, not quite right. "I wasn't sure, but he really is dead."

Wasn't sure? I wondered. "Did you get a chance to talk to him?" I asked, keeping my voice kind and soothing. Tara looked like she might bolt if someone were to make a loud, sudden noise.

Tara shook her head in that unsettling, jerky way. "I went looking for him where I last saw him," she said, almost dreamily. Her gaze drifted down the hall, over everyone's heads. I wasn't sure she was actually seeing anything at this point. "But he wasn't there."

"He was in the ballroom."

"He was." She blinked three times quickly before her gaze drifted back to me. "But I didn't know it at first. I couldn't find him."

I rested a hand on her shoulder. She was shaking. It seemed odd to me that she'd react so badly to learning someone she didn't like had died. I didn't expect her to be jumping up and down in joy, but she was acting like she'd just lost her best friend.

She could have killed him. Or know who did. It would explain why she was acting so strangely.

"What happened, Tara?"

"I went back there," she said, waving her hand vaguely down the hall. "There's a hospitality room for those of us who are presenting. Charles stopped by there after the tasting, and I thought he might still be there."

"But he wasn't." I knew for a fact that he'd left,

since I'd seen him with the redhead not too long before he was found. *Another suspect?* I wondered, before focusing on what Tara was saying.

"No, he wasn't." She swallowed with some diffi-
culty before going on. "I decided to take a few minutes to cool down, since I was so ramped up and
angry. I was afraid I might punch him if he started to
taunt me or act like he was better than me. While I
was there, some woman came in, close to tears. I
asked her if she was all right and she cursed Charles's
name. When I asked her about him, she told me
where I could find him."

She sucked in a trembling breath and hugged herself.

"Did you know this woman?" I asked, wondering if
it was the woman I'd seen him with earlier.

"No. I don't think so." She frowned. "I might have
seen her around, but there's so many faces here, it's
hard to say for sure. I honestly wasn't paying too
much attention, so I couldn't even tell you what she
looked like." She closed her eyes and shuddered.

I squeezed her shoulder. Tara leaned into my
hand as if it was the only thing keeping her upright.
She took another deep breath and sighed.

"So, you went looking for Charles," I pressed when
she didn't go on. If Tara had killed him, I was betting
it hadn't been planned. She could have found him,
and he could have started in on her, gloating over his
victory. She might have pushed him. He could have
lost his balance, fallen just right. Accidents like that
happen all the time.

"I . . . He . . ." Tara's eyes became unfocused, but
then they firmed on me. "I found him," she whispered.

"He was lying there and I panicked. I should have told someone, but I was too scared." Tears leaked from the corners of her eyes, causing her dark mascara to run.

"You saw him?" I asked. "In the ballroom?"

She nodded, wiped at her nose. "He was lying there, not moving. I couldn't tell if there was blood or anything like that. I walked in and just froze." She reached out, crushed my wrist in a bone-breaking grip. "I didn't know what to do. I thought he might have fallen or, I don't know, had an attack of some kind. I left him there. I might have been able to help him if I would have checked him."

"You don't know that," I said, pulling my wrist free and rubbing at it. The woman was small, but she had a grip like a vice.

"I left him," she repeated. "He was lying there, in need of help, and I just walked away."

"Did you tell anyone?" I asked. "Did you see anyone before going in who might have done it? Or afterward? Was anyone else in the room with you? In the hall outside it?"

"No." She ran her thumb beneath each eye, smearing her mascara more. "If someone was there, I didn't see them. I left, and while I was trying to decide what to do, I heard the scream. I should have done something!"

I considered what to do. Tara was obviously distraught over Charles's death. I wasn't sure if she was telling the full truth, but it was clear she was scared out of her mind. And while I could condemn her for not calling the police immediately, or at least checking Charles to make sure he wasn't just unconscious,

I knew from experience that finding a body isn't pleasant. It would be easy to lock up and panic.

"You should go to the police," I said. "Tell them what you told me."

"But what if they blame me for his death?" she asked. "I found him and didn't do anything. Could they arrest me for that?" Her eyes widened farther. "What if they think I killed him? They wouldn't, would they?"

"It'll be fine," I said. "You're likely in shock. People do strange things all the time when that happens. They'll understand that."

Tara resumed hugging herself. Her gaze moved to where the police were questioning people near the ballroom doors.

"Talk to them," I urged. "Tell them everything. If you didn't do anything, then there's nothing for you to worry about."

"Are you sure?"

"I am," I said. "I've done this before. If you don't tell the police now, they'll wonder later why you withheld information from them." I was about to gently urge her forward, when a new question sprang to mind. "Did you see Thomas before you joined us in the hallway earlier?"

"Thomas?" Tara asked. "Why?"

"Just curious. He spilled some coffee on his shirt." I wasn't sure how to go on from there without point-blank asking if she thought he might have killed Charles Maddox.

"We spoke briefly after the tasting, but I finished my cleanup before he did and left," Tara said. "I didn't see him again until I saw the two of you together."

I forced a smile in the hope that it would ease her mind, though my own mind was racing. How many people were still in the room after Tara had left? How long after I'd seen Charles with the redheaded woman did he die? Could Thomas have been waiting in the ballroom for Charles to return? Was the woman to blame for Charles's death? Was she a witness?

"All right," I said. I needed time to think. I didn't want to accuse anyone of anything without knowing more. "Go tell the police what you know. If you need to talk afterward, come find me."

She gave me a look, as if wondering why I cared so much, before making her slow way over to where the cops were interviewing other convention guests. She glanced back once, managed a scared smile, and then walked up to the nearest cop to tell him her story.

I sucked in a trembling breath and let it out in a huff. A man was dead. At least two women were likely traumatized after finding the body. And there was an entire convention's worth of suspects who could have easily slipped into the room through one of the multiple entrances without anyone noticing.

And to make matters worse, I was due to have dinner with my number one suspect later that night.

Chapter 6

The excitement died down a short time later. Life, for those of us still living it, went on. Ballroom A, and the surrounding area, was off-limits, but the police were letting the con goers mill about on their own, albeit with a watchful eye. No one had announced the end of JavaCon, so I assumed it would continue—at least for a little while.

I waited in the main hall, hoping Thomas would return and reassure me that he was completely innocent of the crime, but I saw not hide nor hair of him. It worried me that he'd made himself so scarce after a murder. He might have already slipped out the door and was working his way to Canada, while the rest of us were still trying to figure out what was going on.

Everyone was buzzing about the murder. There were quite a few people who were concerned for their own well-being. At least two dozen had already

made for the checkout line, and I was sure more
would follow as the day went on.

Of course, the police weren't letting them get
away without talking to them first. A pair of grim-
faced officers stood by the exit and questioned everyone who tried to leave. The chaos had to have been
making the investigation a struggle. It wouldn't have
surprised me if, before long, the cops separated
everyone into two rooms—one for those they've already talked to, and one for those they still needed to
interview.

I was one of the latter and was hoping to keep it
that way for as long as I could. I wasn't just looking
for Thomas, but for the redhead I'd seen Charles
with before his death as well. They were my two best
suspects—not that I was investigating—and I didn't
want either of them to slip away before I had a
chance to point them in the direction of the police.

I was quickly learning that finding two people in
the masses was next to impossible. There were hundreds of people here, including people who were
staying at the hotel who weren't attending JavaCon.
It was likely why the police hadn't attempted to cor-
ral everyone together; it would be, quite simply, un-
feasible.

Vicki found me still standing in the same place
nearly twenty minutes later.

"What do you want to do?" she asked. "It seems
like they're trying to ramp things up again, but I'm
not so sure we should stay."

A handful of people were making for one of the
other ballrooms in preparation for an event. Carmine
Wright was in the lead. His head was bowed, hands

stuffed into his pockets. He met no one's eye as he vanished into the ballroom, the group right behind him.

"I think we should stick it out for a little longer," I said. "At least for today. If it doesn't feel right, we can always leave in the morning."

"I was thinking the same thing." Vicki glanced around, then scooted a little closer to me. "Do you think it's safe?"

I didn't have to ask to know she was referring to the possibility that a murderer was lurking the halls of the convention center. "There's police everywhere," I said. "I think as long as no one wanders off alone, nothing else will happen."

She didn't look convinced, but nodded anyway. "I'm going to check out the seminar over there." She indicated the ballroom where Carmine and the others had disappeared into. "Do you want to come?"

"I think I'll stay here for a bit," I said. "You go ahead."

Vicki didn't argue. She flashed me a worried smile, then wandered over to the ballroom, head constantly on a swivel, like she thought the murderer might spring out of the crowd at any moment.

A part of me wanted to put the murder behind me and go with her, but I doubted I'd manage to sit through a seminar or workshop. My mind was spinning, and my fingers were itching to be doing *something*. Rita wasn't wrong when she said I had experience with this sort of thing. What would a little casual conversation with a few suspects hurt?

I just had to find one of them.

I continued scanning faces and listening in on

snatches of conversations in the hope that someone would let something slip. Quite a few people were concerned about the con, but weren't ready to leave.

"It's not cost-effective," one woman said. "I flew in. Do you know how much it'll cost me to change my return flight?"

Her companion gave her a grim nod. "Maybe we can convince the organizers to pay for it for us," he said.

The two walked off together, presumably to find said organizers.

My phone buzzed in my pocket. I pulled it out and checked the screen. My chest tightened when I recognized the number.

What now? I wondered as I put the phone to my ear. "Hello?"

"Krissy? Thank goodness you answered."

"Mason," I said. "Is everything all right?" He was calling me from Death by Coffee, so I knew it wasn't, but remained hopeful. How much could go wrong in one day?

"Define 'all right.' "

I groaned. "What happened?"

"It's nothing, really. Well, I mean, it's something. But the place isn't burning down or anything."

"That's good to hear."

Mason made a sound that might have been a laugh, albeit a nervous one. "I probably shouldn't have bothered you, but quite frankly, I'm not sure what to do."

"Why not call Vicki?" I asked, curious. I mean, she *was* his wife. "Is her phone off?"

"I don't know," Mason said. "I didn't try her. I

called you first, hoping you might, I don't know, tell
me something that might help. I don't want her to
think I don't know what I'm doing."

I was genuinely curious now. Mason didn't sound
like whatever was happening was a big deal, yet he
wouldn't have called if it wasn't. And since he'd
called me, it had to do with Death by Coffee.

Even though Mason had promised to help out
with running the bookstore café, he wasn't fully up
to speed with the ins and outs of the business. I was
hoping his call had to do with where we kept the
hazelnut coffee, not that he'd misplaced the money.

"Is everyone okay?" I asked, suddenly worried
there had been an outbreak of some kind that left
Mason the only one available to work in the store.
"You're not alone, are you?"

"No, Lena and Jeff are here." He took a deep
breath, paused, and then laid it on me. "It's Dad."

"Your dad?" I asked, though who else could it be?
Both my dad and Vicki's dad were in California.
Mason's father, Raymond Lawyer, lived right there in
Pine Hills. In fact, his insurance company was housed
right across the street from Death by Coffee. "Is he
okay?" I asked. If he was sick, then Vicki would need
to get back to Pine Hills as soon as possible.

"No. Well, not sick in the way you're thinking."
Something came into his voice then, a disdain that
often marred his words whenever he spoke of his difficult father. "He's created something of a situation."

"What kind of situation?" I asked, dreading the answer. Raymond Lawyer wasn't a nice man. He mistreated pretty much everyone he came in contact
with, other than his girlfriend, Regina Harper. Even

his son couldn't avoid his wrath. I could only imagine what sort of trouble he'd caused that would make Mason call me instead of Vicki.

"One sec." There was a rustle, and then the thump of a door closing. "Sorry. I'd rather no one overhear."

"Is it that bad?" I asked, heart sinking. "What happened?"

"So, you know how you hired Beth Milner?" he asked.

"Yeah?"

"And you know how she used to work for Dad at Lawyer's Insurance?"

A hollow space opened up in my gut. "I do."

"Well, Dad just found out she's working here. Suffice it to say he's not too happy."

"How 'not too happy'?" I was imagining hand grenades and police with riot gear.

"She was up in the books when he came in," Mason said. "I was in the back, so I didn't see him until it was too late. I would have stopped him if I'd known what he planned to do."

"Mason, what did he do?" I was breathing hard, almost frantic with worry. Raymond Lawyer had a temper. A bad temper. I wouldn't put it past him to threaten or coerce Beth into quitting, or worse, fleeing Pine Hills altogether.

"He made a scene," Mason said. "He yelled at her and trapped her in a corner. Jeff didn't know what to do, and Lena was on her break. By the time I got to Beth, she was in tears and he'd scared Trouble half to death. The cat was nearly climbing the walls to get away from him."

Anger at Mason's father broiled just beneath the surface when I asked, "Is Beth okay?"

"Physically, yeah," Mason said. "But mentally . . ." I could almost see his shrug. "She's near inconsolable. I managed to wrangle Dad out of there, but the damage has been done. I'm not sure she's going to stay."

Crap. "Is she there?" I asked. "Can I talk to her?"

"I told her to take a walk, clear her head," Mason said. "I'm thinking I'll let her go home once she's back and after Jeff gets his break. I don't know what else to do."

"You did all you could," I said. When I got back home, I was going to have to have a serious talk with Raymond Lawyer. I'm sure Mason would have one of his own, as would Vicki, but they were family. They wouldn't want to ruin what relationship they had with him.

I, on the other hand, had nothing to lose.

"There were quite a few people here when it happened," Mason went on. "I'm worried it's going to hurt business, especially after some of the stuff Dad said about Beth. You know how people around here gossip."

Oh, I knew, all right. I so didn't want to know what Raymond had said, or whether any of it was true. I was going to kill him when I saw him next.

Well, maybe not *kill* kill, but I was going to give him a pretty big piece of my mind, and I wasn't going to do it kindly.

And then, as if the fates had decided things weren't bad enough, I heard Rita's "There she is, Detective!" I looked up to see her coming my way, an annoyed-looking man with a badge clipped to his belt in her wake.

"Tell Beth to call me if she wants to talk," I said. "Insist on it if she seems like she needs it. I've got to go. You've got this."

"I really hope so," Mason said. "I feel like this is all my fault somehow. I should have done something sooner."

"You did what you could. I know you'll make things better." With Beth, maybe. I didn't know how anyone could reason with Raymond.

We clicked off just as Rita and the cop reached me.

"Where have you been, dear?" she said, wiping phantom sweat from her brow. "I've been looking all over for you for the last fifteen minutes!"

From the look on the detective's face, I didn't doubt it.

"You said she might know something?" he asked. He was a big, dark-skinned man who had an intense gaze that made him seem intimidating even before he spoke. His deep, rumbling voice only added to the intimidation factor.

"Of course she does," Rita said. "Tell Detective Kimble, Krissy."

"Tell him what?" I asked, wishing there was a table between us so I could kick her in the shin.

"About that man's murder!" She crossed her arms and shot me a smile, as if she thought I was going to launch into a well-told tale of murder and deceit.

"I barely knew the guy," I said with a shrug.

Rita's mouth fell open as the detective frowned. He looked from me to Rita, and then, I swear, he rolled his eyes.

"Did you see anything?" he asked. He sounded like this wasn't the first time someone had dragged him off on a wild-goose chase.

I opened my mouth to speak, but hesitated. Should I tell him about Thomas's coffee stain? What if Thomas was telling the truth and it had been an accident? Could I really sic a detective on him?

If not Thomas, what about the redhead? Or the woman Tara had talked to? I was pretty sure Tara had already told the police about the latter, so did I really need to mention the former when I didn't even know *why* they'd been speaking?

"I wish I could help," I said, knowing that somehow, I was going to regret holding out on the detective. Hadn't I warned Tara about the same thing earlier?

Kimble's mouth pressed into a tight line. "Well, if you do think of something, let one of us know." He shot Rita a look and then stormed off.

"Why did you do that?" Rita asked.

"Why did you bring him to me?" I retorted.

"Because, well, it's you!" It was her turn to frown. "You have to have some idea as to who did it. You could have told him, and then offered to help in the investigation."

"Rita, I'm not getting involved." At least, not any more than I already had.

"But . . ." She trailed off, brow collapsing. She looked as if I'd just told her she couldn't have puppies and ice cream.

"I know you want to help," I said. "But we don't know these cops. This isn't Pine Hills. We need to let the police do their jobs and stay out of it."

"I suppose you're right, dear." Rita pointedly looked at her watch. "I guess I should go find something to eat."

As she said it, my stomach grumbled. I hadn't actually eaten anything for breakfast, other than coffee, and it was already past lunchtime.

But before I could tell her I'd join her, I caught sight of one of the people I'd been looking for.

And he wasn't alone.

"I'll catch up with you later," I said, putting my grumbling stomach—and the troubles at Death by Coffee—out of my mind.

Rita said something, but I missed it. I was too intent on watching Thomas as he hurried down into a mostly empty hallway, a nervous-looking Tara in his wake.

"What are you up to?" I muttered as Rita wandered over to one of the stations selling pastries. Ignoring how my mouth watered at the thought of a sugary snack, I followed after the two retreating figures to find out.

Chapter 7

The hallway was quiet as I snuck to the door Thomas and Tara had vanished into. Well, by "quiet," I mean no one was there with me. The sounds coming from the main convention floor echoed down the corridor, making it impossible to hear anything through the closed door in front of me.

A sign by the door read EMPLOYEES ONLY but had no other markings indicating what might be inside. Thomas and Tara had no reason to be here. Something was up—something that could very well have to do with Charles Maddox's murder.

My instincts were screaming at me to turn around and walk away. Did I really want to know if Thomas was a killer? What about Tara? I liked them both, yet they weren't acting like innocent people. Innocent people didn't sneak down hallways and enter rooms they had no business being in.

I glanced back the way I'd come. No one was paying me any mind. There were no members of the hotel staff nearby as far as I could see, and the same went for the police. I was alone and, for the moment, free to make up my own mind on what to do.

It's none of your business, Krissy. Thomas and Tara might have something important to discuss, something they didn't want anyone to overhear. It didn't have to be anything sinister. Paul and I did that sort of thing all the time back home, though he was a cop, and our conversations often involved who might or might not be involved in a murder. Who knew, maybe Thomas and Tara were trying to come up with Charles's killer on their own and needed a quiet place to think it through.

But could I really walk away without at least checking to make sure? If their secret chat *was* about Charles, but how one of them was responsible for his death, walking away now might let a killer get away.

But what if they aren't talking?

The thought was oddly upsetting for someone who claimed she wasn't looking for a relationship. Just because Thomas had said there was nothing between him and Tara didn't make it true. And you didn't go sneaking off into unoccupied rooms with people you barely knew either, not unless something underhanded was going on.

Taking a deep breath, I reached for the door, but caught myself before pulling it open. I'd told Mason to tell Beth to call me when she got back to Death by Coffee. Knowing my luck, the moment I opened the door to eavesdrop, she'd make that call. I so didn't want to get caught listening in on Thomas and Tara's conversation, especially if it could have been prevented.

I took out my phone, set it to vibrate, and then slid it back into my pocket. That done, I reached for the door and eased it open.

"Are you sure no one knows?" Thomas asked. His voice came from deeper within the room, which was filled with folded tables and with chairs stacked atop one another.

"I'm positive," Tara said. "Wynona would have said something if she knew, and she never said a word. You know what she's like."

"She was more worried about Charles at the time," Thomas said. "She could be waiting for the right moment, especially if she thinks she'll get something out of it when she does."

I eased forward, half in and half out of the door. I couldn't see either of them from where I stood. I was hoping to catch a glimpse of the two to see if they looked as anxious as they sounded. Something was definitely going on here.

"Believe me, she'd have said something already if she knew," Tara said. "I talked to her a little while ago to see what she had to say about this whole mess. She was angry about Charles, and despite his death, she didn't appear inclined to let up on him. She showed no signs that she has anything on either of us."

"What if she pokes around too much?" Thomas asked. "If she keeps at it long enough, she'll surely find something. We might think we were careful, but what if someone knows?"

"I'm not as worried about Wynona as I am the police," Tara said, her voice rising in pitch. "They're the ones asking everyone questions now. All it takes is one person to say the wrong thing."

"If you're right and Wynona doesn't know, then I'm sure no one else does." Thomas heaved a huge sigh. "I think . . . I think we'll be okay."

"I wish I could be that certain."

"Trust that it'll all work out," Thomas said. There was a long stretch of silence. My mind conjured an image of him taking her in his arms and hugging her close. My chest tightened at the thought.

Stop it, Krissy. I go a few months without a boyfriend, and suddenly I'm jealous of people I hardly know.

Still, I eased forward as far as I could without taking my hand off the door. I didn't want it to close behind me, just in case it made too much of a sound. Behind a set of chairs, I could just make out a small patch of red and black that I took for Tara's shirt. I couldn't see where Thomas was standing.

"I'm still worried," Tara said. "If they start looking into us, they'll find out. Charles knew. That's why I had to go to him to keep him from talking."

I sucked in a shocked breath, which was thankfully obscured when Tara made a choking, disgusted sound.

"That came out wrong. I didn't mean it like that," she said.

"I know." Thomas sounded as if he was standing right in front of Tara. "If he'd spoken up, this whole trip would have been for naught." He sighed. "It's not like it matters now anyway."

"I still can't believe this is happening," Tara said. "Everything we've worked for . . ."

"What are you doing?"

A scream caught in my throat and I nearly smashed

my face into the door as I spun to face the source of the voice.

The man looked to be in his sixties, bald head speckled with age spots. He was carrying a broom and a bucket and wore the uniform of hotel staff. He was frowning as he looked at me over a pair of spectacles resting at the end of his nose.

"Nothing," I said, easing back out into the hall. I pulled the door closed behind me as I went, vainly hoping that Thomas and Tara hadn't heard the man's booming voice. "I was looking for the bathrooms." I grinned and shrugged. "Wrong door."

The man didn't look convinced, but he pointed down the hall and said, "They're that way. Ladies' is on the right. Can't miss it."

"Thank you," I said. "This place is a maze!"

He grunted and shuffled down the hall to another door. He paused there, gave me a warning look, and then vanished inside.

I watched him go, just barely suppressing the urge to wave, and then spun around. If I hurried, I might make it back to the main hall before Thomas and Tara poked their heads out of the room to see what all the commotion was about.

"Krissy?"

I closed my eyes briefly before turning to the now open door. "Thomas?" I asked as if I was shocked to find him standing inside the room. "What are you doing in there?"

By the look in his eye, I could tell he didn't buy my act of innocence.

"Okay, fine," I said, slumping. "I saw you two sneaking down here and was curious."

His face reddened as Tara peeked around a stack of chairs. "What did you hear?" His voice wasn't hard or angry, which surprised me. If I caught someone eavesdropping on me, I'd be livid.

"Enough," I said, keeping my voice level. "We should talk."

He checked the hall both ways before he motioned me to join them in the room.

A panicked *What if they killed Charles?* shot through my head, but I clamped down on the thought. If they had, I was hoping my years of chasing—and running from—murderers would serve me well. I wasn't as easy a target as I was once was.

Or so I hoped.

Taking a calming breath, I entered the room. Thomas held the door open for me and then closed it behind us. Not wanting to have someone at my back, I waited for him to take the lead.

Thomas slid around me and walked back behind the stacks of chairs to where Tara was waiting. I was glad to note she was still fully dressed and didn't look any more rumpled than the last time I saw her. Not that it mattered. If she and Thomas were sneaking off for some necking, it was none of my business.

Thomas moved to stand next to Tara. I stopped well short of them, just in case they did have violent intentions toward me. I crossed my arms and raised my eyebrows at them. "Well?" I asked, as if I had every right in the world to know what they were doing skulking about.

"Well what?" Thomas said. "We were just talking."

"About?"

"I don't see how that's any of your business," Tara

said. Any goodwill she might have had toward me was now gone.

"It might not be," I said. "But if it had to do with Charles's death, then I'm pretty sure someone would be quite interested." I didn't have to spell it out for them; they both knew I was talking about the cops.

Tara's eyes widened, while Thomas's narrowed.

"Is that a threat?" he asked.

"No." I let my arms fall to my sides and sighed. "I'm just concerned. With everything that's going on, I'm on edge, and I don't want people I like to be involved in something they shouldn't be."

"There's no need to be worried about us," Thomas said. "What's between Tara and me has no bearing on what happened to Charles."

"Are you sure?" I asked, unconvinced. If it didn't have to do with the murder, then why did they feel the need to sneak away to talk about it?

Tara looked to Thomas, questions in her eyes. She didn't look like a killer, but she was definitely upset by something. Then again, she *had* found Charles's body, and had left it there to be discovered by someone else. It would be stranger if she *wasn't* upset.

"It was about the competition," Thomas said, speaking slowly, as if he was measuring his words before saying them. "And what Wynona said."

"About Charles cheating?"

Thomas nodded. "I was thinking about it, and of what I knew of Charles, and I realized he was likely guilty of everything she accused him of." He glanced at Tara, who shook her head minutely. I noticed anyway. "I think he stole his entry."

"You mean his café mocha recipe?" I asked.

"I swear I've tasted that exact blend before," Thomas said. "If not, it was really close. If I'm not mistaken, it won a small competition somewhere. I just can't place where."

"But wouldn't that be easy to prove?" I asked. "I'm sure they keep a record of winning blends or something, right? I mean, they'd have to, wouldn't they?"

"Probably," Thomas said. "But really, who would care enough to look into it? Even if he did steal it, he'd use his own beans, his own flavoring, so it would be hard to know for sure without finding the recipe hidden in his room with an 'originally crafted by' sticker with someone else's name on it."

"There are people who take this stuff seriously," Tara said. "If he stole someone else's blend and they found out . . ."

They might kill him over it.

"Do you know who made the original coffee?" I asked. "If it is indeed the same one you remember from before, they might have had something to do with his death."

Thomas glanced at Tara, who shook her head. "I don't remember," he said. "It was at least a year ago, probably longer. You go to so many of these things, they all start to blend together."

I clung to the hope that his memory was right and that Charles *had* stolen the recipe from someone else. If that person was at JavaCon and tasted Charles's winning café mocha, they'd realize it was their creation. They might have confronted him about it, and then killed him when he refused to admit it.

"I see you got changed," I said to Thomas, trying to ease some of the tension that had filled our conversation. I really didn't want to make enemies of the only two people I'd befriended since arriving at Java-Con.

He glanced down, face reddening. "Yeah. I'm kind of glad I did when I did. I can't imagine what would have happened if the police had seen me in a coffee-stained shirt after Charles was found like he was."

A new question sprang to mind. I almost didn't ask it out of fear of angering him, but decided it was important for me to know for sure—if not for my peace of mind, then to at least help set a timeline of the events leading up to Charles's death.

"You were in the ballroom when you had your accident, right?" I asked. Thomas nodded. "Charles was found in the same ballroom sometime later. Did you see him there?"

Thomas and Tara shared yet another look. Were they still hiding something from me? I really didn't want to believe either of them capable of murder, but if they weren't honest with me, what else was I supposed to think?

"He was there briefly," Thomas said. "Then he left with some woman, I think. Honestly, I wasn't paying much attention. I spilled my coffee while I was cleaning up, and then I left. I didn't see him again after that first glimpse."

"Did you recognize the woman he was with?" I asked, wondering if it was the woman I'd seen Charles talking to or if it was the one Tara had seen. *If they aren't the same person, that is.*

"Never seen her before today," Thomas said. "She might have been there for the tasting, but if she was,

I didn't recognize her. There were so many faces, it would be hard to remember a specific one from the crowd."

"Did you see her?" I asked Tara.

"Sorry," she said. "I wasn't paying close attention to Charles at the time."

It sounded plausible enough, and it jibed with what little I'd seen. "Do you remember what color the woman's hair was?" I asked, turning back to Thomas.

He thought about it a moment and then shook his head. "I don't. I think it might have been a darker color, but like I said, I really wasn't paying them much mind. I only noticed them because Charles laughed."

"Could it have been red?" I pressed.

He spread his hands and gave me an apologetic look.

"We didn't do anything wrong," Tara said. From her tone, I could tell she was done with the conversation. "I don't understand why you were stalking us."

"Stalking you?" I asked. "I . . ." How did I explain my interest in their private conversation without sounding like, well, a stalker?

Thomas must have seen something in my face, because the corners of his mouth quirked in a hesitant smile. "We weren't sneaking away together for any reason other than to talk without having to shout over everyone else," he said.

I hated it, but I felt my face warm. "I didn't think you were," I said.

Tara looked from me to Thomas, as if confused, and then a light bulb seemed to go on. "Oh!" she said. "You thought we were together, as in *together* together?"

"We're not," Thomas said.

"No, we're not," Tara said with an odd lilt to her voice. "Not in that way."

I was too embarrassed to say anything, though I did wonder what exactly she meant by "not in that way." What other way was there?

"Let's talk about it later," Thomas said. "We're still on for dinner tonight?"

That panic from before was back, but I swallowed it before it could make me blurt out something stupid, like *As long as you aren't a murderer.* "Yeah," I said. "Sure."

"Dinner?" Tara asked. "After this, you're going to *dinner?*"

"We're just going out for a bite to eat," Thomas said, before glancing at his watch. "But really, we'd better go before someone catches us. I've got somewhere to be."

Tara, who wasn't wearing a watch of her own, glanced at Thomas's. "Oh, crap! I'm going to be late."

We hurried out of the room. Thankfully, the hotel employee who'd caught me eavesdropping was nowhere to be seen, and we escaped without further witnesses. Tara rushed off with barely a goodbye, while Thomas lingered a moment.

"I get why you did what you did," he said. "If it had been me, I'd probably wonder the same thing."

"I still feel guilty," I said. "I should have trusted you more."

"Why would you?" he asked, smiling. "We barely know one another."

And by the sound of it, it appeared he wanted that to change.

"I hope the police catch who killed Charles and things can get back to normal," he said before I could come up with a response that wouldn't make me sound like an idiot.

"Me too."

"I'll see you later, then, all right?"

"Sounds good."

As Thomas walked off, I couldn't help but wonder why he was so forgiving about my eavesdropping. Was it like he said—he realized I was concerned, and he might have done the same thing himself?

Or was he hoping to ease my mind before he could get me alone at dinner that night so he could silence me once and for all?

Chapter 8

My stomach grumbled, reminding me it was past lunchtime, but after my encounter with Thomas and Tara, I wasn't sure I could keep anything down. Some of it had to do with the murder, of course. Nerves have a way of making everyday activities seem near impossible, including eating.

And let me tell you, I was nervous.

I'd eat eventually, but for now, I decided to go ahead and do what I'd originally come all the way to Maryland to do—I went to a seminar.

The room had seating enough for a good hundred people, but most of the chairs were empty when I entered. The con still might be happening, but many of the guests who hadn't left yet were playing it safe and staying in their rooms. If I was being honest with myself, I should have joined them and waited for this entire thing to blow over, but that sort of thing simply isn't in my nature.

Carmine Wright stood behind a podium at the

front of the room, shuffling notes. Every so often, he'd glance up, brow pinched, as if worried. About how many people were going to attend his session or about the prospects of the murderer popping up again, I wasn't sure. It was likely some combination of both.

I took a seat near the front, figuring I might as well get a good view. The seminar was entitled "The Principles of Flavoring," and I had hoped Carmine, who was presenting, would have samples, but from the look of things, he was simply going to talk.

"Kristina Hancock, is that you?"

I glanced across the aisle to find a face I found vaguely familiar but couldn't quite place staring back at me. She was wearing a wide smile, so I was hoping our previous interactions were positive. The woman was about my age, thin as a pole, with hair spritzed and sprayed like it was still the eighties. Her skirt was short, exposing an impressive length of leg.

"Hi," I said, smiling in what I hoped was a friendly way while my mind raced to place the woman. I knew I'd met her somewhere but wasn't sure if it was in one of the events here at JavaCon or if it was somewhere else. "Call me Krissy. Everyone does."

"Krissy. Of course." She rolled her eyes. "You don't remember me, do you?" Her smile faltered briefly before coming back full force.

The hair. I knew that hair. "It's been a crazy day," I said, as if that explained my mental lapse. "I'm sorry."

"It's Valerie. Valerie Middleton. Well, it was. I divorced my husband a few months back, so it's Kemp again." She tittered. "I keep forgetting. Not about the divorce, mind you, but the name thing. After spending so many years as a Middleton, it's easy to say the wrong thing. I guess I should call myself Valerie Kemp, formerly Middleton. I think it has a ring to it, don't you?"

I stared at her, mouth agape, as she babbled. *Valerie Kemp?* Here? I'd grown up with her. She'd lived just down the street from me while I was a kid in California, and for the most part, she'd made my childhood a living hell.

Valerie had always believed she was the center of the universe. She was the popular kid in school, the girl all the guys wanted to date—or, at least, claimed they did. She had the looks for it, that was for sure, but her personality had left a lot to be desired.

She never paid much attention to anyone outside her clique most of the time. She treated many of the other kids in school like dirt, hardly worth being trod upon. I think most people were invisible to her.

That was, unless you caught her eye at the wrong time.

I was one of those she'd targeted.

"Valerie?" I asked, still not quite sure I believed it. I hadn't seen her since we'd graduated high school. "Why are you here?"

"To learn about all of this." She waved a hand around the room. "I was thinking of opening my own little place, something trendier than what we have back home."

"In California?" I asked. Last I'd heard she was still living in the same old neighborhood after marrying her high school sweetheart, Aaron Middleton—who was apparently now her ex.

"Of course," Valerie said, with an exaggerated eye-roll that might have won her an Oscar if this wasn't real life. "I couldn't imagine anyone wanting to leave the weather and beaches back home." Her implication was that I was stupid for following in Vicki's footsteps and vacating the sun and fun for the bitter winters of the Mideast.

"I opened a place of my own with Vicki," I said, doing my best to play it cool, even though just the sight of Valerie brought back horrible memories of skinned knees and gummy hair. I think this was the first time she'd ever spoken a civil word to me. "You remember Vicki Patterson, right?"

Valerie shrugged. "It sounds familiar." She glanced around the room. "I can't believe so many people left after spending the money to get in here. It's such a waste."

"Someone *did* die."

"That sort of thing happens all the time. I don't see why it should change anything for the rest of us." Valerie sighed and crossed her legs. She was wearing heels that probably cost more than what I made in a month and a blouse to match.

Some things never change.

The doors in the back of the room closed. Valerie turned her attention away from me to focus on Carmine, who cleared his throat at the microphone before tapping it twice.

I stared at Valerie a moment longer before putting her out of mind. She hadn't changed a bit in the years since I'd last talked to her. I hoped that after this little seminar, it would be another fifteen or twenty years before our paths crossed again.

"Welcome to 'The Principles of Flavoring,'" Carmine

said. He glanced around the room once, sighed as if disappointed in the meager showing, and then began speaking.

The next hour was a struggle. Perhaps at another time, in different circumstances, Carmine's lecture—and that's what it was; a lecture—might have been interesting. But as the minutes ticked slowly by, I found myself thinking about my empty stomach or about the murder, not about what he was saying.

And I wasn't the only one who'd lost interest. By the time Carmine wrapped up the seminar and the doors opened again, nearly half the room was yawning. As soon as he said, "Thank you," Valerie and the ten other people in the room popped up and were out the door as if they feared he'd start talking again if they didn't make a run for it.

That left Carmine and me alone. I'd be remiss if I didn't take advantage of the situation.

"That was a good presentation," I said, rising and stretching. At least I managed to suppress the yawn, lest I contradict my own words.

"It was a disaster." Carmine shoved his papers into a briefcase and snapped it closed. "I was so preoccupied about what happened, I found myself droning on like my old college history professor."

From his shudder, it was obvious that wasn't a good thing.

"Charles's murder has put a damper on things, that's for sure."

"It has." He sighed and leaned against the podium. "If I hadn't dumped so much money into this convention, I would have called the entire thing off already. But since we're still up and running, that means no one can demand a refund." He gave me a worried look. "Right?"

"I don't think anyone will," I said, though I wasn't too sure about that. "And I'm pretty sure things will pick up tomorrow after everyone calms down."

He nodded. "Most of the big events are being held tomorrow anyway. Today was all about the tasting, and we all saw how that turned out." He paled slightly before going on. "It should be better tomorrow once everyone realizes that the thing with Charles was a one-time deal."

"I'm sure it will." I paused, switching gears. "Have you heard anything from the police? If they catch whoever killed Charles, then JavaCon can go on like normal." Or, at least, as normally as it could, since someone *had* died. You couldn't simply forget that.

Carmine rubbed at his temples as if thinking about it hurt his head. "They aren't telling me anything." He glanced down at my badge. "Krissy Hancock from Pine Hills."

"That's me." I smiled.

He didn't return the smile. "I know I should be more concerned about what happened to Charles, but I can't help but worry that this whole thing is going to ruin JavaCon's reputation. Our first year and someone dies on the premises. Why couldn't he have . . ." He glanced at me and reddened, as if realizing what he had been about to say and how it might make him look.

"It's all right," I said. "His death has put a lot of pressure on you and the other organizers. Do you have any idea why anyone would want to kill him? I saw you two enter the hotel together, so I assume you knew him pretty well."

"Not really," Carmine said. He ran a finger along the top of the podium as if looking for dust. "He is—was—an acquaintance. Since we'd met at other cons and gatherings, it seemed natural to say hi when I saw him in the parking lot."

"So you weren't friends?" It would explain why he wasn't all that broken up about Charles's death, but somehow, I wasn't buying it.

"No, I'd think not."

I stared at him in silence. Carmine rubbed his fingers together and stared at the top of the podium. After a few seconds, he gave in and went on.

"Charles Maddox was a hard man to like. He always wanted things done his way and would do anything in his power to make sure it happened."

"Like bribing judges?" I asked.

Carmine's eyes went hard. "I take offense to the suggestion I would take a bribe from anyone, let alone Charles Maddox."

"Wynona Kepler seems to think you did."

"Winnie Kepler thinks a lot of things," Carmine said. "She's always been a conspiracy theorist. Every time something happens that she doesn't like, it has to be because someone cheated, not because her stuff wasn't good enough."

"She said Charles stole his coffee blend."

"I know what she said," Carmine snapped. "She has no basis for her argument, just wild accusations." He cleared his throat and smoothed down his shirt as he composed himself. When he spoke again, he was calmer. "I can vouch for the validity of Charles's café mocha. It was his own creation, made from his own blend. No matter what anyone says, it was legit."

I wondered how he could be so sure if they weren't friends. Charles may not have bribed Carmine, but I was definitely getting the impression that there was something more between the two of them.

Could they have been working together?

I wasn't sure if there was much monetary reward in the award, just the exposure the winner would garner afterward. Could Carmine and Charles have come up with the blend together, and that was why it won? Did Carmine plan on capitalizing on it now?

"What's going to happen with the coffee?" I asked. "It was supposed to be featured for the con, right? Does anyone else know how to make it?" I was fishing, but I didn't know how else to ask without coming right out and accusing Carmine of cheating for Charles.

Carmine shook his head. "Charles kept that information close to his chest. No one knew what he was going to bring until he presented it at the tasting. His was the first café mocha I truly thought deserved an award. And now . . ." He closed his eyes a long moment before picking up his things. "If you'll excuse me, I'd best go. There's still much to do."

"Of course." I stepped aside and let Carmine pass. He paused at the door to look back at me. He stared for a pair of heartbeats, then he exited the room.

Carmine was definitely worried about something. Was it solely the fate of JavaCon? Or was there more to it? Like, were my questions hitting a little too close to home? It was something to consider.

I was standing alone in the room, wondering whether Carmine and Charles had been working together all this time, when I realized my pocket was buzzing. I snatched up my phone, but before I could accept the call, the line went dead.

I checked the screen and immediately recognized the number.

It was Beth.

"Crap." I redialed and pressed the phone to my ear. It rang four times before it went to voice mail.

I tried three more times, to the same result. On the last attempt, I left a brief message, apologized for missing her call, and asked her to please call me as soon as she could. I kept my phone in hand in the hope she'd call me right back, but it didn't ring.

Worried that I might have missed something important, I left the room. Carmine was long gone, and the remaining con goers were walking in groups of three or more, as if they were all afraid to walk around without someone to watch their backs.

Shoving my phone back into my pocket, I realized I should be doing the same thing, lest the next time I found myself alone in a room with someone, they turned out to be a killer.

Chapter 9

"I can't believe you saw Valerie Kemp," Vicki said with a shocked shake of her head. "And she and Aaron got divorced? I thought they'd end up together forever. Did she say why?"

"She didn't," I said, taking a bite of my salad. "And I didn't ask."

"I don't blame you. She never was very nice." Vicki shook her head again, this time in wonder. "Valerie Kemp. Wow."

The three of us were sitting in our hotel room, huddled around a small pull-out table eating lunch. Rita absorbed my tale, listening as if she was gearing up to tell someone every last word. Who would she tell? I had no idea. The only people in Pine Hills who knew Valerie were Vicki, me, and my ex, Robert Dunhill.

"I talked with Carmine Wright too," I said, putting all thoughts of Valerie away—hopefully permanently.

"I guess he dumped a lot of money into JavaCon and is worried Charles's murder is going to ruin him."

"I guess that explains why we're still here," Vicki said. "If it had been me, I'd have canceled the whole thing the moment he was found."

"Me too." What really shocked me was the fact that so many people were sticking around. On my way to the room, I passed quite a few people heading toward the convention center. I wasn't sure if it was because they wanted to see who'd killed Charles or if the initial fear and panic had passed.

"That's all fine and dandy, but I heard something that will blow both of your minds," Rita said, leaning forward. "When I heard it, I was downright shocked!"

"What did you hear?" I asked with some trepidation. Rita had a tendency to overreact to most everything. And since she likely felt left out of the gossip, this was her chance to reestablish herself as the gossip queen of our little group.

"Well, I was minding my own business, you see," she said, "when this woman barged straight through the doors as if she owned the entire hotel. She nearly knocked the young man I was talking to over in her haste to get to the cops!"

"She went to the cops?" I asked.

Rita nodded. "Went straight for them the moment she was inside the door, like someone had lit a fire under her and a police officer was the only one who could put it out."

"Was it about Charles?" I asked. I wasn't sure what other reason anyone would have to go to the police here, but I supposed it was possible something else had happened.

"Now, I didn't hear everything, mind you." From the way she said it, I assumed that wasn't entirely true. "The woman was spitting mad and didn't seem to care who heard her. She claimed to be Charles Maddox's wife, if you can believe it!"

"His wife?" Vicki asked. "I didn't know he was married."

"What did we really know about him?" I wondered out loud. I'd only seen the man a handful of times. He hadn't come to the con itself with a woman, as far as I was aware. Had he left his wife at home while he came to the con? It wasn't out of the question, considering Vicki had done the same thing with her husband.

"She demanded she be allowed into Charles's room so she could look through his things," Rita went on. "When the cops tried to get her to calm down, she only yelled louder. And then, when they wouldn't take her to his room, she stormed away, though she didn't leave the way she'd come in."

"Huh." I understood why his wife would be upset about his death, but something about Rita's story didn't sit right with me. Wouldn't she be sobbing instead of yelling? Or was Charles really such a bad person that not even his wife mourned his passing?

"Do you know where she went after she left the cops?" Vicki asked.

Rita smiled. "Let's just say she wasn't too hard to follow. I excused myself from my young suitor and used the skills bestowed upon me by a higher power to see where she was headed. I had a feeling the drama wasn't over. And wouldn't you know it, she went right up to hotel management and demanded a key to Charles's room as if the police hadn't just told her no."

"Did she get one?" I asked.

"They refused, of course," Rita said with a dismissive wave of her hand. "No one is allowed in the room, not even his wife. If I were to guess, the police aren't done in there and don't want an important piece of evidence to up and walk away."

I chewed slowly on a tomato, thinking. Why was Charles's wife so intent on getting into his room?

"What did she look like?" I asked, thinking back to the woman I'd seen him with before his death.

"Well, let's see." Rita tapped her chin. "She was medium height, perhaps a little on the thick side, if you know what I mean." She tapped her hip and gave me a pointed look. "If I were to guess, I'd put her in her forties, but you know how that goes. Some people just don't age properly."

"Red-haired?" I asked. "Wearing a white dress?"

Rita nodded. "Though I do have to wonder if red is her natural color. It looked dyed to me." Another look, this one disapproving. "And she shouldn't have been wearing white, not with that skin. It washed her right out."

My mind was racing. I was positive I'd seen Charles with this woman, though it was possible there were two redheads in white dresses running around. I hadn't gotten the impression they were married, but not all married couples act the same.

Still, it seemed odd to me that she didn't have a key to his room. She might not have come to the con with him, but I know if I was married and my husband showed up, I'd share the room with him. It would not only be cheaper, but far more convenient. Were they fighting, and that was why they were staying somewhere separately? Was she even an official JavaCon guest? Or had she merely stopped in to check on her husband when I'd seen her earlier? If so, could her visit have been a surprise, as in, a concerned wife checking in on a husband she didn't quite trust?

The word "affair" drifted through my mind. Could Charles have been having an affair, and his wife caught him in the act? Tara had said something about running into a woman who was upset with Charles. Could that have been his wife just after she learned he'd been cheating on her?

It would explain why she didn't have a key to his hotel room.

It might also explain why he was murdered.

"I know what you're thinking," Vicki said, eyeing me from across the table.

"I don't know what you mean," I said.

"Uh-huh." She gave me a knowing smile. "You're thinking the wife had something to do with his death. Either she killed him or her presence got him killed."

I shrugged one shoulder and shoved lettuce into my mouth. "Maybe," I said between bites.

"You're hoping it exonerates your man."

"My man?" I nearly choked on the lettuce. "I don't have a man."

Rita and Vicki shared an amused look.

"What are the two of you laughing at?" I swallowed before I choked for real.

"I've seen how you look at that Thomas fellow," Vicki said. "And while he's cute and all, I think you might want to be careful."

" 'Careful'?" I asked. "You're the one who told me to go for it and have some fun."

"Yeah, I did. But that was before someone got murdered."

"He could have done it, dear." Rita rested a hand on my wrist and gave it a gentle squeeze. "A lot of otherwise good men don't know how to control their tempers when they get into a heated argument, you know? It might not have been planned, but it could have happened."

"Didn't you say he had coffee on his shirt?" I'd told Vicki about that earlier and was now regretting it.

"He said it was an accident." The excuse sounded weak, even to my ears.

"It might have been," Vicki allowed. "But what if it wasn't? Do you really think you should be going out with him tonight?"

"It's just for dinner," I said. "We're going to be in the middle of a restaurant with dozens of other people around us. He wouldn't do anything to me with witnesses, even if he *was* the killer." Which I was hoping he wasn't.

"I don't like it," Vicki said. Her good humor had evaporated. She looked worried. "He might seem okay now, but what happens if you do or say something that sets him off? Rita's right; some men can't handle their tempers. What if Thomas can't control his and lashes out at you when you say the wrong thing?"

"I'm sure that won't happen." Though now, my

stomach was churning at the thought. Just because I wanted him to be innocent of the crime didn't mean he was. I mean, I'd caught him sneaking off with Tara Madison. And there *was* the stain to think about. None of that screamed "innocent" to me.

"I'd feel better if I knew you were safe," Vicki said. "We don't know anyone here well enough to let our guard down. It's not like back home where you can call Paul or John to come to your rescue if things get out of hand."

"I don't need them to save me." In fact, Officer John Buchannan would be the last person I called if I needed help. He'd be just as liable to arrest me as look for the real culprit, thanks to our less than stellar relationship. Paul, on the other hand . . .

I sighed, giving in. They were both right, as much as I hated to admit it. "I get your point. It's not safe." Or smart, when you got right down to it.

"If the police catch the killer, then I'm all for you going out on a hot, steamy date," Vicki said. "But until then, it might be better if we stick together."

My heart sank. I hadn't realized until then how much I was looking forward to dinner. There was no possibility of anything long-term happening, yet I felt that if I didn't go, I'd be missing out on something special. It wasn't every day a cute guy asked me out. Who cares if nothing could come of it? It's nice to feel wanted every once in a while.

"I could go with you," Rita said.

I turned to her. "As in a double date?" I asked, wondering who she could find on such short notice. I had a feeling the young man she'd mentioned earlier wasn't much more than some poor sap she'd trapped in a corner.

She shook her head, smiling. "Of course not, dear. I'd go secretly. That way, you could talk to him and do that thing you do to see if he'll tell you anything. If he tries anything he shouldn't, I'll be there to step in and put him in his place."

"Or you could call for help," Vicki said with a pointed look at Rita. "You know, it's really not that bad an idea."

The more we talked about it, the more I warmed to the plan. Having someone watching my back would make me feel a whole lot better. And if she was hiding in the shadows watching, it would keep Rita out of the line of fire if something *did* happen.

"I could choose a place and tell him that's where I want to go," I said. "You could get there before me and find a spot where you can keep an eye on us."

Rita was beaming. "He won't even know I'm there."

I pulled out my phone and did a quick search. "There's a restaurant not far from here called City Perch. I saw it on the way here." I skimmed the website, grimacing. "It's a bit pricey, though."

"What time are you supposed to meet him?" Vicki asked.

"Seven, in the hotel lobby," I said. "If Rita gets there a little before then, she'll have time to get into place before we get there." I had some concerns that with the con going on, it would be packed and we wouldn't be able to get a seat, but if that was the case, I could call the whole thing off and we wouldn't have to worry about it.

Rita was practically bouncing up and down in her chair. "This is so exciting!" she said. She finished off her fries and shoved her trash into a bag. "It's almost like a real stakeout."

Vicki stood. "I'm going to head down and check out more of the con," she said. "You want to come?"

"I'd love to, dear," Rita said. "There's a few things I'd like to do before tonight, if that's okay?"

"Fine by me," Vicki said, before turning to me. "Krissy?"

"You two go," I said. "I want to make a call before I head back down." I'd considered telling Vicki about what was going on at Death by Coffee, but opted against it for now. If things got out of hand back home, Mason would tell her. No sense worrying her now. As far as I knew, the call I'd missed was Beth telling me everything was okay and that Raymond had backed off and apologized.

I'd never known the man to do any such thing, but there's always a first time for everything.

I picked at my salad until both Vicki and Rita were gone. As soon as the door swung closed, I grabbed my phone and dialed.

"Drat," I said as it went to voice mail yet again. I was worried that Beth was avoiding me for some reason. Or worse, that things had escalated and she hadn't been just verbally assaulted by Raymond Lawyer, but physically as well.

I was imagining overturned tables, books everywhere, and food and coffee splattered against the walls.

Needing reassurance, I tried to call Death by Coffee's landline, but no one answered. "It's lunchtime,"

I muttered, glancing at the clock. Okay, so it was past lunch, but if Beth hadn't come back, that left only two or three people to handle the rush and the cleanup afterward. It was no wonder no one answered the phone.

Doing my best to remain calm, I dialed yet another number. This time, my call was answered.

"Phantastic Candies, this is Jules speaking. What sweet can I get you today?"

"Jules," I said, breathing a sigh of relief. I didn't know what I'd have done if no one had answered. Not only was Jules Phan my neighbor, but he was also one of my best friends.

"Krissy! I'm so glad to hear your voice. How's the con?"

"Not bad," I said. There was no way I was going to bring up the murder and worry him needlessly. "How's Misfit?"

"Lance just called me five minutes ago about him," Jules said, laughing. "Apparently, your cat trapped Maestro in the bathroom for twenty minutes before Lance realized what was happening." Maestro was Jules's white Maltese.

"Oh no, I'm sorry," I said. "I'm sure he wouldn't hurt him."

"It's all right. It's kind of funny, actually. Maestro wants to be friends and barks at Misfit constantly, but your cat is having none of it. It's kind of cute to watch."

"That's good," I said, though I was still worried that Maestro would push a little too hard and end up with claw marks on his nose for his effort.

"So, why are you calling?" Jules asked, tone growing serious. "I have a feeling it's not just because you wanted to check up on your cat. You sound worried about something."

"It's Death by Coffee," I said. "With both Vicki and me out of town, I'm concerned."

"Don't be," he said. "It's in good hands."

"I know, but I'd love it if you could check in for me? I tried to call, but no one answered." I left out the trouble with Raymond Lawyer in the hope that it wouldn't amount to anything. "If you could stop by and have someone there call me, I'd really appreciate it."

"Well, I was thinking of taking a break here soon anyway. I could put a sign on the door, head on over to Death by Coffee, and grab something to eat."

"If it wouldn't be too much trouble . . ."

"No, of course not. I completely understand. You worry about your babies when you're away."

If he only knew the half of it. "Thank you, Jules. I'll make it up to you when I get back."

"No need. Your company is enough."

We hung up and I was able to breathe a little easier, though I was still worried something had gone horribly wrong.

But there was nothing I could do about it now except wait. I polished off my salad, deposited the trash in the trash can by the desk, and then gathered my things so I could return to the convention floor.

Chapter 10

The hotel lobby and the convention center were once again hopping by the time I returned downstairs. I doubted people had forgotten about the murder, but since JavaCon was going to continue, it appeared most of the guests had decided to stick around for a little while longer.

I walked the hall with no real direction in mind, hoping to bump into Charles's wife. I hadn't really paid all that much attention to her when I'd seen her with Charles earlier that day, but with Rita's description on top of my hazy memory of her, I thought I'd recognize her if I saw her again.

Unfortunately, there were quite a few redheads in attendance. If she'd changed out of her white dress, there was a good chance I'd look right past her without knowing it.

I wandered aimlessly for a bit but saw no sign of the woman in white; nor did I see Tara or Thomas. I caught a glimpse of Rita once and moved to join her, but I lost her in the crowd before I'd made it much more than a couple of steps her way.

Feeling mildly put out, I decided to put my time to better use.

The vendors' room was small and was packed wall to wall with people selling coffee and coffee-related products. There were pots and cups, of course, as well as shirts and kitchen items decorated in coffee themes. Like the rest of the convention center, the room smelled heavily of coffee, and I found myself browsing each and every table, breathing deeply as I did.

I was debating on whether or not to buy a wall hanging of a grumpy-looking cat holding a mug that said "Talk to me after my coffee" when I heard a voice I recognized.

"I'm thinking of filing an official complaint." Wynona Kepler was standing only a few feet away with two other people I recognized as other competitors from the tasting, but had yet to officially meet. Like always, Wynona looked spitting mad.

"It's not going to matter now," a short, stocky woman with thick glasses and an extremely short haircut said. "They won't take an award from a dead man. It would be just as bad publicity as giving it to him in the first place, so why bother?"

"He doesn't deserve the honor," Wynona said loud enough that everyone in the room could hear. "He cheated. Everyone knows it. I don't understand why everyone is letting it slide!"

I couldn't help it. I wandered over closer so I could hear them better.

"I don't know, Winnie," the man of the group said.

He was short, like the woman, but was thin and had shoulder-length hair in the back. The top of his head was completely bald. "I think Lisa is right. They're not taking the award back and giving it to someone else, no matter who complains. It'd be bad press to take it from a dead man. You should let it go."

"Let it go?" Wynona's face reddened. "Just because he up and died? It's not fair to the rest of us! We worked hard for this, and to have it go to that no-good cheat?" She made a frustrated sound that was nearly a growl. "It's a catastrophe!"

I considered hanging back, but decided I'd get nowhere if I just stood there listening. Gossip is fine and good, but what I needed were facts. The only way I could get them would be to ask direct questions.

"Are you talking about Charles Maddox?" I asked, acting as if I'd simply wandered by and overheard their conversation, which in some ways, I had.

Wynona scowled harder than ever, though she didn't tell me to go away. "Did he cheat you too?" Before I could answer, she did for me. "He probably did. The man cheated every chance he got."

It was clear Wynona truly hated Charles, and I feared I wouldn't be able to get anything useful out of her because of it.

Still, I wasn't going to let this opportunity pass without trying. "I didn't know him," I said. "I met him at the tasting, and I saw him around, but I didn't get the chance to get to know him before he died."

"Lucky you," the man muttered. When I glanced at him, he coughed and looked away.

"His coffee was pretty good," I said, turning my attention back to Wynona. "But I don't think it was good enough to win. Something did seem fishy about the whole thing."

"See!" Wynona nearly shouted it as she threw her arms up into the air. "Everyone sees it! Why won't anyone do anything about it?"

"I think I remember seeing you at the tasting," the woman, Lisa, said. "I never caught your name, though."

"Krissy Hancock." I extended a hand. Lisa hesitated, but ultimately shook. "I own a bookstore café called Death by Coffee."

"Lisa Mitchell, coffee maker." She had an infectious grin. "That's an interesting name for a coffee shop."

"It's from a book, actually." I didn't tell her that the book in question was one of my dad's. I was proud of him, but didn't like feeling like I was riding his coattails. "The name does seem to draw attention to the place." And not always in a good way.

"I bet."

"Horace Yoder," the man said, sticking out his hand. "Like Lisa, I make coffee. If you're in the market for a new supplier . . ." He raised his eyebrows in question.

I shook with Horace. "It's why I came."

He grinned. I could see the glimmer of a potential sale in his eye.

Next to us, Wynona glowered about the room as if searching for someone to blame since Charles was no longer around to accuse.

"Did you know Charles well?" I asked the group in general.

"I didn't know him at all until he won the competition," Horace said. "I never expected to win myself, so I didn't pay him much mind, to be honest. I came here for the experience, and the hope that a few people might be interested in my coffee after tasting it."

I tried to remember what Horace's coffee had tasted like, but came up blank. "I'd love to try another sample sometime," I said.

"I can make that happen." He beamed.

I turned to Lisa. "How about you? Did you know Charles?"

"My wife and I met him once before," she said. "It was at another convention, a year or so ago." She frowned as she thought about it. "It might have been two years now. Seems like time flies by faster and faster the older I get."

"Tell me about it," Horace said, running a hand over his bald pate.

"What was your impression of him?" I asked.

Lisa grimaced. "Let's just say he didn't care that I was with another woman at the time. The guy was rude, and didn't take no for an answer."

"You mean, he . . ."

Her eyes widened briefly, then she smiled. "No. He was all talk. He kept flirting, asking if I'd come back to his room with him so he could show me something. I didn't have to ask to know what he meant, and had no intention of following him anywhere. Once I walked away, I think he forgot all about me, because he never bothered me again."

I glanced at Wynona, who was just about grinding her teeth. She looked like a dog in desperate need of something to chew.

She noticed me looking and grouched, "Of course

I knew him. The man was everywhere. He showed up at any and every coffee event he could find, much to the annoyance of everyone involved. He always tried worming his way into the good graces of all the people who mattered, but I think most everyone saw through him."

I took a step away from Wynona. Every sound out of her mouth was harsh and full of venom. Spittle flew as she snapped off each word like it offended her. I don't know if it was too much coffee or if she was naturally high-strung, but I felt as if she could use some serious relaxation time.

"You claimed he bribed the judges," I said to her. "What makes you think that?"

"Bribed them, extorted them." She glanced around, then mercifully lowered her voice when she continued. "I think he had something on a few of the judges and used that to get them to vote for him."

"Are you seriously saying he blackmailed them?" Horace asked. "You can't truly believe that."

"Would you put it past him?" Wynona asked, looking from face to face. "You saw what he was like. I saw him cozying up to the judges ahead of the event. And we're not talking friendly banter either. There was something going on, and I bet it had to do with whatever he knew."

I thought back to when I had seen him with a couple of the judges. It was hard to say if he'd been bribing them or simply trying to win them over, but I never got the impression that he was blackmailing any of them.

Then again, I hadn't known who any of them were at the time. And neither Clint nor Carmine had appeared happy about their conversations with Charles. *Could it really be blackmail?* It was something to go on, at least.

"Come on, Winnie," Lisa said. "You're grasping. I agree that he shouldn't have won, but different people have different tastes. Maybe the judges liked his coffee best. It doesn't have to be a big conspiracy."

Even as Lisa spoke, Wynona was shaking her head. "There's more to it than that. He was blackmailing them." This time when she said it, she sounded far more convinced of the fact. "The award should be stripped from him and given to someone who actually deserves it."

Horace laughed. "Like who? You?" He shook his head and started to walk away. "I think I'm going to find somewhere to sit down. This is far too much drama for me."

Lisa looked like she wanted to join him, but decided to remain. "Even if he bribed them or blackmailed them, I think we should leave it alone," she said. "You don't have proof of anything, and stirring it up will only make everyone miserable. I'd like to enjoy the last few days of the con if at all possible."

"Besides," I added. "There's Charles's wife to think about."

Both Wynona and Lisa looked at me. It was Wynona who spoke. "His wife?"

"That's what I was told," I said. "She showed up a few hours ago, demanding to be let in to Charles's room. I guess she wants to get his things, but the police won't let her."

"I didn't know he was married," Lisa said, a thoughtful expression on her face. I could tell she was wondering if he had been married when he'd hit on her all those years ago. "I guess I did see him talking to a woman before we set up. Maybe it was her."

"A redhead?" I asked.

"No, this one was a brunette. Pretty. They were standing really close, noses nearly touching. I didn't pay close enough attention to them to know if they were flirting or kissing or were just whispering. Heck, they could have been arguing, for all I know. It was none of my business, quite frankly."

I wondered if this was the same woman Tara had seen in the hospitality room, the one who'd been angry with Charles after the tasting, or if this was yet another woman he'd been cozying up to.

"I wouldn't put it past him to cheat on his wife," Wynona said. "I didn't even know he was married." She crossed her arms and scowled all the harder. "To think, he had the nerve to flirt with *me!*"

"He flirted with you?" I asked.

She must have heard the disbelief in my voice, because she said, "It wasn't here at JavaCon, but at the last event we both attended. This was, I'd say, about three months ago. He tried to convince me to go to his room, as if I'd simply jump into bed with him. I didn't even *like* him, yet that didn't stop him from trying."

I studied her, wondering how much truth there was to her story. Just because she didn't like him now didn't mean she hadn't been fond of him before.

"He was always hitting on someone, I suppose,"

Wynona said. "Why, I remember a con a few years back when I caught him in a dark corner with another man."

"Flirting?" Lisa asked.

Wynona shrugged. "Probably. I didn't think much of it then, but who knows. The guy was as sleazy as they come. If he thought it would get him ahead somehow, I wouldn't put it past him to try to sleep with everyone here."

I wondered if that was true. Could Charles have been sleeping with multiple people and his wife found out? Could Wynona, for all her complaints about him, be jealous? Just because she acted like she hated Charles from the start, that didn't necessarily make it true. If she'd found out he'd been sleeping around, *and* that he was already married, she could very well have killed him in a jealous rage.

"I'd better get going," Lisa said. "Chloe is probably looking for me. She's paranoid after what happened, and honestly, I don't blame her."

"It was nice to meet you," I said, and I meant it. Lisa seemed like a genuinely nice person.

"You too, Krissy." She glanced at Wynona, who didn't seem inclined to say goodbye, before she walked away.

"No one ever wants to do what's right," Wynona said, eyes searing holes into Lisa's back. "They're willing to let things slide, just as long as it doesn't interfere with their petty lives."

"But that's not in your nature, is it?" I asked.

Wynona shot me a look. "No, it's not."

Her threat to Charles once more drifted through my mind. "You said Charles would regret cheating to win." I tried not to make it sound like I was accusing her of anything—yet how do you say something like that and *not* make it an accusation?

Wynona didn't catch on. "He got what he deserved." Her jaw worked a moment before she added, "Though I suppose murdering a man for cheating does take it a bit far."

Ya think? I remembered something else she'd said before she'd stalked off the stage. "What about the recipe for his café mocha?" I asked. "Do you truly believe he stole it?"

"I know he did. Charles never did anything the honest way in his life."

"But do you have proof?" I asked. When she glared at me, I added, "If you did, you could take it to Carmine. With proof in hand, he'd be more likely to consider revoking Charles's award. He'd almost have to."

Wynona's expression turned contemplative. "Do you think that'd work?"

"It couldn't hurt to try," I said. "If you have proof that he cheated, what else could he do?" And I was hoping that the proof would also lead to whoever murdered him.

"Proof." Wynona tapped a nail on her chin. "I need to find proof."

I found it both disappointing and unsurprising that she didn't already have anything on him. I had a feeling Wynona Kepler often leapt to conclusions based on nothing more than bad feelings.

Which made me wonder if any of her theories held any merit or if she was, as Charles had put it, "a sore loser."

"I need . . ." Wynona looked at me, eyes narrowing, like she'd just realized I was still standing there. "Thank you for your input." She abruptly spun and walked away.

"Glad to have been of help," I muttered. I wasn't sure if I was happy about putting an idea into Wynona's head, but it was too late to do anything about it now. I only hoped she wouldn't go and do something stupid. I knew without a shadow of a doubt that it would somehow come crashing back down on my head if she did.

Still, I was glad we'd talked. I was getting a better grasp on who might want to kill Charles and why.

That wasn't to say I knew who did it. There were quite a few suspects, many of them with multiple reasons to be angry with Charles.

The more I learned about the man, the more I realized that finding his killer wasn't going to be easy.

I left the vendors' room, feeling as if there was no chance anyone, let alone little old me, would ever figure out who killed Charles Maddox. There were too many suspects, too many reasons to kill the man. I didn't envy Detective Kimble in the slightest.

I stepped into the main hall and debated on what to do. I wanted to find Vicki and Rita and spend some time with them, but wasn't sure where they were. I supposed I could text one of them, but if they were in a seminar or workshop, they wouldn't answer their phones.

It was then that my eyes fell on a redheaded woman talking to one of the cops in a way that was anything but friendly. She was wearing a white dress,

and by the way she was flailing her arms about, it
looked like she was about to explode.

Charles's wife? I wondered. It was the same woman
I'd seen him with earlier, so I found it likely.

She stomped a foot when the cop shook his head.
The man was clearly exasperated by her, but was
doing a good job of not losing his cool. Though I
could tell by the way his hand kept inching toward
his gun that if she continued to press him, he would-
n't keep his calm for much longer.

The woman shouted something at the cop, and
for a second, I thought she might rear off and slap
him. She seemed to think better of it at the last moment, then she spun on her heel and stormed away.

I thought about what to do for half a second before I gave chase.

Chapter II

"**E**xcuse me, I'm sorry," I said, bumping into a couple walking side by side, taking up nearly the entire hallway.

Charles's wife was ahead, smoothly sliding past other con goers without touching anyone, yet I seemed to run into every single one as I followed in her wake.

The couple glared at me as I passed. At least they didn't say anything nasty like the last woman I'd bumped into. Some of the things she'd said would make a sailor blush.

Much to my relief, Charles's wife came to a stop in the hotel lobby. She whipped out her phone, dialed, and then pressed it to her ear, foot tapping impatiently as she waited for someone to answer.

I hurried to catch up to her in the hope of eavesdropping on part of her conversation. It was none of my business, really, but I wanted to hear, just in case it had something to do with her husband's death.

"Watch it, lady," an old man said, poking me in the side with his cane as I tried to slip past him.

"Sorry," I said, though I hadn't bumped into him. He must have seen me bouncing around like a pinball and decided to be proactive in preventing the same from happening to him.

Charles's wife said maybe five words before hanging up. By the time I reached her, her phone was already back into her purse and she looked as if she might restart her power walk.

"Excuse me," I called, nearly out of breath. "Ms. Maddox!"

The redhead took a few steps before her name seemed to register. She turned to me. "Yes? Is this about Charles's things? If you could have them brought to my room, it would be much appreciated."

"I don't work here," I said, only mildly offended. I supposed someone might mistake my con badge for a name tag and my semi-dressy shirt and pants as work attire.

No, scratch that. Even the densest person would be able to tell the difference. We were wearing the same badge around our necks, though hers was turned so her name faced inward.

"Oh." She frowned. "Then you aren't here to help me."

"No," I said. "But I did know Charles briefly," I hurriedly added as she was about to turn away.

"I see." She glanced past me, brow furrowing. "No one here understands what I'm going through. They treat me like an outsider." She huffed. "I deserve some respect, you know? He was my husband, after all."

"I truly am sorry for your loss," I said. I might not have liked Charles all that much, but that didn't mean I was happy he was dead. Nor did I think his wife should be mistreated because of her husband's misdeeds. Who knew what she'd gone through living with a man like that?

"That's all well and good," she said. "But that doesn't help me one bit. Sorry means nothing when the police refuse to release his things to me."

"Ms. Maddox . . ."

"Tatiana, please."

"Tatiana," I amended. "Did they say why they weren't releasing them to you?"

She shrugged. "I wish I knew. I'm his wife!" She said the last loud enough so everyone could hear. "You'd think that would mean something. I have every right to his things. In fact, since we are married, they are rightfully mine as it is. The police are keeping *my* things from me! Can you believe it?"

"Don't you have access to his room?" I asked. Something about her bothered me. It was like she was trying especially hard to convince me she was Charles's rightful heir. I once more wondered if their marriage was on the rocks, or if they were recently divorced and she was trying to backtrack on it now that he was dead.

She blinked at me, a condescending smile on her face. "Why would I?"

"Because you two were married?"

She laughed, as if I'd told an uproariously funny joke. "Why should that matter? This is a *hotel*, not our home. It's not like I can just walk in whenever I want."

"I know that," I said, trying hard not to grow angry with her. "I just figured that the two of you would share a room."

"Me? Here?" She laughed again. "I don't think so."

It was my turn to blink at her. "You're here now."

"True. But Ms. . . . ?" She frowned, as if just now realizing I hadn't introduced myself.

"Hancock. Krissy," I provided.

"Ms. Hancock, I did not come to this event. I never go to these things with him if I can help it. I am only here because of what happened to Charles. As soon as I get what I want, I'm leaving."

"You have a badge," I pointed out.

"A necessity if I want to remain." She put a hand on it, as if making sure it was still there.

"Do you live in town?" I asked, thinking it strange how quickly she'd gotten here if she hadn't come for the con.

"No," Tatiana said. Her gaze darted around the room. "I was staying at another hotel. I got a room here *after* he died."

"Why not just stay here if you're staying in town?" I asked, genuinely curious. If she'd traveled to Maryland with Charles, then it made sense they'd stay in the same hotel, even if they were doing different things. Why pay for two rooms when you can just get one?

"There's nothing suspicious about it," she said, as if reading my mind. "I had matters of my own to attend to. Staying here would have been a hassle. Charles would have wanted me to come with him to his silly events. Honestly, I don't have the interest."

I wasn't buying it. Tatiana was lying to me, and I

had no idea why. I really wanted to ask her if she and Charles were having marital problems, but figured it would be pushing my luck. The police could ask that sort of question and get away with it. Me, not so much.

"I was absolutely shocked when I heard someone killed my poor Charles," she went on. "He was very dear to me." She put her hand over her heart, despite the hollowness of the words. "He'd called me earlier to tell me he won the taste test, and he was in such good spirits at the time. I can't believe someone would hurt him." This time, she wiped away an imaginary tear. "If only I'd been here, perhaps he would still be alive."

It was all an act. Nothing out of her mouth was genuine. No wonder the police weren't letting her anywhere near his room.

I could have let it go, but I decided to press her in the hope she might crack.

"I'm pretty sure I saw you with Charles earlier," I said. "Before his death."

"Me?" Her face reddened to match her hair. "It couldn't have been me. I didn't arrive until after Charles died."

My memory might not be top-of-the-line, but I could have sworn she was the woman I'd seen talking to Charles after he won the competition. I might not have gotten a close look at her, but the outfit was the same, as was the hair.

The question then became, why continue to lie?

The obvious answer was, of course, that she'd killed Charles and was doing a poor job of covering her tracks. If she had indeed been here earlier, she had to realize that other people would have seen her, not just me. It wasn't like they'd been tucked away in some dark hallway where no one would see them. They'd been standing right out in the open. Even Clint had seen them together.

While it was entirely possible there could be another woman running around the con somewhere with red hair and a white dress who knew Charles Maddox well enough that they'd walk off together, I doubted it.

"I must have been mistaken, then," I said, not wanting to push her *too* hard. "Since he won, I thought that maybe if it *was* you, you were here to celebrate his win with him."

"It wasn't me." Then her face darkened. "It should be mine." Tatiana stomped a foot like a petulant child. "That's how marriage works, doesn't it? What's his is mine and so forth? Do you know how much money he could make off of his coffee blend now that it won a competition? It shouldn't go to waste just because he's dead. How does that honor his memory?"

Now we're getting somewhere. Money has a tendency to bring out the worst in people, and it appeared Tatiana Maddox was no different. "Do you plan on selling the recipe?" I asked.

"I would if I had it." Her eyes darted to the desk, where hotel staff were watching us. She raised her voice. "But they won't let me into his room to retrieve it."

"Wait," I said. "You don't have a copy of it back home?"

She shook her head and gave one more good

glare to the staff before turning back to me. "Charles kept that part of his life separate from me. He preferred to work alone and didn't tell me much of anything; not that I asked him about it all that much. It's why I'm so upset that they're not letting me have his things. What if someone else comes along and steals it?"

"I'm sure that won't happen."

"How do you know? The police steal things all the time. That coffee blend is mine by right. Everything Charles owned belongs to me!" She moved as if she might stomp her foot again, but caught herself. "I think these people are trying to keep it for themselves, to prevent me from capitalizing off of my husband's success."

Or his death, I thought, none too kindly. I was starting to think of Tatiana in the same light as her late husband.

"I'm sure it'll all come to you in time," I said. "The police need to go through his belongings just in case there is evidence in them. Once they determine whether or not anything in his room will help find the killer, they'll turn his things over to you."

Tatiana huffed. "What could possibly be in his room that would help? He died in the ballroom, didn't he? The evidence would be there."

I didn't want to bring up the fact that if he'd been sleeping around, there'd likely be evidence in his room, and quite possibly on his bed, so I remained silent.

"You know what?" Tatiana said, her gaze returning to the desk. "I think it's time I really put my foot down. I've been ignored long enough." She glanced at me, sniffed, and then walked toward the front desk. "Excuse me," she said. "I'd like to speak to your manager."

"Again, ma'am?" one of staff said. He was young, and looked about as excited to talk to Tatiana as he would an ax murderer.

"Yes, again!" Tatiana's hands found her hips. "Don't make me get a police officer over here to make you do your job. I'll do it, you know!"

The staff member heaved a sigh and said, "One moment." He turned and slipped into a room behind the desk. Tatiana tapped her foot while she waited.

Dismissed, and with no reason to hang around the lobby, I returned to the convention floor, leaving Tatiana to harass the staff. My mind, however, was on anything but coffee.

Well, that's not entirely true. I wondered about Charles's coffee. Had he stolen the blend, like Wynona insisted? Did his wife know about the theft? Was that why she was so intent on getting hold of the recipe? Not because she wanted to make money off it, but because she wanted to destroy evidence that Charles wasn't on the up-and-up?

I was finding it hard to feel sympathetic toward her. It was obvious their marriage wasn't a close one. And while I understood her desire to get her hands on Charles's things, she didn't seem like she cared all that much about what had happened to her husband.

I spent the next hour milling about, not sure what to do. I didn't think I could sit through a seminar or workshop without my mind wandering, and when I walked up to a tasting station, I found I couldn't bring myself to try the coffee, since it was a café mocha.

There was something going on here at JavaCon, and there was more to it than just a murder.

I was headed back toward the hotel lobby, thinking it might be time to go back to my room to get ready for my dinner date with Thomas, when I noticed Tara sitting alone by one of the big windows. She was staring outside, both hands balled into tight fists.

I veered off and headed her way. "Hey, Tara," I said. "How are you holding up?"

She jumped and sucked in a sharp breath. "I'm sorry," she said. Her entire body eased, though her fists remained bunched. "I was lost in thought and didn't hear you approach."

"It's all right. I think we're all a bit jumpy right now."

She gave me a weak, thankful smile. "It's hard. Every time I close my eyes, I see Charles lying there and wonder if I could have done something to help him."

I sat down in the chair next to her and rested a hand on her arm. I gave it a gentle squeeze. "You can't think like that," I said. "Chances are good that when you found him, he was already dead."

"I know, but . . ." She shook her head. "I keep wondering if I saw something. Like, when I was going in, was someone else leaving? Or was there someone else in the room?" She made a frustrated sound. "They could have still been in there. If I would have taken my time and checked him, then perhaps I would have seen the killer."

"And then they might have come after you," I said, causing Tara to pale. "I don't say it to scare you, but to let you know that I don't hold any of this against you. No one does."

Tara gave me another weak smile. "Well, I'm glad someone doesn't."

"What do you mean by that?" I asked. "Is someone blaming you?"

Tara looked out the window. She was silent for a long few moments, then she shrugged. "I don't know. I guess not. It just feels like everyone is staring at me, judging me. I don't know what to do. I keep thinking I should get on a plane and just get out of here, away from everyone's accusatory eyes, and away from all of this." She gestured toward the milling con guests.

"I totally understand. I feel the same way sometimes." And then, just to see how she'd react, I said, "I talked to Charles's wife."

Her brow knit together and she glanced at me out of the corner of her eye. "He was married?"

"Everyone keeps asking that," I said. "No one seemed to know he was married until his wife showed up."

"If he was, I never knew about it." Tara frowned. "Then again, I didn't know him well enough to care. He was just one of those people you met, but never truly got to know. Never wanted to, really."

"His wife seems more concerned about obtaining his coffee recipe than she is about his death," I said.

"I'm not surprised. Charles was a hard man to like. What little I knew of him told me that he didn't have a lot of close friends."

I'd gotten the same impression. I might have seen him talking to quite a few people, but none them had seemed happy about it.

"You said you saw a woman who told you where to find Charles," I said. "Now that you've had some time to think about it, do you know why she was upset with him? Did she say or do anything that would give you a hint?"

"No," Tara said. "But I did get the impression it was personal."

"Could they have been sleeping together?" I asked. "Maybe she found out about his wife and they fought."

"Couldn't say for sure, but with how she was crying and cursing his name, I wouldn't doubt it. She was really upset."

"Did you ever learn the woman's name?" I asked. "Or have you run into her since then?"

"No, I haven't," Tara said. "All I remember was she had brown hair, was about my height, and was wearing a guest badge. I hadn't seen her before, so she wasn't one of the taste test competitors."

I wondered if the police had talked to the woman yet. She might have been the last person to see Charles alive. And while that didn't mean she had killed him, she might have seen or heard something that would point to the person who had.

Tara's gaze drifted out the window, to the falling leaves. I decided it best to leave her to it.

I stood. "I'd better go," I said. "I'm due to meet Thomas in a little over an hour and need to get ready."

Tara actually managed a smile, though it didn't

quite reach her eyes. "Thomas is pretty excited about dinner," she said. An air of melancholy hung over the words. "He's talked about you all day."

I blushed, flattered. "We're just getting something to eat," I said. "I told him he could invite you if he wanted."

She glanced up at me, her smile turning sad. "That's all right. I don't think I could eat much anyway." Her hands moved to her stomach as if she might be sick.

"I'll see you later, okay?" I said, keeping my voice gentle. Tara seemed especially fragile, and I was afraid that if one more thing happened to her, she might break.

"Have fun." She looked back toward the leaves.

I hesitated a moment more, wondering if there was something I could say that would make her feel better, and then I turned and walked away. I could spend all day trying and only make things worse.

I got onto the elevator. My eyes found Tara across the room. As if she could feel my gaze, her head turned my way, and I could swear I saw a tear in her eye. Before I could be sure of it, however, the doors slid closed, and I was on my way upstairs to prepare for my dinner date with a man who very well might be a cold-blooded killer.

Chapter 12

My foot jiggled up and down at a pace that was quickly becoming exhausting, yet I couldn't stop. There were only a few people in the lobby of the hotel, and none of them were paying me any mind. Somehow, that only made my nervousness worse.

It was five until seven, and I had yet to see Thomas. Rita had left nearly fifteen minutes ago. She'd promised me she wouldn't let anything get by her, but I knew Rita. It wouldn't take much to draw her attention away from me, especially if it was a juicy piece of gossip. I had to trust she'd keep an eye on me, but I had my doubts. I might have been excited about it before, but now that the time was here, I was reconsidering our plan, and most of all, the dinner date.

And it wasn't just because of the murder. I was single, that was true, yet I felt like I was cheating on someone by going out with Thomas. My last boyfriend, Will

Foster, was in Arizona for a new job, and whenever I thought about him, I found I missed him, but I wasn't unhappy. He deserved that shot, even if it meant the end of our relationship.

No, it wasn't the thought of Will that made my stomach do slow flips and my heart throb painfully.

It was Paul.

Paul Dalton, Pine Hills police officer. We went on one date, one that ended up as an unmitigated disaster, yet I held that date close to my heart. Every time I saw him, I felt like I'd missed out on something with him; like if I were to finally give him a chance, things could work out. And now that both of us were single, it appeared as though we *could* try again if we wanted to.

This is just a friendly date. I had to keep reminding myself of that. Nothing could come of any relationship with Thomas. I didn't even know where he lived, let alone what he did when he wasn't making coffee. We were merely going to go out, have dinner, and then go our separate ways. There was nothing wrong with that.

Unless he was a murderer, of course. That'd put a damper on any relationship.

I stood up and stretched. My legs were stiff from all the walking I'd been doing, yet I found myself pacing. Thomas had yet to arrive and I was starting to wonder if there was a reason for that.

Something could have come up and he could already be miles from the convention center. He didn't have my number, let alone my room number, so it wasn't like he had any way of letting me know he had to bail. It had been hours since I'd last seen him at

JavaCon. Anything could have happened in that time.

The elevator dinged, causing my gaze to swivel that way. A man got off, but he was older than Thomas, and not nearly as good-looking.

I deflated, my heart resuming a more normal pace.

Calm down, Krissy. I wanted to believe Thomas innocent of Charles's murder, yet there were so many questions, I was having a hard time dismissing him as a suspect. Did he really spill coffee on himself, or had it gotten there when he'd struck Charles? Where was he between the spill and when I saw him afterward? Why did he really sneak off with Tara, and what were they actually talking about? I wasn't convinced they'd told me the whole story.

Voices broke through the questions running through my head. I looked back and noticed two of the judges, Pierre Longview and Dallas Edmonds, walking toward the elevators. They were deep in conversation, but were keeping their voices low. Neither looked happy.

Glancing around, I checked to make sure Thomas still wasn't there, and then I made a snap decision.

I hurried over to the two judges before they could reach the elevators. "Hi, Pierre, Dallas," I said in my peppiest voice. "My name's Krissy Hancock. I was at the tasting earlier today."

Both Pierre and Dallas grimaced at the same instant. "A pleasure," Pierre said in a way that was as much a dismissal as it was a greeting.

Dallas didn't respond other than to give me the slightest of nods.

"It's crazy what happened, isn't it?" I asked, playing it off like I was merely an overexcited guest. "The guy who wins up and dies." I tsked. "And they're saying it's murder."

"It is a tragedy," Dallas said, though she didn't sound too upset by Charles's death. She was far from the first person who'd acted that way.

"And I'm sure it won't happen again," Pierre added. "You should have nothing to worry about. Enjoy the rest of the con."

Both he and Dallas moved as if they might slip past me and to the elevators, but I stepped in front of them, barring their path.

"I was surprised he won, to be honest," I said. "His coffee wasn't bad, but I thought there were a few others that were better."

"You don't say," Pierre said. He shared a look with Dallas, as if my thoughts confirmed what they'd both been thinking.

"I preferred a couple others myself," Dallas said. "But since it wasn't our decision alone, Mr. Maddox emerged victorious. These things happen when you have a panel of judges rather than just one or two."

I glanced back. Still no Thomas. "Can you believe how some of the competitors reacted?" I asked, still playing it off like I was half-clueless. My eyes were wide, as if the mere thought of Wynona's reaction shocked me to the core. "I thought Ms. Kepler was going to attack him right then and there."

Pierre cleared his throat and once more looked at Dallas. It was obvious my line of questioning was making them both nervous. Nervous because they knew something? Or nervous because we were talking about a man's death? It was hard to tell.

"Not everyone agreed with the decision," Dallas said. She spoke slowly, carefully, as if measuring each word.

I'm onto something, I realized. And there was something in their expressions, the way they answered, that told me that if I asked the right question, in the right way, they'd tell me exactly what I wanted to know.

"I sure didn't," Pierre said. "I was partial to Wynona Kepler's coffee myself, as much as it pains me to admit it."

"Do you think it's true what she said?" I asked. "Did Charles cheat?"

Yet another shared look. Pierre's expression hardened when Dallas gave him a quick, subtle shake of her head.

Okay, fine, play it that way. I dropped the act. "I was told by a few people that Charles bribed the judges," I said. "I saw him talking with both Clint Sherman and Carmine Wright before the tasting. Wynona saw one of those conversations as well, and she wasn't happy about it. She swears Charles must have gotten to the both of them, if not all the judges."

Pierre looked upward, as if looking for strength. Dallas's jaw worked a moment, and then she relented.

"Charles Maddox did attempt to bribe us," she said. "He came up to each of us individually, asking for our backing."

"We refused," Pierre said.

"I thought the others had more sense about them and would turn him down out of hand," Dallas went on. "But apparently I was wrong."

"Did he have a lot of money to offer?"

"It wasn't about the money," Pierre said. "He offered me a pittance, really."

"And it wasn't *just* money he offered," Dallas added with a grimace.

From her expression, and from what Wynona and Lisa had told me earlier, I could guess what it was he'd offered her. It made me wonder what exactly he'd used to convince the other judges to vote for him. I had seen him with Carmine and Clint, and I assumed he'd gotten together with Evaline as well. Had he slept with Evaline to earn her vote? Or had money been involved?

"What about blackmail?" I asked. "Wynona thinks he might have had something on some of the judges, pressured them into voting for him."

Dallas sighed. "He had nothing on Pierre or me, which was why he couldn't sway us," she said. "Evaline wouldn't have been hard to convince, not if he offered her the right thing. She's been . . . lonely."

Pierre shook his head sadly. "It's a shame, really. Her husband was such a nice man."

"He died?" I asked.

"A long time ago," Dallas said. "She still mourns him, though many of us think it is time she moved on."

"But with Charles?" Pierre said with a shudder. "I can't imagine."

I hadn't gotten a chance to talk to Evaline Cobb yet, but from what little I'd seen of her, she seemed nice enough. I couldn't see her with Charles either. "What about Clint and Carmine?"

Pierre leaned past me and pressed the button for the elevator. "There's not much to say about them."

"Didn't all five of you organize JavaCon together?" I asked.

"We did," Dallas said. "But this whole thing is really Carmine's baby. He planned everything from the start, but couldn't do it on his own. He needed extra support, so the rest of us jumped in with him."

"He has more at stake than the rest of us when it comes to JavaCon's success," Pierre said. "He dumped everything he had into it."

Which jibed with what he'd told me. "But why accept a bribe from Charles?" I asked. "If people found out about it, it would tarnish the con's reputation."

"Exactly," Dallas said. "It's why I was so shocked when he let Charles sway him. I know for a fact Carmine doesn't care for café mochas. He doesn't like chocolate of any sort, actually. It makes him sick to his stomach."

"I don't even think he tasted it, to be honest," Pierre said.

Which meant Wynona was right; Charles *had* used underhanded tactics to win. It was possible Carmine had played favorites, not because he thought Charles's coffee was better, but because they were friends. Bribes and blackmail didn't need to play into it at all.

While that might have been the case, I was having a hard time believing it. Nothing in either man's demeanor when I saw them together told me they were friends. And I had a feeling that if they were, Wynona would have screamed favoritism the moment Charles's name came out of Carmine's mouth at the tasting.

The elevator pinged and the doors slid open.

"What do you think happened to Charles?" I hurriedly asked. A small group of people were making their way off the elevator, which meant I had only a few moments left.

Pierre chose not to answer. He waited for the car to empty and then stepped inside.

Dallas followed him in, but she at least responded. "If you want to know that, you'll have to talk to someone who was there."

The doors slid closed, and they were gone.

I stared at the doors, mind racing. It appeared Charles *had* cheated. Did that mean Pierre and Dallas had a reason to kill him? If JavaCon's reputation was dinged, it would inevitably come back on all of them, not just Carmine.

But was that enough of a reason to kill a man? It sure didn't seem like it.

"Krissy! Don't go. I'm here!"

I jumped about a foot into the air and spun to find Thomas jogging into the lobby from the direction of the convention center.

"I wasn't getting on," I said, stepping away from the elevator as if to prove it. "I saw some people I knew and wanted to say hi."

He smiled, seeming to accept my explanation. "I'm sorry I'm late. I was setting up and lost track of time."

"That's okay," I said. His late arrival had given me a chance to talk to two people I otherwise might not

have had the chance to meet. "I haven't been waiting
long."

"That's good." He looked me up and down. "You
look great."

I blushed. When I got changed for the dinner
date, I'd considered dressing down as a way to prove
to myself it wasn't a *real* date. I'd even pulled a Death
by Coffee shirt on before changing my mind and re-
placing it with a nice light blue blouse. I was glad I
had made the switch.

"You do too," I told him, and I meant it. Thomas
was wearing a button-down shirt and slacks that went
well with his eyes.

"Are you ready to go?" he asked. His smile was
wide and a bit mischievous.

"I am," I said. "There's a restaurant called City
Perch not far from here. It sounds interesting and I
thought that it might be fun to give it a try."

Thomas glanced toward the doors leading out
into the night, then shook his head. "Actually, I have
a better idea."

My heart just about stopped in my chest. "What do
you mean?"

"Well, I had a chance to think about it earlier
today. It's not like we're going to get another chance
to do this once the con ends. I know this is just dinner, no strings attached, but I thought it would be
nice to make the meal special."

"Special?" My mouth went dry. "I thought we were
going to get dinner."

"We are," Thomas said, gently taking my arm. "But
why wait half the night for a table at a place that's

likely packed when we can go somewhere where we'll get seated right away?"

He led me past the doors, toward the convention center. My brain was screaming at me to stop him, to pull away and demand he take me to where Rita was currently waiting for our arrival.

Yet my mouth refused to work. I let him lead me from the lobby without so much as a word of protest.

"I've got it all worked out," he said. "No crowds, no noise."

"Sounds great," I said.

He glanced at me, one corner of his mouth lifted in a grin. "Where we're going, no one will disturb us."

Chapter 13

"Here we are," Thomas said, ushering me over to a table that had been set up in one of the large rooms in the convention center. It was covered with a white tablecloth and held a bowl of salad, two wineglasses, and a corked bottle of wine.

"No one else is here," I said, my nervousness growing. Only a few of the room's lights were on, giving us enough light to eat by, but leaving everything else in gloom. I supposed I should be glad he hadn't opted to dine by candlelight only.

"That's the point," Thomas said, pulling out a chair for me. "I figured after spending the day around so many people, you might like something more private. I know I could use a little quiet after today's madness."

I hesitated only a moment before sitting.

A napkin lay folded on the table. I picked it up and spread it over my lap to hide my nervousness. Even if there hadn't been a killer running around, I

would have been on edge. This was definitely looking more like a real date than I'd anticipated.

"What's on the menu?" I asked. I was happy to
note there was no tremble to my voice, despite the
way my heart thudded in my chest.

Thomas beamed as he rounded the table. He
scooped salad into a bowl in front of me, and then
some into his own bowl. "I figured we'd start with
salad, obviously," he said. "Wine?" He picked up the
bottle.

"Water, if you have some." I didn't want to cloud
my judgment by drinking. I rarely drank as it was,
and wine often hit me hard. And while a glass might
not affect me too much, it was probably best to avoid
it entirely, just in case.

Thomas's face fell briefly before his smile returned. "Of course. I'll be right back." He turned
and hurried across the room, to a door opposite
where we came in. He paused to flash me a nervous
smile before he vanished into the other room.

As soon as he was gone, I leaned forward and
sniffed my salad. It smelled like, well, salad. I wasn't
sure what I'd been expecting, honestly. Did I really
think Thomas would try to poison me?

He won't, I assured myself. He had no reason to
want to hurt me. He didn't know my history with
murder investigations; almost no one here did. He'd
simply wanted to get me alone. Whether it was like
he said and he wanted the peace and quiet, or if it
was because he hoped I might spend the night with
him, I didn't know. A part of me was kind of excited
to find out.

Checking the door to make sure Thomas wasn't returning yet, I tugged my phone out of my pocket and shot Rita a quick text, telling her where I was. I might hope that Thomas's intentions were pure, but I couldn't take the chance that they weren't. And besides, who knew what Rita would do once she realized we weren't going to show up at the restaurant?

Thomas returned just as I put my phone away. He was carrying a pitcher of water in one hand, and a towel was draped over his forearm. He paused at the table, frowned briefly, and then filled both our wineglasses with water. "I should have brought cups," he said by way of apology.

"This is fine." I picked up my glass and took a sip. The water was clean, refreshing, and tasted nothing like poison—not that I knew what that tasted like.

Thomas sat down and fidgeted with his napkin a long moment before speaking. "When I came up with this plan, it sounded romantic and exciting. Now I'm starting to realize how ridiculous it was."

"No, it's not ridiculous," I said. "It's sweet." I picked up my fork and stabbed a tomato. "You were right; it's nice to get away from all the people and the noise. How did you manage to do it?"

"It wasn't easy," Thomas said, taking a bite of his own salad. He chewed and swallowed before speaking, which earned him a few points in my book. Some men talk through their food, and I was glad to see he wasn't one of them. "Well, I guess it was, but it'll cost me."

"If this was expensive, you shouldn't have done it," I said. "Don't get me wrong, I appreciate it, but you

really didn't need to spend so much money on me."
Especially for what was only supposed to be a dinner
between friends.

"No, I don't mean expensive that way." He took a
drink and set his glass aside. "A friend of mine knows
someone who works at the convention center. When
I asked about reserving the room for the night, he
made it happen."

I noted he used the word "he" and not "she." So,
his friend wasn't Tara. I don't know why that relieved
me so much, but it did.

"I'll have to do my friend some favors down the
line," Thomas went on. "Knowing him, he'll make
sure I earn every bit of it." He smiled when he said it,
so it wasn't all that bad. "But I'm sure it'll be worth it."

His eyes met mine. His gaze was intense, and there
was an interest there, one that went beyond mere
friends. I felt a flush coming on, so I quickly took a
drink and looked around the room lest he see it.

It was dark, but I could still tell there were other
tables pushed up against the walls. Chairs were
stacked up next to them. I assumed this was going to
be the room in which the JavaCon dinner would be
held tomorrow night. If that was the case, the door
Thomas had gone through to retrieve the water
likely led to the kitchen. Sniffing, I realized I could
smell something mouthwatering coming from that
direction.

"Is someone back there?" I asked, indicating the
kitchen door. "A cook, I mean. It smells great."

He shook his head. "I cooked dinner right before
I met with you." He actually blushed. "I hope you like

chicken. There weren't many other options available to me on such short notice."

"I love chicken." And from the smells of it, I was going to really enjoy what he was serving. "You didn't have to go to all this trouble. I would have been fine with a small meal at the cheapest place in town. This . . . this is beyond amazing."

Thomas tried to shrug off my comment, but I could tell he was pleased. "I wanted to do it. It's been so crazy lately, I needed to get away, and figured you might need to as well. Besides, I like to cook; it calms my nerves. This sounded like the perfect opportunity to clear my head and to make a good impression on a pretty lady."

This time, the blush hit me full force, and there was no way I could hide it. If Thomas Cole was a murderer, he was an awfully romantic one. There were worse ways to go than to be killed by a romantic, I supposed.

Not that I was looking forward to getting murdered, mind you. But you get what I mean.

"You know, I'm kind of surprised you didn't have coffee waiting for us," I said. "We *are* at a coffee convention."

He laughed. "I thought about it, but realized we've both probably already had enough. I'm so pumped full of caffeine, I'm not sure I'll be able to sleep for a week."

"You're probably right," I said, smiling. I was quickly warming to this private dinner idea. Thomas was turning out to be a genuinely nice guy. "Sleep is overrated anyway."

The smile that spread across his face then made me realize how that must have sounded. I considered correcting myself, lest I give him the wrong impression, but I let it stand. It wasn't like flirting had to lead to anything, so why not do as Vicki said and have a little fun?

We took a few moments to eat our salads in companionable silence. I wanted to ask him all sorts of questions regarding Charles's death, but was afraid I'd ruin the mood if I did. This was nice; a whole lot nicer than I'd expected. I was reconsidering my decision on the wine when Thomas set his fork aside and stood.

"Let me get the main course," he said. "Don't go anywhere."

"I wouldn't think of it."

He hurried to the kitchen, a skip in his step.

While he was gone, I checked my phone. Rita hadn't replied to my text or tried to call. I didn't know if that was a bad sign or a good one. I was afraid she'd turned her phone off and was still sitting there, watching the door, waiting for Thomas and me to arrive. How long would she wait before she called the cops, claiming I'd been abducted? I wasn't looking forward to *that* conversation, if and when it happened.

Thomas returned, this time carrying two plates. He set one in front of me, and my mouth immediately started to water. There was the chicken, of course, and sides of green beans and roasted potatoes. The smell coming from the plate had my stomach growling.

"This is too much," I said, even as I picked up my fork and dug in.

"It's not enough, actually," he said, resuming his seat. "Think of it as both dinner and an apology."

"An apology?" I asked between bites. The food was good. No, scratch that, it was amazing. Thomas was apparently not only a good coffee maker, but an outstanding cook as well. He was easing on into perfect guy territory, which was a real shame since I already had one of those back home.

"I haven't been entirely honest with you," he said. While his food looked just as good as mine, I noticed he had yet to take a bite.

My fear of poison instantly returned, and I very nearly spat out a mouthful of potatoes before I swallowed them and asked, "What do you mean?"

Thomas propped his elbows on the table and folded his hands in front of him. He pressed his forehead to them a moment before meeting my gaze. "Tara and I didn't meet here at JavaCon by chance."

My fear went from poison to his relationship status. *I knew there was something between the two of them!* "You're dating?" I asked.

"Dating?" He laughed. "No, it's nothing like that." He took a deep breath and sighed. "Tara and I have known each other for about ten years now. She was the one who got me into coffee."

"I see." Though, honestly, I didn't really. Why was that such a secret? I imagined a lot of coffee makers knew one another, especially if they hit up a lot of cons.

"We are planning to form our own company," Thomas said. "We don't want anyone to know about it yet. The plan was to come to JavaCon and enter the tasting competition as individuals. While it pits us against one another, the hope was either Tara or I would win. If that happened, we could use that success to help promote our business endeavor."

Okay, that made sense, to a point. "But why make it secret?" I asked.

"JavaCon rules." When I only stared at him blankly, he explained. "Anyone who works for the same company must enter the competition together. Even though our coffees were different, and were our own blends, we'd be listed as one organization and would only be allowed to enter one coffee for the tasting."

"So, to increase your chances of winning, you held off starting your business and entered separately."

"Exactly," he said. "We could have entered together, but that would have given us one less chance to win. We needed this." He lowered his eyes. "We really did."

I wondered how important the win was to their chances of success. Was it important enough to kill for? I'd figure the quality of their coffee would have more to do with their company's success than a win would, but the attention they would have garnered for that win might have pushed them over the top.

"You could have told me," I said. Disappointment marred my words despite my effort to hide it. "I wouldn't have told anyone."

"I didn't know that at first." Thomas finally picked up his fork and took a bite of his food. "We'd just met, and as far as I knew, you had ties to other competitors. I couldn't take the chance you'd tell one of them."

"Is this what you and Tara were talking about when I bumped into you earlier?" Never mind the fact that by "bumped into," I really meant when I'd eavesdropped on them.

Thomas chewed a moment as if considering his answer before speaking. "It was," he said.

For some reason, I didn't quite believe him.

I didn't call him out on it, however. He was willing to talk, and I had a feeling there was nothing malicious in what he was holding back. He was thinking about his company, and I'm sure there were things about it he wished to protect.

"Charles's victory must have put a damper on your plans, didn't it?" I asked.

"It did." He wiped the corners of his mouth, folded his napkin, and set it aside. "When he won, it made me question the chances of us being successful. I mean, if we couldn't beat him . . ."

"But he might have cheated," I said. "Everyone thinks so."

"Everyone might, but it doesn't change the fact that Tara and I can't use a JavaCon victory to promote our company. Do you know how many people are out there making coffee, coming up with new flavors, new blends?"

I shook my head. I might work in the coffee industry, but I just sold it. Vicki was the one who chose the coffee brands we sold, so she'd have a better idea of how many were out there.

"Let's just say there are a lot." Thomas leaned back in his chair. He'd left most of his meal untouched, yet he appeared to be finished. "What makes me think we can be successful when hundreds of others fail every year?"

"You have good stuff."

"Maybe." He didn't look convinced. "But the loss did make me reevaluate some things. I need to figure out how to make our brand stand out, how to get the company name out there so that people will know we exist. I think I banked on this win far too much and didn't really consider what we'd do if we didn't have it to lean on."

Thomas fell silent. I continued to eat, letting him think. As I chewed, I considered what he'd just told me and how it might relate to Charles's death. If either Thomas or Tara realized Charles had cheated to win the tasting, and if it was going to adversely affect their fledgling business, it gave both of them motive for murder.

I hated to think it, but I couldn't dismiss it out of hand. Just because I liked the both of them, it didn't make them innocent.

"I've been talking to some others," I said between bites. "Many believe Charles might have bribed some of the judges to get his victory—and I'm not just talking about Wynona. There are some who think he even resorted to blackmail."

Thomas didn't appear surprised. "It's too late to worry about it now," he said. "Even if I wanted them to void the award and give it to someone else, the entire thing is tainted. I wouldn't want to be associated with it now."

"Wynona still insists he stole the blend as well," I said, not willing to give up so easily. "Maybe if the truth comes out, it'll vindicate your loss." I knew I was reaching, but I wanted Thomas to feel better. He'd started the evening looking excited, and he was now so glum; it made me feel bad, like it was some-how my fault.

Thomas reached for his water, eyes meeting mine. He held my gaze a long moment before he took a large drink. "Wynona should just drop it," he said. "There's no sense in starting something now."

"But Charles did die," I said. "Maybe finding out who he stole the blend from would help catch the killer."

"Or it might cause more problems," Thomas said.

"What do you mean by that?"

Just as he was opening his mouth to answer, the door flew open and Rita burst in.

"Krissy!" she shouted. "I'm here. Are you safe?" She jerked to a stop just inside the door. "Oh! You are."

Thomas was staring at her, mouth agape, hand hovering near his water. It would have been funny if I wasn't so embarrassed. I closed my eyes and wished I'd sink right into the floor.

Rita's hands found her knees. She was panting, which made me wonder if she'd run all the way from City Perch to the convention center the moment she'd gotten my text.

"Well, now," Rita said, between gasps of air. "When you texted me, I thought he might be dragging you away to kill you, but instead you're *eating*!"

"Rita!" I glanced at Thomas. "That's not what I meant when I told you where we were."

"Why would I kill you?" Thomas asked, brow fur-rowed. Then it dawned on him. "You think I killed Charles?"

"No, I don't!" I glared at Rita. "I was just being

careful. People tell their friends where they're going all the time."

Thomas pushed away from the table. "I see. If you were frightened, you should have told me."

"I'm not frightened." I stood, my napkin falling to the floor, forgotten. "Tell him, Rita. It wasn't my idea."

"Of course it wasn't, dear." Rita said it like I'd never had a good idea in my life.

I didn't care; I ran with it. "See!" I turned to Thomas. "I told her where we were going, that's all. And when you brought me here, I told her where I was. In this day and age, you can't be too careful." I could feel my face burning.

Thomas studied me a long moment before he glanced at Rita. "I suppose you can't be."

"I didn't think she'd come bursting in like this," I said. "I didn't ask her to."

Rita harrumphed and crossed her arms. "That's how you're going to thank me?" Her eyes drifted to the food on the table.

Thomas noticed it too. "If you'd like some, I'm finished." He stepped away from the table and swung an arm toward it in invitation.

"No, she . . ." I tried to protest, but it was already too late. Rita crossed the room and plopped down into my recently vacated chair.

"I knew I should have ordered something while I waited for you," she grumbled. "I just about starved myself, and for what? To be stood up for no good reason? I swear . . ." She shoved a large helping of potatoes into her mouth, still grumbling.

Putting Rita out of mind the best I could, I turned

to Thomas. "I'm so sorry about that," I said. "She really was only looking out for me. She didn't mean anything by it. Neither of us did."

"I understand." He smiled, though his eyes were sad, and a little disappointed. "It's good to have friends who care."

"It is," I said. "Even if they sometimes make a mess of things."

"I heard that," Rita said through a mouthful of food.

Thomas chuckled, some of his good humor returning. "If you want to join her, I could go. I wasn't all that hungry anyway. Nerves have really gotten to me lately."

I shook my head. "No, I'm done." And then, because I felt horrible about what had just happened, I said, "If you wouldn't mind, I could use some fresh air. We could take a walk."

Thomas's smile returned. "A walk sounds lovely." He glanced at Rita. "But what about her?"

Rita was making short work of the remains of my meal. I had a feeling she'd wolf down Thomas's as well when she was done. She'd even poured herself a glass of wine.

"She'll be all right," I said, and knew it to be true. "Let's go."

Thomas held out his arm, and I took it gratefully. He might still be unhappy about Rita's sudden appearance—and the suspicions it represented—but at least he didn't appear to hold it against me.

Maybe, despite how it had started, this evening would turn out all right after all.

Chapter 14

I wish I could say important revelations came out of my walk with Thomas Cole, but they didn't. Thomas didn't reveal any more secrets, nor did he admit to any wrongdoing. He *did* forgive me for texting Rita, so I supposed that was something.

After we left Rita to polish off our dinner, there wasn't much talk of Charles—or of JavaCon, for that matter. We talked briefly of Death by Coffee and of his business, and spent the rest of the walk in companionable silence. All in all, it was relaxing, and was something I hadn't realized I needed until it was over.

We returned to the hotel lobby, a part of me wishing our stroll could have gone on longer. I was only slightly winded from the walk, though the fresh air had me feeling energized. I probably could have stayed up and talked to Thomas for the rest of the night, but I knew our time together this evening had come to an end.

Thomas started for the elevator doors, but stopped when he noticed I wasn't following. "Are you heading up?" he asked.

"I will soon," I said. My pulse was racing, which was both exhilarating and terrifying, because I knew exactly what it meant. "I think I'm going to stay down here a little while longer."

He took a step my way, which caused my heart to skip a beat. "Would you like some company? I don't have any other plans tonight."

I shook my head, unwilling—and unable—to speak. If I was around Thomas much longer, who knew where it would lead? It was why I didn't want to get into the elevator with him. A small space, our body heat; no thank you. I had enough on my plate at the moment. I didn't need to add stress over my relationship status to the mix.

"All right then," he said. The look in his eye was heartbreaking. "It's probably for the best anyway. I'll see you tomorrow?"

"Sure thing." I managed a smile. "Bright and early."

He stared at me a moment longer, as if trying to figure me out, before he turned and headed for the elevators. He pressed the button, then stepped into a car when the doors opened. As they closed again, he waved.

I returned his wave, one hand clenched into a fist behind my back. I was torn between running to him and running the opposite way. I blamed Vicki for that. She shouldn't have told me to let loose, because darn it, I *really* could have used the company right then, and while I thought I could be good and we could sit and have a nice chat, I was afraid of what *could* happen. As soon as the elevator started moving, I sagged into a nearby chair, hands going to my face. *What are you doing, Krissy?* My hormones were doing their best to interfere with common sense. There was no way it would ever work between Thomas and me. I knew that, he knew that.

Yet why did it feel like I'd made a huge mistake by turning him down?

I pulled my phone from my pocket and stared at the blank screen. Of course, I knew why I didn't go with him. If I'd gotten on that elevator, chances were good I wouldn't get off on my floor. Nothing might happen, but would that really matter? I knew if I so much as considered spending the night with him, I'd regret it.

It was late, but not too late. Most of Pine Hills was closed up by now, and many of its citizens were likely tucked away in bed or were relaxing in front of the TV, feet up, eyes heavy. I could call Beth and check on her, could call Jules and find out what he saw when he went to Death by Coffee, since he hadn't called me back, but they weren't the voices I needed to hear.

A night clerk was at the front desk, watching me. Wilting under his stare, I rose and stepped outside. I wasn't going to do this with an audience, but I *was* going to do it. I *needed* to do it.

I dialed.

The phone rang once. Twice.

And then an answer. "Hello? Krissy?"

"Hi, Paul." I leaned against the wall. The sound of his voice made my knees go weak. Either that, or I was far more tired than I realized. "I thought I'd call and see how you were doing."

"I'm good," he said. "Honestly, I'm glad you called."

A warm feeling spread through me then. *This* was why I couldn't spend the night with Thomas, even if all we did was talk. We weren't dating, but I still felt something for Paul Dalton. It might never amount to anything, but right then, his friendship was more important to me than a night with a good-looking guy I barely knew.

Why can't you have both?

I mentally pushed the little devil off my shoulder and asked, "How is everything in Pine Hills?"

"It's good." There was a rustle on the other end of the line. I couldn't tell if he'd simply switched ears, or if I'd caught him in bed. I had to fight to keep an image of the latter from slipping into my head. "I stopped in at Death by Coffee today. Everything seems to be running smoothly."

"That's good to hear." I hoped that meant Beth's trouble with Raymond had been taken care of. I'd have to check in with Mason tomorrow to be sure. It irked me that no one was letting me know one way or the other.

"How's the con?" Paul asked. He sounded genuinely interested.

"Not bad." I bit my lower lip as I debated on how much to tell him, then decided it best to be honest with him. It was inevitable that tale of the murder would reach Pine Hills. Rita would make sure of it. "Well, it started out great. And then someone was murdered. It kind of put a damper on things."

"Murdered?" He reverted to cop voice. "Tell me they caught who did it."

"Not yet," I said. "But the police are looking into it. I'm sure they'll have it figured out by morning."

There was a long pause. I knew what he wanted to say, but I wasn't going to help him along. I remained silent, praying he'd move on without comment.

Finally, he spoke. "Please tell me you aren't getting involved."

"I'm not," I said. "Not really."

"Krissy . . ."

"What? It's not like I'm actively looking for the killer." *Keep telling yourself that.* Sure, I might have talked to a few people involved with the deceased, and I tended to bring up Charles's death in conversation, but that didn't mean I was going to chase after the person who killed him.

No, really; I swear I wasn't.

"That's what you always say." I could hear both disapproval and amusement in Paul's voice.

"I do not!" Okay, maybe I did. "I can't help it, Paul. Someone died. I met the guy before it happened. He wasn't too nice, and it's starting to look like he was pretty corrupt and had a lot of enemies, but he deserves justice."

"The police can handle it."

"I know, but—"

"No buts," he said. "If you feel the urge to get involved, you should get on a plane and come home instead. I don't want anything to happen to you. I can't help you if things get too hot while you're there."

That warm feeling was back. "It won't," I said. "I'll be

careful." My mind flashed to my dinner with Thomas and our walk. If he'd been the killer, that was about as far from careful as you could get.

"What is it?" Paul asked.

"What do you mean?"

"Something is bothering you. I can hear it in your voice."

"It's nothing." My face heated up. There was no way I was going to speak Thomas's name, not to Paul, not even in passing. "I should probably get back to the room. Vicki and Rita are probably wondering where I am."

Thinking of Rita, I wondered if she'd finished with the meal, and who was cleaning it up. Thomas had gone upstairs, so I doubted he'd do it. It was unlikely Rita would do it herself. It was possible Thomas had forgotten all about it after our walk, but still.

His friend is probably taking care of it. Or the staff member who let him use the room. There was no reason for me to worry over something so insignificant.

"All right," Paul said with a weary sigh. "I need to get to bed anyway. I have an early shift tomorrow."

"Get some sleep," I said. "I'll see you when I get back to Pine Hills."

"First thing, okay?"

"First thing," I promised.

"Good night, Krissy."

"Good night, Paul."

We hung up.

I drifted back into the lobby, feeling light on my feet. I don't know why it surprised me so much, but I couldn't believe Paul was actually concerned about me. It made my decision not to follow Thomas upstairs feel like the right one.

I glanced down the hall that led to the convention center and the room Thomas had taken me to. If Rita was still there, it would be a good idea to go get her. There was still a killer out there somewhere. Wandering the halls alone could be dangerous.

But if she was already in the room with Vicki, I'd be the one without someone at my side.

Besides, I could hear other voices coming from down the hall. Thomas and I had passed a few people when we'd left for our walk. All the events might have wrapped up for the day, but that didn't mean everyone had to retire to their rooms.

The night desk clerk was watching me again, so I made for the elevators. I pressed the button and turned my back on the clerk while my mind returned to Paul. I wondered if I should tell him how I felt about him. Maybe then I'd stop having all these uncomfortable encounters and conversations. If he wanted to remain solely friends, I'd be okay with that. It would allow me to move on without wondering if I was making a mistake.

The elevator doors opened and I stepped into the car. They were about to slide closed again when I saw Clint Sherman coming my way. He looked exhausted, and a little rumpled. He held up a hand as he rushed toward the elevator.

I stuck my foot in the door and held it open for him.

"Thanks," he said, getting into the elevator with me. "Tenth floor, please."

I pressed the button for him as the doors slid closed.

"It's been quite a day, hasn't it?" I asked him. He looked like he'd been run over, trampled, and then sprayed clean by a high-powered hose. I supposed helping run a con could do that to you.

"It's been awful," he said, leaning against the elevator wall. "If I had realized how difficult this would be, I never would have done it."

"And since Charles Maddox got murdered, it has to be even worse." I watched him to gauge his reaction.

Clint closed his eyes tight. "Yeah. I can't believe someone would do something like that here, of all places."

"I saw you talking to him," I said, keeping my voice light. "Did you know him well?"

He glanced at me. I noticed his eyes were bloodshot. From being tired? Or from something else? I wouldn't blame him if he'd stopped by the hotel restaurant and had a few drinks before calling it a night.

"Well enough, I suppose," he said. "Charles made the rounds with all of us. He thought he could get ahead by rubbing elbows with anyone important."

"I heard he wanted to do more than rub elbows."

Clint straightened, eyes going hard. "What do you mean by that?"

"You heard what Wynona Kepler said." When he didn't react or say anything, I went on. "She said he cheated, that he stole his coffee blend."

"That had nothing to do with me."

"I didn't say it did."

Clint stared at me. There was no kindness in that gaze, no compassion. "What exactly are you implying?" His voice was cold, almost threatening.

"Nothing." I shrugged, tried to play it off as idle curiosity. "Wynona has been talking a lot about how Charles might have bribed some of the judges, and it makes me wonder. Every time I see her, she's trying to convince someone new to do something about it."

Clint shook his head. "That's ridiculous. Even if Charles did try to bribe us, none of us would have gone for it. The reputation of the entire con is on the line." He scowled. "Wynona needs to keep her mouth shut. Nothing untoward happened between Charles and any of us; I can promise you that."

"That's not what everyone thinks."

"I don't care what everyone thinks!" Clint's shout boomed in the small space.

I took a quick step back from him, but there was nowhere for me to go. I'd been prodding him for a reaction, but I hadn't expected such anger from him.

Clint seemed to realize what he'd done. He cleared his throat and sagged back against the wall. He rubbed at his eyes. "I'm sorry, I didn't mean to shout. I'm tired, and I don't like having my integrity questioned, especially after today."

The elevator stopped on the tenth floor. Tense silence filled the air until the door slid open. Clint pushed away from the wall, nodded to me, and then stepped off. As the doors slid closed, he glanced back in time for me to see the anger that still simmered there.

Ruffled some feathers, I think.

The question was whether Clint was angry that I had questioned his integrity, as he said, or if he was mad that I was asking questions he didn't want to answer because there was some truth to Wynona's claims.

Chapter 15

I was running down a long dark hallway that didn't seem to have an end. There was no light at the end of the hall, no door.

And someone was chasing me.

Some part of me knew I was dreaming, yet it didn't stop my heart from pounding, my body from breaking out into a cold, terrified sweat.

I never saw my pursuer, couldn't even hear them, yet I *knew* they were there. I kept thinking that if they caught me, it would all be over. What, exactly, would be over? I wasn't sure. But it was enough for my dream self to be in a full-blown panic as I hurtled down the hallway at a pace I'd never be able to sustain in the waking world.

I kept running, on and on, seemingly forever.

And then a thump from behind caused me to not only scream in the dream, but to startle awake, a barely suppressed scream on my lips.

I shot up in bed, body bathed in sweat. Both Vicki

and Rita were still soundly asleep. If I'd made any noise in my sleep, it hadn't been enough to wake them, though it sure felt like I'd screamed my heart out. My throat and mouth were dry, as if I'd been panting.

I swung my legs over the side of the bed and leaned forward, head in my hands. My heart was pounding in my ears, and I took a few moments to catch my breath. My head was swimming, so I looked at my feet as I tried to reorient myself. The curtains to the hotel room were closed, but the light in the bathroom was on, so it wasn't pitch-black. The door was open but a crack. The sliver of light revealed only a tiny bit of the room, but it was enough for me to see the three of us were still alone.

I licked my dry lips with a likewise dry tongue. I reached for a water at the bedside, but the glass wasn't there. I didn't remember returning it to the tray in the bathroom, but I must have done it before falling asleep.

Glancing at the clock, I saw it was three in the morning. I couldn't imagine many people were up at this hour. Though we were in a hotel and guests often came in at all hours of the night, it was eerily quiet. Could that have played into my nightmare somehow?

No, more than likely, it was Charles's murder and Paul's warning to be careful that had done it. My overactive imagination was playing havoc with my head, and I doubted it would get any better until I was safely back home.

I rose on shaky legs, slid my feet into slippers I'd brought so I wouldn't be walking around barefoot on

hotel carpet—who knew what might have been
spilled on it—and tiptoed across the room to the
bathroom. I slid inside the tight space and closed the
door most of the way behind me. I picked up a glass
and filled it with water from the tap. I chugged the
entire thing down in one go.

A thump not unlike the one I'd heard in my
dream came from somewhere out in the hall.

I froze halfway to putting the glass back on the tray
and listened. I heard nothing else, but was almost
positive I knew from which direction the sound had
originated. If I didn't miss my guess, it had come
from the room directly across the hall from my own.

Charles's room.

I set the glass down and exited the bathroom. I
snagged a robe off the back of the chair by the door,
and then, careful not to wake anyone, I made my way
to the hotel room door. Breath held, I peered through
the peephole and into the hallway.

Nothing.

At least, nothing I could see. The view was hazy, as
if the lens was dirty, making it hard to see much of
anything. You'd think making sure safety features
were well-maintained would be a priority in a hotel,
but apparently, it wasn't at this one.

Checking back to make sure Vicki and Rita were
still asleep, I gently took hold of the door handle.
Turning it slowly, as not to make a sound, I pulled
the door open. No one was standing outside the
room, so I took a step out into the hall . . .

. . . and just barely caught the door before it
closed behind me.

"Stupid," I muttered to myself as I slipped back into the room and made for the bedside stand where I'd left the keycard to the room. It would be just my luck to get locked out with everyone else fast asleep.

Hurrying back—carefully, mind you—I opened the door again and stepped out into the hall.

The muffled sound of a television came from somewhere a few doors down. A heavy snorer slept in the room next to mine. Otherwise, the floor was silent.

You imagined it, I thought, unconvincingly. I *had* heard the thump, both in my dream *and* in the waking world. There was no disputing that.

But the source of the sound? I couldn't be sure it had come from Charles's room; not yet anyway.

I crossed the hall to the door. It appeared to be tightly closed, but I checked the doorknob to be sure, moving it slowly and giving it a gentle push.

It was, as suspected, locked.

So far, so good. On a hunch, I pressed my ear to the door, held my breath, and listened.

There was a faint clunk from within. It was followed by the sound of shuffling papers.

Someone's in there!

I wanted to believe the police had decided to give Charles's room another good look, or that it was housekeeping cleaning up the room for its next occupant, but not at three in the morning. Since it was unlikely it was either one of them, I was leaning toward it being someone who was most definitely not supposed to be there.

My hand went for my pocket, but I wasn't wearing

my clothes, just my pj's and a robe, which meant my phone was sitting on the nightstand by the bed in my hotel room.

But who would I call? I didn't have the number to the police here. And while I could use the hotel phone to call down to the desk, I was afraid the intruder would get away in the interim. I couldn't even hide in my room and watch through the peephole, since it was so dirty I doubted I'd make anyone out well enough to identify them.

Mind racing, I pressed my ear back to the door. If I could discern exactly what the person inside was doing, then perhaps I could figure out who it was, and why they were there.

Whoever it was, they were going through the room quickly, but were trying to be quiet about it. Nothing slammed closed, and I didn't hear the fluttering of pages as if they were throwing things around. I could, however, hear their quick, sliding steps, and the way they seemed to be rifling through papers so quickly, it was likely some of them were falling free.

That meant whoever it was in there wasn't concerned that the police would know someone had been inside. Either that, or they were in such a panic, they weren't thinking straight. I doubted the intruder would take the time to set the room to rights after finding whatever it was they were looking for.

Would the killer be so careless?

If they were afraid evidence of the crime might be somewhere within the room—and that the police, who'd already been inside, could have missed it—then I thought they just might be.

A new sound came from the room, one that seemed completely out of place against the backdrop of a theft in progress.

It sounded like wind chimes.

I froze, my mind playing over the sound. *What in the world?*

Footsteps neared, and I realized that whoever was inside the room must have finished their search, because they were heading my way.

I jerked back from the door and hurried back across the hall, nearly tripping over my slippered feet in my haste. I waved my card in front of the reader, but the indicator stubbornly remained red.

"Come on," I hissed, pressing the card against the reader and removing it slowly in the hope I'd simply moved it too quickly the first time.

Still red.

The door behind me opened. Images of a cold-blooded killer holding a gun flashed through my mind. Panicked, I spun, ready to use my hotel key-card as a weapon if it came down to it.

The person exiting the room froze on the threshold. She was dressed in all black and was wearing a mask that hid not just her face, but her hair. The clothing was loose-fitting, as if made for someone else, but was tight enough around the chest for me to tell it was indeed a woman.

"Hey!" I said, unsure what else to say. I stepped away from my hotel room door, as if I hadn't been frantically trying to get inside. I noted the thief didn't have a weapon immediately evident, just a phone she slid into a back pocket. I moved even closer to her, ready to leap if she made any sudden moves. "The police are on the way, so you should probably wait here."

At mention of the police, the woman's eyes widened and she sucked in an alarmed breath. There was a heartbeat where she didn't move, and I thought that she might comply. Then, in a flurry of movement, she rushed forward so quickly, I didn't have a chance to react.

"Oof!" I grunted as her elbow connected solidly with my stomach. I staggered back and made a belated grab for her, but she'd already slithered out of my reach. The woman was already three doors down by the time I had righted myself.

A couple of things flashed through my mind then.

The thief might simply be someone who was taking advantage of Charles's death, who thought they could steal a few valuables no one would miss.

Or it could be Charles's killer.

There was no way I could let a murderer get away, not when I was this close to them.

"Sorry, Paul," I muttered.

And then I gave chase.

The woman was quicker than I was, but there wasn't really anywhere for her to go. She started toward the elevator, but then, upon realizing I was huffing down the hall after her, she veered off, toward the stairwell. She blasted through the door and hit the landing hard, never slowing her stride.

I reached the door just as it started to close. I entered the stairwell and immediately started down. Not only could I hear her pounding down the steps, but I could see her hand on the railing below.

"Stop!" I called, my voice echoing in the tight space.

Unsurprisingly, the woman didn't listen.

Knowing I was going to regret it in the morning, I started down the stairs. My pace was a lot slower than the woman's, since I was wearing slippers and, well, I wasn't in the world's best shape. While I might want to catch her before she got away, I also didn't want to break my neck by pitching headfirst down the stairs.

Why couldn't I have the same stamina I had in my dream? Even after such a short run, I was already winded, and a stitch in my side made every step hurt.

I kept hoping someone would hear us pounding down the stairs and would investigate. If I was lucky, they'd stop the woman before she got away.

But if anyone heard, they weren't making themselves known. The woman's rapid footfalls were growing fainter, and I was quickly running out of steam. By the time I hit the fourth-floor landing, I was panting, sweat pouring down my face as though I'd run two miles.

A door opened beneath me, then closed. The footfalls vanished, telling me she had left the stairwell, but I couldn't discern how far down she'd gone.

My best guess was she'd made for the lobby, since exiting on any other floor would give her nowhere to go, so I rushed down the last few flights of stairs, pushing myself well beyond my normal limits. If she exited there, then it was likely the night desk clerk would see her and inform the police. I doubted they'd be okay with a woman in a black mask running around the hotel.

I reached the lobby floor, gasping. I couldn't hear anything at all anymore, other than a buzzing that seemed to originate somewhere within my own head.

Ignoring the sound, and whatever warning my body was trying to give me, I threw open the door and burst out into the lobby . . .

. . . and directly into someone's waiting arms.

Chapter 16

I screamed and immediately lashed out blindly in my panic, connecting a solid hit on my attacker's shoulder. He grunted, and then his hold on me firmed.

That, of course, made me thrash all the harder.

"Stop it!" the man holding me commanded.

Without thinking, I complied.

"Are you going to hit me again?"

The panic-induced blindness wore off and I saw that I wasn't being held by a deranged killer, or by the woman I'd been chasing. Instead, it was a very annoyed-looking Detective Kimble who held me tight in his grip.

"I'm sorry, Detective," I said, sucking in a shuddering breath. "I thought you were someone else."

He hesitated a moment before letting me go. I rubbed at my arms where his fingers had dug in to keep me from smacking him. I would likely have bruises, but I could deal with bruises. I didn't want to know what he'd have done to me if I'd punched him.

"Ms. Hancock, right?" Detective Kimble asked. He looked me up and down, an expression of mild amusement on his face. "Did you get lost on your way to your room?"

I pulled my robe closed and fought furiously not to blush, but it was to no avail. I could feel my face warming. "I was sleeping in my room when I heard a noise," I said. "I decided to investigate."

His eyes narrowed. "What do you mean by 'investigate'?"

"My room is on the fifteenth floor," I said. "Right across the hall from Charles Maddox's room. I went over to see what was going on and heard someone poking around inside. She caught me outside the room, and when she ran, I chased after her." I reached up and smoothed down my hair, which was sticking up every which way.

"Someone was in his room?" Kimble asked. When I nodded, he took me gently by the arm and led me toward the elevator. "Show me."

I let him guide me into the car and pressed the button for the top floor myself. As we rose, I took a moment to give him a once-over. He was still wearing his suit; still looked like the professional detective he had earlier.

Yet there was a tiredness about him, one that told me that he hadn't been getting much sleep. I'd seen the same look on Paul whenever there was a murder. For some reason, it made me trust Kimble that much more.

"Why were you downstairs?" I asked, curious. Perhaps the intruder hadn't just snuck into Charles's room, but other rooms at the con. It was awfully late for him to be investigating otherwise.

Kimble glanced at me out of the corner of his eye and then resumed watching the numbers scroll by. "When something like this happens, I tend to not get much sleep. My mind doesn't shut off, and I dwell. Can't sit around when that happens."

"You handle a lot of murders?"

"Too many, if you ask me." He sighed. "I figured I'd take a walk around the scene, see if something new jumped out at me."

"Did it?"

He shook his head. "There's not a lot of evidence to be had. The murder weapon—a coffeepot, if you can believe it—shattered on impact."

"Did the glass . . ." I shuddered at the thought.

"No." A faint smile. "When he was struck, the glass shattered, but it was the fall that did him in. He hit his head on the corner of a metal table, and that's what got him."

"It sounds horrible."

Kimble nodded and sighed. "There were just too many people in and out of there at the time of the murder. Even if there's some sort of evidence lying around, it's not going to be easy to find."

"That's too bad," I said. "The killer needs to face justice."

"I agree," Kimble said. "Though I do think it's *my* place to look for him or her, not a would-be Nancy Drew, don't you think?"

"I do," I said. "I promise, I wasn't trying to stick my nose where it doesn't belong." At least not then, I wasn't. "I could have sworn the woman I was chasing entered the lobby before me. You didn't happen to see someone run by, did you?"

"I didn't." He made it sound like I was making the whole thing up as an excuse for my appearance. "You say it was a woman?"

"I'm pretty sure it was," I said. "She was wearing a mask and was covered head to toe in black, so I didn't get a good look at her or anything."

"How do you know it was a woman, then? Did she speak to you?"

"No," I said. "But I can tell."

When he gave me a questioning look, I pulled my robe tighter, which in turn gave him a better look at my figure.

"Ah," he said. I was surprised to note a ring of red creep up his neck and shade his ears a little darker. Kimble was standing awfully stiff. That's when I noticed his hands were clenched tight behind his back.

"Don't like elevators?" I asked him.

"Not particularly." He didn't look at me as he said it.

"You know, you don't look much like Harrison Ford," I said in an attempt to lighten the mood.

Kimble glanced at me. "What?"

"Detective Kimble. Like in *The Fugitive.*"

"He wasn't a detective in that movie." Kimble faced forward again. "You're thinking of *Kindergarten Cop.*"

"Well, you don't look much like Arnold Schwarzenegger either."

Kimble grunted, but didn't otherwise reply.

We reached the fifteenth floor a moment later. As

soon as the doors opened, Kimble stepped off. His
shoulders eased and he took a deep breath before he
started forward. I followed in his wake.

The hallway was quiet and still. If anyone had
been disturbed by my chase, they'd gone back to
bed. I didn't blame them. The adrenaline was wearing off and exhaustion was starting to weigh on me. I
wasn't used to being awake at this hour.

I stifled a yawn as we reached room 1528—Charles's
room. The door was closed, which meant it was also
locked. I was about to say something about not having
a keycard when Detective Kimble produced one from
his pocket. He held it over the reader, and the light
flashed green.

"Stay out here," he said, pocketing what I assumed
was a keycard the hotel had given him for his investigation. I wondered if it worked on every room, or
just Charles Maddox's old room. "This will take just a
minute."

Kimble opened the door wide enough for him to
slip through. The door started to swing closed, but I
caught it at the last second. There was no way I was
going to let this opportunity pass, even if it earned
me a firm reprimand from a police detective. At this
point, I was used to it.

I slid in after Kimble, moving as quietly as I could.
I kept my hand on the door so that when it closed, it
did so quietly.

Charles's room was in shambles. His suitcases were
open against the far wall, the clothes that had been
in them tossed to the floor. His bed was likewise a
mess. The covers were pulled back and were piled on

the floor. A briefcase lay on the desk in the corner. Papers were scattered around it, as were a couple of broken pencils.

Kimble was standing just inside the room, hands on his hips as he surveyed the scene. It was clear someone had been searching for something—I'd figured as much when I'd listened at the door. I had a feeling I already knew what the intruder was looking for, but the big question was did she find it?

Kimble turned, and he yelped when he saw me standing there. His already harsh expression turned into a glower.

"I thought I told you to stay outside."

"You did," I said. "But I didn't want to be alone." My eyes were wide and hopefully looked frightened. "The intruder might come back, and if she was Charles's killer . . ."

He stared at me long and hard before giving me a sharp nod. "I suppose you're right, though if you were so concerned about a killer getting you, then you probably shouldn't have chased after whoever did this."

"Point taken," I said. I scanned the mess of the room, wondering how anyone would ever know if something actually *was* missing. "Who do you think did it?"

Kimble surveyed the room. The bathroom door next to us was open but looked as if no one had bothered it. Either the intruder had found what they were looking for or had had to leave before checking. "If I were to guess, I'd assume Charles Maddox's killer. What was she looking for?" The last was clearly more to himself than me, but I answered anyway.

"His recipe," I said. When Kimble glanced sharply my way, I explained. "Charles won a coffee taste test competition this morning." Actually, I supposed by now, it was yesterday, but that was splitting hairs. "Whoever did this was probably looking for the blend he used."

"Who would kill someone over a coffee recipe?" Kimble asked.

It was a rhetorical question, but once again, I answered. "Someone who has something to gain from it. They might think that since the coffee won the tasting, it could be valuable to the right person. Java-Con was planning on featuring the coffee, so if the thief had the blend, they could turn around and profit off of its success."

Kimble grunted and shook his head. "It still seems insane to me, but I suppose people have killed for less." He produced a phone from his pocket and pointed toward the door. "Out. I'm going to call this in and then we're going to have a little chat."

I took one last glance into Charles's room before doing as the detective said. He was dialing even before the door had closed behind me.

The hallway felt oppressively quiet as I stood out there alone. I couldn't even hear the resident snorer anymore. It was as if everyone in the hotel was holding their collective breath, waiting to see what would come of this whole mess.

I paced the short distance between Charles's room and my own. Thankfully, Detective Kimble's call wasn't long, and after only a few minutes, the door opened and he stepped outside. He crossed his arms over his chest and looked at me expectantly.

"What?" I asked, wilting under his stare. "I told you what happened."

"True," he said. "Now tell me what you're holding back."

"What do you mean?"

"I can see it on your face. You think you know something."

"I don't *know* anything. Not for sure. But I have suspicions."

"Okay. Tell me."

"I do believe the woman who broke into his room was after the winning recipe. She's likely hoping to cash in on it."

"Okay, but who would do that? As soon as she tried to collect on it, we'd know who broke in. She'd be hard-pressed to talk her way out of it then."

I considered it only a moment before I said, "His wife, Tatiana, might. I ran into her earlier today."

Kimble grimaced. "I've had the pleasure."

"She was pretty adamant about being allowed into Charles's room to collect his things. I bet she was after the coffee blend then, and when the hotel wouldn't allow her in, she decided to break in."

"That would still make it easy to identify her as the perpetrator."

"Maybe," I said. "But she could claim she already had the blend and had nothing to do with the break-in. Since she was Charles's wife, it'd be easy to convince others that she had a copy of it already."

Kimble's brows drew together. He clearly didn't like what I was saying, but I went on anyway.

"The woman I saw was the right height for Tatiana." It could also have been Tara or any number of other women I'd seen—other than Wynona, who was too tall. "When she ran, she wasn't carrying anything, so she might not have found what she was looking for."

"Not unless she pocketed it," Kimble said. "A recipe wouldn't take up much space, I wouldn't think."

He had me there. "What I don't understand," I said, glancing past him to the door, "is how she got in."

"What do you mean?"

"When I talked to Tatiana earlier, she said she didn't have a key. The hotel staff refused to give her one, and I doubt they'd suddenly change their minds. And if they *did* give her a key, why sneak into his room in the middle of the night? With a key, she could have walked in anytime she wanted and wouldn't have had to dress up like a thief in doing it."

Kimble turned back to the door. He leaned down and ran his hand along the frame. "It wasn't jimmied open," he said.

"Which means whoever broke in had a key, right?"

"Or some way to fool the device into thinking they had one."

"Does something like that exist?" I asked, alarmed. If that was the case, there was no way I was going to be able to sleep in a hotel ever again.

Kimble shrugged. "Not that I know of, but anything is possible in this day and age."

Not exactly reassuring, but it would have to do. "Did Charles have his key on him when he was killed?" I asked. "Maybe the murderer stole it before fleeing the scene."

"No, he had it," Kimble said. "It's the one I have

now." He patted his pocket as if making sure it was still there.

"Do you know if the hotel gave him more than one key?" I asked. "Maybe he had a spare."

"I'll have to check with them," Kimble said, producing a small notepad. He jotted down a few notes, closed it, and shoved it back into his pocket. "Shouldn't I be asking *you* the questions here?"

"Sorry," I said. "Habit."

He didn't look amused. "Your friend was right about you. You have a sharp head on your shoulders."

"Thanks."

"But you'd best give up chasing after possible murderers, okay? It would be a shame for you to lose that head of yours because you stuck it somewhere it didn't belong."

"You're not the first person to tell me that."

Kimble actually laughed. It was a rich, pleasant sound, and it made me like him a little more. The detective might be serious about his work, and tend to be a little rough around the edges at times, but he did appear to be a good man.

"I'm going to go find out about the key and do some digging," Kimble said. "I want you to go into your room, go to sleep, and keep your nose clean. No more chasing people down hallways, and definitely no more investigating strange noises. This is a dangerous situation, and I won't stand for you or anyone else getting killed over it. Got it?"

"Got it," I said.

He studied me a long moment and then shook his head. "You're going to be one of *those*, I can feel it."

I didn't know what he meant by that, but I took it as a compliment nonetheless.

"Go to your room," he said again. "If I need you, I'll be in touch. You do the same." He handed me a card.

"I will," I said.

Kimble ran a hand over his jaw and let loose a yawn. He rolled his shoulders twice, then turned to walk slowly down the hall toward the elevator.

I watched him go, thinking he needed to get some rest, just like the rest of us. Actually, probably more than the rest of us. He did have a murder to solve.

He paused at the elevator, stared at it a long moment, and then turned to the stairwell. He pushed open the door, gave me one last warning look, and then vanished inside.

Once he was gone, I let loose a yawn of my own and slipped back into my hotel room, and, despite my own worries about not getting to sleep again, as soon as my head hit the pillow, exhaustion overwhelmed me, and I fell promptly to sleep.

Chapter 17

Sleep might have come easily, but it didn't take much to yank me out of it. It seemed like every hour or so, a noise would wake me. Sometimes it would be a door closing somewhere down the hall. Other times, a snort from Rita would cause me to jerk upright in bed, certain someone was in the room with us.

When morning came, I wasn't ready for it. Still, I crawled out of bed and started on my morning routine well before the others were up.

"You feeling okay?" Vicki asked as I trudged my way out of the bathroom. A shower had helped wake me somewhat, but barely. What I needed was a major dose of caffeine to get my mental gears running properly.

"I'm fine," I said. "Just tired." I punctuated that with a yawn. "It was an odd night."

"Rita told me," Vicki said. "Thomas actually took

you to a private room? How could he even think that's a good idea after what happened?"

"It was a room in the convention center," I said, feeling the need to defend him. "There was lots of space if I needed to run." I glanced at Rita. "She saw it. How was dinner, by the way?"

Rita paused midway through working on her hair. "It was very good, dear. I honestly don't know why you two didn't finish it."

I didn't want to tell her that it was because of how she'd barged in on us like an overprotective mother on her daughter's first date, so I changed the subject. "Besides, dinner with Thomas wasn't what I was talking about."

"Oh?" Vicki had her clothes folded over one arm. She was ready for her own shower, yet she already looked perfect. I don't know how she did it, because whenever I wake up, I look as if I've been dragged six miles through a field of static.

"Someone broke into Charles's room last night." I said it with a dismissive shrug, hoping they wouldn't make a big deal out of it.

"What?" Vicki's eyes widened in alarm. "Isn't his room right across the hall?"

"It is. I saw the woman leave, but she got away before I could figure out who exactly it was."

"You saw her and you didn't wake us?" Vicki asked, before narrowing her eyes. "And what do you mean by 'got away'?"

Crap. "I might have chased her downstairs." I didn't look up as I said it, choosing instead to focus especially hard on my shoelaces as I tied them.

"You chased her?" Vicki asked, voice flat. "And didn't wake anyone just in case the person you were after was a killer?"

"I didn't want to disturb you."

Vicki looked at the clothes in her arms and then raised a finger at me. "Stay here," she said. "I'm going to shower and then we're going to talk about this."

She entered the bathroom and closed the door. I could hear her moving around, muttering, and knew she was questioning my sense of self-preservation. I didn't blame her; I sometimes questioned it myself.

A moment later, the shower started up.

I finished tying my shoes and stood. "What?" I asked when I noticed Rita was still staring at me.

"Well now, what do you think?" she asked, putting an indignant hand on her hip. "I thought we were all friends here."

"We are."

"Then why are you running off chasing people down hallways without us? That's the sort of thing friends are for!"

It made me question what kind of life I was living that she thought I needed people to help me chase after thieves and killers.

"I'm sorry," I said. "The next time a thief or murderer is near, I'll be sure to tell them to hold on while I go get you so we can confront them together."

"You'd better," Rita said, not catching the sarcasm. That, or she was choosing to ignore it.

I sighed and slid my badge on around my neck. I knew why Vicki and Rita were upset with me, yet they had to understand why I hadn't wanted to risk getting them hurt. As far as I knew, the killer could have been in there, armed to the teeth. Putting myself in harm's way is one thing; I wasn't going to risk my friends too.

While I wanted to get downstairs as soon as possible for my morning coffee, I waited until Vicki had finished her shower so we could have that chat. There was no sense in frustrating her more by sneaking out before she'd had a chance to say her piece.

The bathroom door opened only a few minutes after the water had stopped.

"Tell me exactly what happened," Vicki said. Her hair was bunched up in a towel, but at least she'd gotten dressed.

"There's not much to say. I got up to get a drink and heard a noise outside. I went to check it out, and the woman came out of the room. She ran. I lost her." I didn't bring up Detective Kimble, or the fact that we went into the room afterward.

"Did you recognize her?" Rita asked.

"No. She was wearing a mask."

"So, you hear a strange sound, while staying in a strange place, and you decide to go check it out on your own," Vicki asked. "Isn't that the sort of thing that gets people killed?"

"It is," I said, as feelings of guilt swept through me. "It's just been so crazy lately, I guess I wasn't thinking. I mean, a guy died. And then there was that dinner with Thomas and trying to make time for the con in between it all. And don't get me started on Mason's call."

"Mason's what?"

Oh, crap. I refused to meet Vicki's eye when I said, "He might have called me yesterday."

"He called you?" Vicki asked. "Why?"

"It's nothing to worry about," I said. "Just a little trouble at the store."

"What kind of trouble?" Vicki's phone materialized in her hand as if by magic. "I've got to call him. I talked to him last night and he never said a word!"

"You don't have to . . ." But it was already too late. She pressed a button and slammed the phone to her ear a little harder than I thought necessary.

"Mason," Vicki said as soon as he answered. "What's this I hear about something happening at Death by Coffee and you not telling me?"

I groaned inwardly. *Now I'm the cause of marital strife.* Mason was going to kill me when I got back home.

"We'd better go, dear," Rita said. "I have a feeling she's not going to be too happy once she ends that call."

"Probably not," I said.

I told Vicki we were leaving, which earned me an impatient wave of the hand while she listened to Mason explain himself. I wanted to tell her to find out how Beth was doing and if everything had worked itself out, but decided it best if I snuck away while I could. She could yell at me later.

I felt like a thief as I followed Rita out of the room. As the hotel room door closed, I heard her say "He did *what*?" and knew that Raymond Lawyer was going to be hearing from a very unhappy Vicki Lawyer soon.

That would be a conversation I wouldn't want to miss.

Rita and I took the elevator, which was empty when

we got on, but made four stops on the way down. No one I knew got on with us, but Rita recognized a middle-aged man from somewhere and proceeded to talk his ear off. He didn't seem happy about it, but he let her babble. He must have realized how futile asking her to stop would be.

We reached the lobby and piled out of the elevator. Rita was still talking to the man, who was making quick time toward the convention center. Rita followed right after. I was seemingly forgotten, but that was okay. There was someone walking across the lobby who I wanted to talk to, and I didn't want Rita listening in on the conversation.

Tara Madison looked a lot like I felt. She had deep, dark circles under her eyes, and her shoulders were slumped. She looked as if she hadn't put much thought into her clothing when she got dressed this morning either.

In fact, she looked like someone who hadn't slept a wink.

Because she was too busy breaking into a dead man's hotel room? I wondered. Or was the stress of the murder weighing on her like it might any sane person?

Maybe talking wasn't the best idea. If she had snuck into Charles's room last night and found the coffee blend recipe, then perhaps she would go to someone to pass it on, a coconspirator, perhaps. I tried really hard not to think of Thomas's name, but couldn't help it. If they were in on it together, it was best that I know.

"Are you even listening to me?" Rita asked, hand going to her hip. "I swear, I don't know where your head is at anymore."

I jumped. I hadn't even realized she'd come back. "Sorry," I said. "I was thinking." I really wanted to follow Tara and see where she went and who she talked to. I wanted to believe she was innocent of any wrongdoing, but I couldn't simply take it on faith.

Unfortunately, Tara knew me by sight and would quickly figure out I was following her. It didn't matter if she was innocent or guilty; I didn't want her to think I didn't trust her.

But she didn't know Rita.

"Would you like to do something for me?" I asked. Tara had stopped to check her phone, but I didn't know how long that would last.

Rita perked up. "This sounds interesting," she said. "Of course I would."

"See that woman over there?" I pointed Tara out as covertly as I could manage. When Rita nodded, I went on. "Can you keep an eye on her and see where she goes, who she talks to? She might be the woman who broke into Charles's room last night, and I'm curious to know if she found what she was looking for."

"You think she might do something if she did?"

"I don't know," I admitted. "But if we're watching her, it'll be hard for her to slip anything by us." And if she tried to sneak back upstairs and break into Charles's room again, Rita would be there to stop her—or to let someone know what was going on.

"I'm on it." Rita folded up a program she was holding and shoved it into her bag. "If she does anything suspicious, I'll let you know."

Tara was on the move again. "Good," I said. "I have my phone."

Rita gave me a sharp nod and then followed after Tara. She glanced back at me once, winked, and then vanished around the corner.

Why did I feel like I'd just made a big mistake?

The elevator slid open behind me as I debated whether to chase after Rita and tell her I changed my mind or to go and find the coffee my body so desperately needed.

"Hey, Krissy. I'm glad I ran into you."

I glanced back to see Thomas Cole stepping off the elevator. Unlike Tara, he looked bright-eyed and ready for anything the day might throw at him.

"Hi, Thomas. Thanks for last night. It was fun."

An older woman who'd stepped off the elevator behind him gave me a startled look before grinning and walking away with an amused shake of her head.

"It was my pleasure." He beamed. "Do you have any big plans for today?"

"Not really." I considered leaving out my adventures last night, but decided that since he and Tara were friends, he deserved to know in case she was indeed the intruder. "But something did happen last night."

I told him about waking up and hearing the sound across the hall, about seeing the woman and chasing her all the way down the stairs. I even told him about Detective Kimble and how we found the room ransacked.

"Wow," he said when I was done. "Sounds like you had an adventurous evening. I'm sorry I missed it."

"Don't be. It wasn't as exciting as I made it out to be." I didn't want to tell him how badly I'd been panting by the time I ran into the detective.

"To think, all I did was a crossword puzzle on my phone before falling asleep."

"Actually, I would have preferred that." I bit my lower lip before asking, "How well do you know Tara?"

"Tara?" He looked confused for a moment before his eyes widened and he shook his head. "You can't possibly think she had anything to do with what happened last night, do you?"

"The woman was about Tara's size," I said. "And I saw her just a few minutes ago. She looks like she didn't sleep last night." I gave him a meaningful look.

Thomas frowned. "It's not possible." He shook his head as he said it. "I know for a fact there's no way she could have done it." He glanced at me, reddening. "I mean, it's not like I was with her last night, but Tara wouldn't do something like that."

"Are you sure?" I asked. "Because she looked like someone who'd just spent her night doing something other than sleeping."

"I . . ." Thomas's frown deepened as he looked past me, toward the convention center, like he could see through the crowded hallways and find Tara. "I'll talk to her," he said. "But I swear to you, there's no way she could have done it."

"I hope not," I said, and I meant it. I liked Tara, even though a part of me was jealous she was going to get to spend more time with Thomas after the con was over. "I really do."

Thomas managed a smile, but I could tell he was still concerned about what I'd said. "Well, I'm going to head in. Are you coming?"

"In a few minutes," I said, though I really did want to follow him. I could do worse than spend my last day in Maryland with a cute guy—one with whom nothing could, or would, ever happen. "I'm waiting for a friend."

Oddly, Thomas looked relieved. "I guess I'll see you inside, then."

"I'll keep an eye out for you." I smiled, hoping he would return it.

Thomas hesitated a moment, mouth parting as if he had something more to say, before he turned and walked away.

I settled back and waited for Vicki to appear. When she stepped off the elevator a few minutes later, she looked like she was in a halfway decent mood.

"Is everything worked out?" I asked.

"Yeah. I'm sorry I snapped at you back there. Mason has everything under control now."

"I should have told you when he first called," I said. "I'm the one who's sorry."

Vicki took my arm and flashed me a smile. "It's all good. But I *am* going to make you spend a little time with me before you go running off chasing after more murderers."

"I'm perfectly okay with that."

We left the lobby and headed for the convention center.

"You know, if we get bored, we can always head to DC," Vicki said. "It's only like thirty minutes away from here."

"Really?" I asked. I'd never been to the capital.

"We could go sightseeing. I mean, I like it here, but after what happened . . ." She shuddered.

"I know what you mean." Though I wasn't too keen on leaving just yet. There was still a killer out there.

Music drifted down the hall, but it didn't sound like something that was coming from a stereo. Vicki and I shared a look and then followed the sound.

We found the source of the music in one of the ballrooms at the far corner of the convention center. A stage had been set up inside, and a band was currently playing to a room that was quickly filling.

"What is this?" I asked over the music. The band was playing an upbeat acoustic jam that had my toe tapping.

"The Coffeeholics," a woman said. "They play these sorts of events often."

"They're good," Vicki said.

I nodded in agreement.

We entered the room and spent the next twenty minutes listening to them play. Many of their songs were coffee-themed originals, but they played a few covers as well, often changing a lyric here or there to throw in a coffee reference. For that short time, I was able to keep my mind off of Charles's murder, but just before they ended their current set, I caught sight of a pair of my suspects, and my brain was right back on the case.

Wynona Kepler stood in the back of the room with Tatiana. They were turned so I couldn't really see what they were talking about, whether it was a heated argument or Tatiana was attempting to convince Wynona to help her get into Charles's room.

The conversation didn't last long. Wynona said something, using a napkin to cover her mouth—a pastry of some kind was in her other hand—and then she turned and walked briskly away. Tatiana watched her go, shook her head, and then left the room through one of the back doors.

The music ended and the singer called for a twenty-minute break. Vicki and I drifted from the room.

She checked her watch the moment we were free of the crowd. "I'm due to meet up with a few people I met yesterday for a workshop," she said. "Want to come along?"

"You go ahead," I said. "There's a few things I'd like to do. I'll catch up with you later."

"All right," she said. And then, right before she walked away, she added, "Stay out of trouble."

"I'll try," I said, which caused her to laugh.

A moment later, and she was gone.

The music had relaxed me, but I was in no way content. With mild regret, I merged with the crowd of people walking the con and went in search of the one thing she'd asked me to avoid.

Chapter 18

I spent the next few hours wandering the con, taking in the sights and smells, and drinking far more coffee than I should have. Jules texted while I was waiting in line for a sample. He apologized for not getting back to me yesterday, but did say that everything seemed fine at Death by Coffee. I shot him a quick thanks, but until I heard from Beth, I was going to be nervous.

While I walked the floor, I kept an eye out for any of the usual suspects, but if they were there, I overlooked them. I figured it was only a matter of time until I bumped into one of them, and honestly, I was counting on it.

I was curious about what Wynona and Tatiana had been talking about. Considering Wynona didn't know Tatiana existed yesterday, I found it strange to find them together.

But I never saw either of them. They, like most

everyone else involved with Charles Maddox, had seemingly vanished.

I did come across Rita once in my wanderings. I caught a glimpse of her following after Tara, who was entering a seminar about the history of coffee. I wished Rita a silent "good luck" she never saw before I continued on.

With no one making themselves evident, I decided to sit in on one of the seminars—this one about making your own flavored creamer. I might prefer my coffee with only a chocolate chip cookie in it, but that didn't mean I couldn't make homemade creamer for Death by Coffee. Making it on-site might help cut down on a few extra costs, which is always a plus.

The room was surprisingly packed. Many of the seats were already full, and a low buzz of conversation filled the air. Many of the conversations were about coffee, of course, but quite a few people were talking about the murder. I caught wind of Charles's name more than once as I looked for a place to sit.

My old rival Valerie Kemp was in the room but paid me no mind, even when she looked up and saw me coming her way. I was okay with that. I didn't wish her any malice, but I wasn't looking to become friends after all this time either. There was an open seat next to her, but I ignored it and headed for another seat, this one beside a woman I was very interested in meeting.

"Excuse me," I said, slipping past an older man in tan slacks and a checkered shirt. He winced as he pulled in his legs so I could slide past him.

I took the seat beside a tall woman with long legs

that bent in a way that reminded me of a bird. Her dark bangs were peppered with gray, and large hoop earrings hung from ears that were just this side of too big.

She glanced at me as I took my seat, a pleasant smile on her lips.

"Hi!" I said, grinning broadly. "Evaline Cobb, right?"

She seemed surprised to be recognized. "Why, yes." She blinked at me, uncertainty crossing her features. "I'm sorry, do I know you? I'm absolutely terrible with faces."

"It's okay, we haven't met." I held out a hand. "Krissy Hancock."

She shook. Her hand was thin and frail, though her skin was extremely soft, like she spent all her free time rubbing lotion into it.

"It's good to meet you, Krissy," Evaline said. "I'm glad you decided to stick around JavaCon. The programing is fantastic."

"It is," I said. "You're one of the organizers of the con, aren't you?"

"I am." She beamed with pride. "It took a lot of work to get this thing off the ground, but we did it. We put a lot of effort into making this the best con for coffee lovers on the planet. We're not quite there, but give us a few years, and I bet we'll get there."

I had no doubt that if they could get through the murder, they very well might. "It shows," I said. "There's so much to do, it's easy to get overwhelmed."

The pleasure in Evaline's eyes made me feel bad about wanting to bring up Charles's murder, so I decided to hold off until after the presentation was over.

We exchanged a few more pleasantries before a rail-thin woman with an extremely long neck stepped up to the podium at the front of the room. I sat back and did my best to focus on the discussion.

Evaline spent the entire talk with her hands folded primly in her lap, one leg crossed over the other. A smile remained on her lips as she listened, and I didn't see her look away once during the entire presentation.

I wondered how a woman like this could have had anything to do with Charles Maddox, as Pierre and Dallas had implied. She seemed so, I don't know, *proper*, like she'd never said a foul word in her life.

Then again, some people have hidden depths. As far as I knew, the moment Evaline was alone, she would break out a leather jacket and a bottle of vodka and tear apart her hotel room like a rock star on a bender.

The talk turned out to be pretty interesting, and I took some mental notes, though most of my thoughts were focused on what I was going to say to Evaline when the seminar was done.

The room erupted in applause as the woman finished. She gathered her notes, bowed, and then scurried away, as if the positive reaction had spooked her.

Once the applause died down, the room started to empty. Evaline was talking to another woman by the wall, so I hung back and waited my turn. The conversation was brief, and the woman turned and walked away with a smile.

Evaline made as if she might follow the woman out, but I deftly cut her off.

"I'm glad you decided not to cancel the con," I said. "So much can be learned at an event like this."

"Oh, I agree," Evaline said, clasping her hands together. "Canceling was discussed, but ultimately shelved. Carmine wouldn't hear of it."

"It had to have been a hard decision," I said. "Someone got murdered." I lowered my voice so none of the other attendees could hear.

Evaline paled, as if the mere thought of a dead person was enough to make her faint. "It was a tragedy, one that I regret with every breath."

"It was," I said, wondering if she regretted it because it had happened, or because she was involved in some way. "I heard you and a few of the other judges knew Charles Maddox rather well."

Her smile slipped, turning uncertain. "In some regards, yes, I suppose we did."

"There's been talk that Charles might not have won the tasting fairly." I kept my voice down, but pleasant, as if I was merely passing the time in conversation, not prying for information. "That he bribed or blackmailed the judges."

Evaline went completely still. "Where did you hear such a thing?" she asked. "Was it from Winnie Kepler?"

"She is one," I allowed. "But there are others who have been saying the same thing. I don't put much stock in rumors, but it's hard not to notice and wonder."

Most everyone who'd attended the talk had left, but a new group was filtering in for whatever event was due to take place in the room next. A man with wild, nervous eyes stood up front by the podium, sorting through papers.

Evaline noticed the influx of people and motioned for me to follow her. Her step was surprisingly
quick as we left the room. She kept looking around
like she thought someone might follow us.

Interesting, I thought as we slipped into a hallway
where there was no one but a pair of women who
were disappearing into the restroom. In moments,
we were as alone as you could get in the middle of a
convention full of people.

"What have you heard?" she asked. There was a
frantic lilt to her voice.

"There hasn't been much in the way of details
floating around," I said. Evaline sagged in relief.
"But people are starting to question the validity of
Charles's win and to wonder what will happen if
Winnie's theories are proven true."

Evaline's hands worked at one another, and she
chewed on her lower lip for a good minute before
she spoke. "People should be questioning what happened," she said. "I'm not proud of it. None of us
should be. In fact, I've gone to both Carmine and
Clint and told them we should come clean."

Bingo, I thought. So, Dallas and Pierre were right,
and Charles *did* buy his win. "Was it money?" I asked.
Money almost always seems to be at the root of cor-
ruption.

"Charles didn't have the money to bribe anyone,"
Evaline said. "But he had other ways of convincing
people to do things his way."

"Like blackmail?"

Evaline nodded. "As I said, I'm not proud of it.
And I don't think the others are either. Carmine has

been inconsolable since, well . . ." She closed her
eyes briefly. "I think he blames himself for Charles's
death."

I was pretty sure there were some people who
thought he was solely responsible for the murder,
but I kept that to myself.

"I want you to understand that nothing like this will
ever happen again," Evaline said, focusing a steady
gaze on me. "I'm only telling you now because rumor
tends to become fact, and I'd rather explain myself
now in the hope that when it does come out, people
won't hold it against JavaCon."

I nodded for her to go on.

Evaline took a deep breath and blew it out in a way
that caused her bangs to flutter before she spoke.

"Carmine and I had an affair."

I blinked at her. That wasn't what I'd expected her
to say.

"I know," she said. "It shouldn't matter to anyone
but those of us involved, but you know how things
are. My husband has been gone for years now, and
Carmine's marriage is a sham, but to have it come
out like this, now . . ." She shook her head. "It would
have ruined him."

"How long ago did it happen?" I asked. "The affair, I mean?"

"Off and on for five years now." A slight blush
crept up her neck. "We've known each other nearly
all our lives, but were nothing more than friends during most of that time. It just sort of happened one
day. And then it happened again a few months later,
and then again, and then so on. We don't love one

another—not like that—but we enjoy each other's company."

"I take it Charles found out?"

"He did." Evaline's brow furrowed. "I don't know how he caught on. We were careful. Carmine's wife, despite their troubles, never knew about us. I'm not even sure she'd really care even if she *did* find out. They barely talk as it is." She sighed, and for a moment looked sad for Carmine before she went on. "We never got together at cons like this, even though we'd have ample opportunity to do so. It was always somewhere where no one who knew us could happen by and see us together."

"Yet Charles discovered it anyway."

Evaline nodded. "He approached Carmine first. It caught him completely by surprise. He called me almost immediately, begging me not to tell anyone and to do whatever Charles wanted. I didn't want to hurt Carmine, or his marriage, so I agreed. It wasn't like we were planning on running away together or anything."

My mind raced. If Carmine had been worried that Charles might reveal his secret, could it have led to him confronting, and eventually killing, the man? It made a whole lot of sense.

"I know what you're thinking," Evaline said. "Carmine wouldn't have killed Charles. He might not want the affair to come out, but he would never stoop to that level. He just doesn't have it in him."

I wondered about that, but I did have to admit that neither Carmine nor Evaline was a fit for the person who broke into Charles's room last night. I found it hard to believe the murder and ransacking weren't connected.

"Do you think Charles had the same kind of dirt on the other judges?" I asked.

"It's likely," Evaline said. "I don't know what that man did in his free time, but it seemed like he spent an awful lot of it spying on other people."

"What about Clint Sherman?" I asked. "Do you think Charles blackmailed him too?"

"I know for a fact he did," Evaline said. "But I can't tell you what it was he had on him. Clint remained tight-lipped on the subject, and quite frankly, I don't want to know."

I wondered if, since Charles had been gathering dirt on the judges, he could have been doing the same to other competitors. It might explain why Tara seemed so off lately. Could he have discovered something about her and confronted her about it, and then she killed him?

"It's not like Charles was a saint," Evaline went on. "The man was apparently married, yet I truly believe he was sleeping with half a dozen people here."

"Really?" I asked, though I'd begun to suspect something similar. "Do you know who he might have been with?"

"Not for certain," she said. "But I did see him arguing with a young woman not long before he was discovered. It wouldn't surprise me in the least if it turns out she found out about his wife and killed him for it."

"What woman?" I asked, wondering if it was the same woman who'd pointed Tara to Charles's body.

"Her name is Misty Rodgers. I recognized her

from other events, though I don't know her all that well personally."

I filed the name away for later. "I'd like to talk to her," I said. "Do you know where I can find her?"

"Around," Evaline said. "She's a small woman. Brown hair, maybe a dark blond, I believe. Mole here." She touched her upper lip. "She was a nice girl when I met her, but Charles had a way of getting under your skin, so who knows?"

I thanked her and started to walk away, but stopped when Evaline called out to me.

"Please don't tell anyone what I told you," she said. "I feel better now that I've told someone, but I don't want it spread all over the con quite yet. While it needs to come out eventually, I'd much rather do it myself, with Carmine's permission. It'll be easier on everyone that way."

I mimed locking my lips and tossing away the key.

She gave me a tight smile and then turned her back on me.

I checked my watch and considered my next move. If all went well, I could find Misty and get her take on Charles, then meet with my friends, hopefully after telling Detective Kimble who had killed Charles Maddox, and spend the rest of JavaCon focused on something other than murder.

Chapter 19

Unsurprisingly, Misty Rodgers wasn't easy to find in the middle of a convention. It wasn't like I had a picture of her, or had anything more to go on than the fact I was looking for a small, brown-haired woman who had a mole on her upper lip. As far as I knew, she was long gone and I was wasting my time.

I decided to grab a light lunch and something to drink and plant myself someplace where I could keep an eye on the main hall, just in case the fates decided to be kind and she wandered by. I stopped at a deli near the convention center, bought a Sprite and a turkey sandwich, and then found a spot to settle in near one of the big windows.

A woman walked by and smiled at me. Another man waved. It was strange; I hadn't talked to any of these people, yet they acted like we knew each other. I supposed mutual interests had a way of bringing people together. They might not have known anything more about me outside of my having a love for coffee, but to them, that was all that mattered.

My sandwich turned out to be dry and unappealing, but I managed to choke down about half of it before tossing it into a nearby trash can. I sipped my Sprite and continued to watch faces as they passed, greeting those who noticed me with a friendly wave or nod.

Unfortunately, no one with a mole on their upper lip walked by. I finished off my Sprite, tossed the can into the trash—there was no recycling container anywhere I could see—and then headed for the hotel lobby in the hope of finding my quarry there.

The lobby was just as busy as the con floor. There were a few people at the front desk checking out, and a large group of women was standing in the middle of the room talking in loud voices about their favorite lattes. Of Misty Rodgers, there was no sign.

"Ms. Hancock."

I turned to find a weary-looking Detective Kimble standing behind me. With all the noise, I hadn't heard him approach.

"Hi, Detective." I flashed him an innocent "I'm not doing anything I'm not supposed to" smile. "Did you get much sleep last night?"

"Some." He said it in a way that translated to "none." "I trust there were no more disturbances last night?"

"Nope," I said. "At least, none where I could hear. Did you find out who broke into Charles's room?"

He gave me a disapproving look, which wasn't a surprise. I *was* prying into a police investigation.

Still, he answered me anyway. "No one has seen or heard anything amiss—no one but you." He made it sound like an accusation. "As far as everyone else seems to know, nothing at all happened last night. No one on your floor heard anything, and that includes the women you're staying with."

"You talked to them?" Why did that worry me so much?

"Briefly. They said they heard nothing, but stand by what you said. It appears you're the only one to have seen the intruder. Not even the staff saw anything out of place that night."

"Lucky me, I guess."

His grunt was punctuated with a smile.

Did that mean he appreciated my help? Or was he merely amused by the nosy woman who kept popping up in his investigation?

I wondered if he'd still feel the same about me after I further involved myself. I was about to find out.

"I was talking to some people about Charles Maddox and some of the rumors going around," I said. "I came across some interesting information, if you want to hear it?" I made the last a question.

Kimble's eyes narrowed briefly before he sighed. "All right, tell me."

I told him briefly about my conversation with Evaline Cobb. I told him there's a chance Charles had something on them, but I left out the details, mainly about her affair with Carmine. While it would be interesting to the detective, I wanted to stick to my promise not to tell anyone until she was ready. If it turned out to be important to the case, I wouldn't hesitate to spill the beans, but for now, her secret was safe with me.

Besides, if he wanted the details, he could always go to Evaline herself. There was no need to tell him more than I had to.

Detective Kimble listened. He had a look on his face that said he wasn't thrilled about me asking questions, but in some ways appreciated that I had.

I knew the look well. The officers at the Pine Hills Police Department often wore the same expression. Eventually, my luck would run out and I'd come across someone less willing to work with a civilian than the cops I've always dealt with, but until then, I plan on doing everything in my power to make my-self useful.

I finished my story. Kimble took a moment to di-gest it before asking, "So you think this Misty woman might have had something to do with the theft?"

"Misty Rodgers," I said. "And she might have. But I'm thinking she also had a pretty good motive for murder. If she's the same woman I'm thinking of, she was with Charles right before he died. I also be-lieve she's the woman who told Tara Madison where to find Charles. And everything points to Misty and Charles having had a falling-out right before his death."

Kimble scratched his jaw. I noted his clean-shaven look was turning into an exhausted-stubble look. "You say she has a mole?"

"That's what I was told. I haven't seen her yet to verify it, so I could be wrong." It wouldn't be the first time someone wore a fake mole as a fashion state-ment. "If Misty is indeed our killer, and if she was the woman who ransacked Charles's room, she could very well have left JavaCon already." Especially if she'd found what she was looking for.

Kimble looked grim at the thought. "I'll keep an eye out for her, but at this point, I'll probably need to find her contact information." As he said it, a group of five people walked out, dragging their luggage behind him. "It's nearly impossible to keep this many people contained."

"Maybe she didn't find anything in Charles's room and is sticking around, waiting for another chance," I said. "I'll watch for her too."

"Well, if you do see her, you contact me." He jabbed a finger at me. "Don't try to talk to her yourself. If she's the killer, I don't need you ending up dead as well. One murder is enough for me."

"I don't plan on joining Charles Maddox, if I can help it," I said. It wasn't quite the promise he was hoping for, but it was as close as he was going to get from me.

Kimble seemed to realize the same, because his gruffness returned. "Is there anything else you've been holding back from me?" he asked.

"I think that's about it." A new thought hit me then. "Did you ever find out whether or not Charles had more than one room key?"

Kimble frowned. I got the distinct impression he was trying to decide whether or not to tell me. I got it; I wasn't a cop. But I'd also helped him out a little with his case already. He had to realize that passing on the information could only help his investigation.

I waited patiently, smiling and acting as if I was

merely asking out of idle curiosity. Nope, there were no ulterior motives here.

He glanced around the room, frowned, and then, much to my relief, answered. "He requested two keys," Kimble said. "But only one has turned up."

"So someone else is running around here with a key to his room. They could get in whenever they feel like it."

Kimble nodded. "Mr. Maddox registered the room in his name only, and I was told he wasn't with anyone when he picked up the key. If he was staying with someone else, he kept it quiet."

"Was there any evidence that someone else was staying in the room?" I asked. I didn't recall seeing anything that screamed he was cohabitating, but not everyone left their personal items lying around in a hotel room.

Kimble spread his hands. "With the mess, it's hard to tell for sure. I'd say no, but can't be certain."

Remembering what I'd been told about Charles and his penchant for sleeping around, I asked, "Could you tell whether or not he'd been with anyone recently?"

Kimble gave me a questioning look.

I didn't know if he was intentionally being dense, or if he enjoyed watching me squirm. Talking about a dead man's sex life wasn't something I enjoyed doing. No, scratch that; talking about *anyone's* sex life was something I had zero interest in, and that included my own.

But there was no way around it this time.

"His wife is around here somewhere," I said. "And

Misty was angry at him, so it might mean he slept with her and then she found out about the wife. I was wondering if you had evidence that he did." I looked away, face flaming like I was a high schooler talking about this sort of thing with her father. "With her, or with anyone else."

If Kimble was amused by my embarrassment, he didn't show it. "If he did, someone disposed of the evidence elsewhere. There was nothing in his trash that indicated he'd had relations with anyone."

"What about on the bed?" I asked. "Were there hairs on the pillow or anything like that?"

"You watch a lot of TV, don't you?" Kimble's smile was teasing.

"Not really." I felt stupid for asking, but I would have thought they'd have done some sort of DNA retrieval since it was a murder we were dealing with. "It just seemed like a logical step."

"We did check," Kimble said, letting me off the hook. "But the staff had already changed his sheets and cleaned his room before they realized he was murdered. If there was once evidence, it was swept away and mixed with samples from dozens of other rooms. It'd be impossible to verify one way or the other at this point."

"Oh." So much for that.

Kimble sighed and straightened. "Enjoy the con, Ms. Hancock. You've been a big help, but I think I've got it from here."

It was a clear dismissal. I appreciated that Kimble had confided in me as much as he had, but wished I'd gotten more. He'd been under no obligation to tell me anything, and in fact, I imagined he could get into a lot of trouble if his superiors found out about our conversations, no matter how innocent they were.

It made me realize how difficult I made things on Paul Dalton back home. Everyone knew I was only trying to help, but there was a line civilians weren't supposed to cross. I'd been walking on the wrong side of that line for years now. It was only a matter of time before someone knocked me back across it for good.

Detective Kimble walked away. Something about his retreating form hit me hard, like I was watching him walk away for the last time. It seemed silly, and honestly, it was probably just the murder getting to me, but it made me sad to see him go.

I left the lobby and headed outside for some fresh air. A strange sense of melancholy had worked its way into me, and I was desperate to hear a friendly voice. I found a quiet spot out of the way, and then I pulled out my phone and dialed.

It rang only twice before it was answered.

"Hey, Buttercup! How's the con?"

"Dad." I closed my eyes at the sound of his raspy voice. Just hearing it was enough to make me feel better. "It's been pretty crazy here, actually."

"Uh-oh. You'd better tell me."

So I did.

As usual, Dad listened without interruption. He knew me, knew how I stressed over things I probably shouldn't. I needed to talk, to get it all off my chest, and he was the perfect man for the job.

Of course, James Hancock wasn't just my dad; he was a mystery writer who longed for the chance to actually solve a mystery or two of his own. He'd do his best to comfort me, but chances were good he'd provide me an outside perspective on the murder. It was part of the reason I called him when I did. I needed direction.

"Are you okay, Buttercup?" Dad asked when I finished speaking. "You sound more stressed than you usually do over these things."

"I'm all right," I said. "I just feel like I should be doing more."

"You aren't in Pine Hills." As if he needed to remind me. "You should let the police take care of things this time. You don't know how they'll react if you get too involved in the case."

"I know." I heaved a sigh. "It's hard, though. I see these people every time I step into a room. I keep wondering if I'm standing beside a killer, or if someone else will end up dead. How do you let something like that go?"

"Honestly, I don't think you can. It's not in your nature."

No, it wasn't. It wasn't in Dad's either. "What do you think I should do?"

"Well . . ." He groaned as he settled back into his chair. I could hear the leather creak. "I think you should have fun, but keep your eye out for anything suspicious. It sounds like you've already done quite a bit of investigating on your own. No sense risking yourself when the detective might already have a handle on things. See if your information pans out. If you come across something else that might help, just call him. Don't try to put it all together yourself."

All sound advice—yet why did I feel like he was telling me to let it go?

"I'll try," I said. "Vicki's told me pretty much the same thing."

"She's a smart lady."

"How's Laura?" I asked, changing the subject.

"She's great." I could hear the love in my dad's voice. Laura Dresden was his girlfriend, who I imagined might soon become his fiancée, if I was reading their relationship correctly. I still missed my mom dearly—she'd died years earlier—but I liked Laura; quite a lot, actually. If and when they finally did tie the knot, I would stand at Dad's side, as proud as could be.

"She's on a hike this morning," Dad went on. "I wasn't feeling up to it, so I told her to go without me."

"Are you feeling all right?" I asked, a sudden worry clutching at my gut. Dad was reaching an age where his health was going to start to become an issue.

"I'm fine; just tired. To be honest, I simply didn't want to go for a walk. I'm allowed to be lazy every now and again." He chuckled.

I was still unconvinced, but I let it slide. If something *was* wrong, I'd get it from Laura later.

"Well, if you—"

A scream from inside the hotel cut me off.

"Buttercup?"

I spun to see a crowd of people just inside the doors, gathering around a central location a little deeper into the lobby. A few people in the back were standing on their tiptoes to get a better view of whatever was happening.

"I've got to go," I said, pulse spiking. "I'll call you later, okay?"

Before Dad could protest, I clicked off. I shoved my phone into my pocket, and then, determined to find out what was going on, I headed inside.

Chapter 20

"Excuse me. Sorry." I pushed my way through the growing crowd, toward the intersection where the hotel met the convention center. A woman was holding her arm, suppressed tears in her eyes. She looked disheveled and pale, and a little angry. She was likely the source of the scream that had drawn my attention.

"What's happening?" I asked her. I couldn't quite see anything, and while I could hear yelling, the noise of the crowd made it impossible to hear what was being said.

"They started arguing." The woman pointed, using her good arm. "One of them shoved the other and knocked me down." She moved her arm and winced before grabbing at her elbow and grimacing. "It might be broken. Or dislocated. I should sue."

With the way she'd moved it, I was guessing it was merely bruised, but I wasn't going to get involved in *that* discussion.

I left her grumbling to the man next to her and pushed my way deeper into the crowd, in the direction she'd pointed. As I neared, I was able to discern two distinct voices; voices I knew.

"You've ruined everything!" Clint Sherman shouted. I reached the front of the crowd just in time to see him shove his adversary, who staggered back a single step.

"I had nothing to do with it!" Carmine Wright shouted right back, shoving Clint in return.

"If it wasn't for you, none of this would have happened," Clint said. He made as if he might shove Carmine again, but it was merely a feint. Carmine jerked back, however, which caused Clint to laugh. "You don't even realize what you've done. You think you know, but you're just guessing."

"Like you know anything?" Carmine retorted. "Rumor and hearsay. Nothing more. You're worse than those old ladies who sit around gossiping all day."

"Rumor?" Clint snorted. "Hearsay? Do you think I'm stupid? I know what I saw, and I know what it means."

"It means you're an idiot." Carmine crossed his arms and grinned, as if he thought he'd won the argument.

Clint's face turned a bright shade of red. He rushed forward and took a wild swing at Carmine's head. He missed badly as Carmine sidestepped him, with his own fists going up in a way that told me he'd never been in an actual fistfight before. He looked ridiculous, but the fact that they were coming to blows made it so no one laughed.

No one was stepping in to stop them either. I considered it, but was afraid I'd somehow end up on the receiving end of one of their wild blows.

Could this be about the murder? I wondered. Both men looked as if they'd already hit the drinks, which, if so, probably contributed to their childish display. I glanced around, hoping to spot Detective Kimble, but if he was there, he wasn't making himself known.

Clint bounced on his feet like a boxer who'd taken a few dozen too many blows to his head, keeping well away from Carmine. "I know," he said, voice a hiss. "I saw you two together, and look what happened. You're a disgrace."

"I didn't do anything wrong," Carmine said. "Unlike you." His grin was feral. "Shall I tell everyone what you have failed to tell your wife? I'm sure they'd all be interested." He glanced around the gathering crowd.

As soon as he took his eyes off of Clint, the other man lunged forward. Carmine barely managed to jump out of the way before they resettled on opposite ends of the makeshift ring.

"Go ahead," Clint said. He was breathing hard. "But if you do, I'll do the same thing to you. We'll see how long that self-satisfied grin of yours lasts once everyone knows what you've been doing behind closed doors."

There was an audible gasp from somewhere within the crowd. Someone else chuckled.

Both men glared at one another for a good long minute with no one saying a thing. Sweat beaded on Carmine's brow, and I noted his eyes were darting around as if looking for someone specific, though he made sure to keep Clint in his sights the entire time.

"You are both corrupt!" Wynona Kepler stood at the far edge of the ring. "Tell them; tell everyone!"

"Shut up, Winnie," Carmine shouted. He dared to take his eyes off Clint to turn his glare onto her. "You're a no-good cheat yourself, so it's not like you have any room to talk."

Wynona gasped, hand going to her chest as if she'd been shot. "I've never cheated on anything in my life. You have some nerve even hinting that I might."

Clint laughed. It sounded crazed. "Is anything about you real, Winnie? You try so hard to act like you're better than everyone else, when we all know you can barely brew a halfway decent pot of coffee without help."

"You stay out of this," she snarled, hands opening and closing. She looked like she was seconds away from leaping into the fray herself.

"You're the one who keeps sticking her nose into everyone else's business," Clint said. "Every time I turn around, there you are, throwing unfounded accusations around like you take some sick pleasure in it. No one cares what you think."

"Ha!" Carmine's mock laugh rang loudly as he turned back to Clint. "Sounds an awful lot like someone else I know."

The room erupted into a shouting match between the three of them. Others in the crowd joined in, but their voices were lost in the cacophony. I tried to keep track of what was going on, but it was too chaotic to make sense of what Clint and Carmine were saying, let alone the twenty or thirty other people who were lending their voices to the arguments.

I turned my attention away from the three stars of the show and instead scoured the crowd, looking for others I might know. If this did indeed have to do with the murder, someone might let something show on their face—a worry that one of those secrets might slip and implicate them, perhaps.

Pierre and Dallas were standing next to one another at the front of the crowd, watching the fracas with horrified looks on their faces. It was obvious they were thinking they were watching the end of JavaCon, and I couldn't say I blamed them. I wasn't sure how the con could survive not only a murder, but a huge rift between two of the organizers.

I didn't see Evaline Cobb anywhere, but a few feet from Wynona, I saw Tatiana Maddox. She kept looking from the two men to Wynona and back. She looked stunned, and for good reason. Her husband had been murdered, and now, people who'd known him were arguing like children in front of everyone.

There were other faces I recognized. Lisa Mitchell was there, holding on to the arm of a woman I didn't know but suspected might be her wife, Chloe. Her friend, Horace, was nearby, shaking his head sadly. I didn't see Rita or Vicki, but had a feeling one of them was likely somewhere nearby. Both Thomas and Tara were also absent.

The shouting was growing louder, and I realized that if someone didn't step in soon, it might erupt into a full-on fight where the punches wouldn't stop flying. I had opened my mouth to say something when my gaze landed on a woman standing just behind a short balding man who was filming the entire thing on his phone.

She was pretty, brown-haired, and of a size with Tatiana. In fact, they very well could have been sisters when it came to their looks. Even their waist sizes were a darn near match, which told me that Charles Maddox had a type, if indeed he'd been cheating on his wife with the other woman.

Misty Rodgers looked absolutely aghast by the fight. Her hand hovered near her mouth, right next to the mole on her upper lip. Her eyes were wide, nearly popping out. When she blinked, I noticed tears forming.

Carmine and Clint were nearly nose to nose by now, but neither had thrown another punch as of yet. Wynona stood nearby, egging them on. A young man who had to weigh no more than a sack of potatoes had moved forward to break up the spat, but got shoved onto his butt by Clint for his effort.

Keeping my eyes on the woman I believed to be Misty Rodgers, I started working my way around the circle toward her. It would have been faster to cross the empty space between us, but I was worried I'd somehow get dragged into the fight if I tried.

"Knock him out!" someone shouted in my ear. It was followed by, "Someone call the police!"

There was no need. The next voice that rose above the crowd was loud and commanding—and just as familiar to me as those of the combatants.

"Everyone step back! Now!"

Detective Kimble was working his way through the crowd, a member of the hotel staff trailing behind him. Onlookers parted as he strode forward, eyes hard. Kimble was in cop mode, for which I was grateful. While it might be interesting to hear what secrets

Clint and Carmine were threatening to spill, I didn't want to see anyone get hurt.

"What is the meaning of this?" Kimble demanded as he stepped into the middle of the circle, which now contained only Carmine and Clint. Wynona had melted back into the crowd to stand next to Tatiana. The innocent expression on her face would have been amusing if it wasn't for the tension in the room.

"He started it," Carmine said. He pointed at Clint like a petulant child who'd just been called out by his parents.

"Like you have room to talk." Clint turned to the detective. "We are having a disagreement. It's nothing that requires the police, thank you very much."

"I think I'll be the judge of that," Kimble said, squaring his shoulders. He appeared to grow two sizes when he did, which caused both men to shrink back from him. "Someone better start explaining exactly what's going on before I haul you both in."

He didn't need to give them a reason as to why he'd arrest them. The mere threat was enough to get both Clint and Carmine babbling excuses. It was a wonder neither man dropped to his knees to beg forgiveness.

The crowd began dispersing now that most of the excitement was over. Quite a few remained, likely hoping someone would say the wrong thing and it would erupt into a live episode of *Cops*. The short, bald guy was still filming on his phone, but I noticed Misty was slowly easing away behind him. She was watching Detective Kimble carefully, as if afraid she'd catch his notice if she moved too quickly.

Innocent people didn't act that way, did they?

"Hey!" I called, hoping to catch Kimble's attention. With the crowd noise, he didn't appear to hear me, or else he was ignoring me. So, I raised my voice. "Hey! Detective!"

Kimble glanced back at me and I swear I saw him roll his eyes, though it could have been a trick of the light.

I pointed toward Misty. "Over there." Her eyes widened, and she ducked back just as Detective Kimble glanced her way.

The balding man paled and shoved his phone into his pockets, hands upraised. "Sorry!" he said. "I didn't realize I wasn't supposed to be recording."

Kimble huffed, shook his head, and turned back to Clint and Carmine.

"No, not him!" I shouted, but Kimble ignored me. It appeared as if I was on my own on this one.

It took only a moment for me to catch sight of Misty weaving in and out of the remaining crowd. I considered grabbing Kimble and dragging him along with me, but realized he'd be more likely to handcuff me to a table than to come along willingly.

So, I did the only thing I could think of to do.

I followed after her.

Or, at least, I tried to.

"Oh my Lordy Lou!" Rita said, snagging me before I could chase after the fleeing woman. "Can you believe what's happening? It's like everyone's gone insane!"

"Not now, Rita," I said, pulling free of her grip, but she wouldn't be put off that easily.

"It's a travesty," she said, moving with me and, since we were in a crowd of people, effectively slowing me to a crawl. "Fighting like that after everything else that's happened? I swear this place is coming apart at its seams! If someone doesn't do something soon, someone else is going to get hurt."

Misty glanced back, a look of relief on her face when she realized the detective wasn't following her. She didn't see me moving her way, or else she might have continued her hurried flight. Instead, she resumed a more normal stroll as she turned down a hallway.

If I wanted to catch her, I needed to hurry. I couldn't do that with Rita grabbing hold of my wrist every couple of seconds. "Where's Tara?" I asked her, keeping an eye on the hall Misty had vanished down. "Aren't you still watching her?"

"I am," Rita said, sounding mildly offended I'd even ask. "Or, well, I was. She's in the ladies' room, so I thought I'd come see what the fuss was about."

"You should probably check to make sure she hasn't left," I said, gesturing toward the ladies' room door. From where we stood, you couldn't see who was going in or out. "You wouldn't want to lose her, now, would you?"

Rita's eyes widened, like she'd never thought of that. "I'd better get back." She said it like it had been her idea. "We'll talk about this later." She hurried away.

As soon as she was gone, I broke into a jog. Most everyone had dispersed by now, and many headed to whatever event they planned to attend next. Behind me, Clint's voice rose. He said something about Carmine and a weasel, but I didn't quite catch the full comparison. It must have been bad enough to sting, because Carmine shouted something right back.

It didn't sound like the argument was going to wind down anytime soon. That meant Detective Kimble would have his hands full for a while, which also meant he wouldn't be around to help in case chasing after Misty Rodgers turned out to be a really bad idea.

As I reached the hallway where Misty had gone, I pulled out my phone. I noticed I had a text from Dad, asking if everything was okay, but decided I'd hold off on replying. I wouldn't know if everything was fine until *after* I talked to Misty.

I did take a moment to shoot Detective Kimble a quick text—I'd added his number to my contacts after he'd given me his card—telling him which way I was going, just in case he managed to extract himself from the argument sometime during this lifetime.

See, I was learning. I still might have been running into what could potentially be a dangerous situation, but at least I'd let a cop know about it beforehand.

I just hoped that it wouldn't be too late by the time he *did* see it.

I shoved my phone back into my pocket and scanned the hallway. There were quite a few people milling around, many talking about what was going on in the lobby. I was worried I'd lost Misty, but I caught a glimpse of her just as she opened a door to one of the convention ballrooms and slipped inside.

I didn't hesitate.

Steeling myself for a potential confrontation with a killer, I followed after her.

Chapter 21

Misty sat in a chair at the front of the room, face buried in her hands. The other chairs were empty, as was the podium up front. Checking the time, I assumed it would be another fifteen minutes before people would start entering for a seminar or workshop, giving us a little time before the room would start to fill.

I closed the door quietly behind me. Misty didn't look up. As I neared her, I noticed her shoulders were shaking. She wasn't making much of a sound, but I was pretty sure she was crying, not laughing. There was an aura of sadness around her, one that made me feel for the woman, despite knowing nothing about her.

"Misty?" I asked, coming to a stop a few feet away. "Misty Rodgers?"

She sucked in a surprised breath and jerked her head upward. She quickly wiped her eyes, which were damp, and tried to put on a brave face. It didn't work. Even before the smile was in place, it cracked, and more tears slid down her cheeks.

"Yes?" she said. Her voice shook slightly. "Who are you?"

"Krissy Hancock." I eased down into a nearby chair. I'd have sat closer to her, but I was afraid that if I did, she'd get up and leave. The woman looked ready to break, and I didn't need to crowd her any more than I already was. "You don't know me, but I've heard about you."

Her face scrunched up in confusion before she shook her head. "You must be mistaken. I'm no one."

"You *are* Misty Rodgers, right?"

She stared at me a moment, as if debating whether or not to admit to it, before she nodded. "Yes, I am."

"I was told you knew Charles Maddox." I put as much compassion in my voice as I could manage. They may have parted on bad terms, but that didn't mean she hadn't cared for him.

Still, despite my kinder tone, at the mention of Charles's name, Misty broke. Tears erupted from her eyes and a tortured groan escaped her lips before she buried her face in her hands again. This time, her sobs weren't silent. They were the big, ugly kind; the sort that often required an entire box of tissues before they are through.

I rose briefly, crossed the short distance between us, and took the seat next to her. I rested a hand on her back and rubbed gently between her shoulder blades. Misty leaned into it, very nearly resting her head onto my shoulder as she cried.

I wasn't sure how to feel about her reaction to Charles's name. A part of me had hoped she was guilty of killing him, because it would clear both Tara and Thomas and would put an end to the tension running throughout JavaCon.

But now, I prayed she was innocent. I also hoped that this would be the last time she cried over a man who'd treated so many people badly. She deserved better.

After a few minutes, Misty sniffed and sat upright. She produced an already ragged, balled-up tissue and wiped at her eyes. "I'm sorry," she said. "It's been a rough couple of days. I didn't mean to blubber all over you."

"It's okay. I completely understand." I took a deep breath and hoped my next question wouldn't set her off again. "Did you know Charles well?"

She shrugged, jaw bunching and releasing over and over. "I thought I did. It appears I was wrong about him."

"Were you two dating?"

She glanced at me, and I thought she might tell me where I could stick my invasive questions, but she relented. "We were. Well, I thought we were." She made a frustrated sound. "It's complicated. With Charles, it was hard to tell."

"Did you know he was married?" I asked. Misty looked so miserable, it made me wish Charles was still alive so I could smack him around a little for what he'd done to her.

"No, I didn't." Misty's eyes went hard for a split second before softening. "He never wore a ring, and he definitely never said anything about it. When I found out, I couldn't believe it."

"Is that what you fought about?" I asked.

Misty looked down at the tissue in her hand. She tugged at it, tearing off small pieces and letting them flutter to the floor. "No. I didn't find out about his wife until after he was dead."

"But you fought?" I pressed.

Misty continued to tear at her tissue without speaking. There was a tension to her shoulders, a stiffness to her posture that wasn't there before.

"You were seen with him on the day of the murder," I said. "And a friend of mine said you told her where to find him. When she got there, he was already dead." I paused, weighed what else to say. "She said you were crying. I take that to mean the fight happened right before his death."

Misty finally looked up from her tissue to give me a hard stare. "It did, but . . ." Her jaw worked some more before she went on. "She killed him, didn't she? That woman? I told her where to go, and the next thing I know, people are saying Charles is dead. It can't be a coincidence that she asked about him."

"I don't know," I said, wishing I did. "She said he was already dead by the time she found him."

"Well, he was alive when I left him." She sucked in a trembling breath and let it slowly out between her teeth. The next came out at a near whisper. "I caught him with someone else. I walked right in on them while they were together."

"In bed?"

She nodded and crushed the remains of her tissue

in her fist. "He wasn't expecting me. We'd made plans to meet before the competition, but were to meet in the convention center, not in his room. I figured I might surprise him. You know, give him a good-luck kiss or whatever." Her face reddened, but she went on. "When I walked in, I could hear them." She shuddered. "The moment I stepped through the threshold, he was out of the bed like a rocket. He pushed me out the door, not bothering to cover himself or deny what I'd seen."

"Did you see who he was with?" I asked.

"No. All I saw was Charles, and then everything went red before he was pushing me out. He kept apologizing, right up until he shoved me out the door and closed it in my face."

"And this was the morning of the tasting?" I asked to be sure. I had to admit, it didn't look good for Misty. Whether she killed him or not, this gave her a pretty big motive for murder, one I was sure Detective Kimble would be interested in hearing about.

"It was," Misty said. "I almost didn't go to the thing, but decided we needed to talk it out. And I guess I was hoping that whoever he'd been sleeping with would show up and make themselves known. I had some words I wanted to say to them. I wasn't sure if I was going to tell them they could have him, or if I was going to fight for him. I guess it didn't matter." The tears were back. She wiped them angrily away. "I guess it must have been his wife he was with."

"Actually," I said, "I don't think it was."

She gave me a questioning look.

"From what I understand, Tatiana—his wife—didn't

show up until *after* he was dead." Or at least, that's what she'd said. I was pretty sure I'd seen her with him before then, but couldn't prove it.

"You mean there was someone else?" Her eyes grew wide. "Someone other than her and me?"

"Apparently."

"I . . ." Misty licked her lips and started breathing quickly. "How could he do this to me? To us?"

"I wish I knew." I rested a hand on her shoulder and squeezed. "Tell me what happened that day. From the start. Maybe you saw or heard something that might point to who killed him. Sometimes the small details are the ones that matter." Especially if whoever had killed Charles was angry with him because of Misty walking in on them. If she had caught a voice, or had seen something that would tell me who he'd been with, then perhaps I'd be able to deduce who'd killed him.

Misty was silent for a couple of moments before she started speaking. "As I said, I caught him with someone, but I couldn't tell you who. I watched him at the tasting, but no one acted oddly, not even Charles. He didn't even seem to care that he'd upset me." Her hands balled into fists.

"So you saw no one you thought might have been his lover?"

She shook her head. "At least, no one obvious. Once the tasting was done and he finished lapping up all the attention for his win, I confronted him. We argued, of course. He tried to deny everything, said he'd been alone, but I knew better. I'm not stupid."

"Was anyone else there?" I asked. "When you two were arguing?"

"There were others hanging around at first. A couple of the judges were standing by the doors talking, but they weren't paying us any mind. I think they left before I did, but I'm not positive. I was pretty upset and wasn't paying much attention, so there could have been others."

Like Tatiana? I wondered. If Charles's wife had shown up early, seen him with Misty, and then heard about Charles getting caught in bed with someone else, then it was likely she wouldn't be very happy. Though when I'd seen them together after the tasting, Charles hadn't seemed too upset; neither of them had. Maybe she hadn't known at the time. Perhaps she still didn't.

"Did Charles leave the room at any point before you talked to him?" I asked, trying to make sense of the timeline.

Misty frowned, thinking it through. "He might have," she said. "I lost track of him for a little while after he won. Everything was so crazy with everyone wanting to congratulate him."

That meant Tatiana might have talked to Charles *before* he argued with Misty. Did that exonerate her? Or did that make her an even bigger suspect? Because if she was lurking when Misty threw around her accusations, there's no telling how she might have reacted.

"I couldn't take his lies," Misty went on. "I wanted to make things right, but Charles refused to accept responsibility for his actions. I told him that I was done with him, and then I stormed right out of the room. I think a part of me hoped he'd chase me down and fix everything somehow. I was so stupid."

"Did you see anyone on your way out?" I asked. "It could be important."

"No." She paused, and then her eyes lit up. "No, wait. There was this other woman outside in the hall, the one who accused Charles of cheating. She wouldn't get out of my way, and I almost walked into her." Her eyes widened. "Do you think she killed him over a silly competition?"

"I don't know," I said, wondering. Wynona *had* been pretty upset. Still was, to be honest. "Did she go into the room after you left?"

Misty bit her lower lip before raising her hands and then dropping them into her lap. "I can't remember. She might have." Her face scrunched up in thought. "The door might have opened behind me, so maybe she did."

"And after that . . . ?"

"I went into a room to calm my nerves, and that woman asked about Charles. I told her where to find him, and then, next thing I knew, someone was saying he's dead." She looked into my eyes. "I told her where to find him, and a part of me wondered if she was the other woman. I mean, why ask after him if you don't already know him, right?" She pressed her palms against her eyes. "Instead, I might have killed him by telling her where he was."

"It's not your fault," I said. "No matter who killed him, it's on them."

"But what if it was her? I told her where he was. How could it *not* be my fault?" She raised a finger, as if an idea had formed. "She knew him. She asked after him like they were more than just friends. She *has* to have been the one he was sleeping with. Why else would she ask me if I knew where to find him? She *knew*."

"We don't know that she killed him," I said, but I really was starting to wonder. Tara claimed to have found Charles, but she had never told anyone until after his body was discovered by someone else. She was also the right height for the woman who'd broken into his room afterward, as was Misty. And when I'd seen her before his death, she'd been pretty darn angry with him.

Misty heaved a sigh, nodding. "You're probably right. It's terrible that this happened, but I should stop beating myself up over it." She sniffed and produced another tissue. "From the sound of things, Charles wasn't worth all the tears I've given him."

I wasn't sure what to say to that, nor did I have any other questions. I was sure Detective Kimble would have a few of his own, and I kind of wanted to be around when he asked them.

Before I could recommend that she find the detective to tell him her story, a sound came from Misty's purse.

Wind chimes.

Misty jumped and then pulled her phone from a bag she'd been carrying. She checked the screen, typed something out, and then shoved the phone back into the bag.

"Sorry. My friend keeps texting to make sure I'm all right."

I stared at her, mouth agape. *She doesn't recognize me*, I realized. It was no wonder. When Misty last saw me, my hair had been a mess, my face had been makeup-free, and I'd been wearing pj's and slippers.

And it had been in the dead of night.

I considered not saying anything, but I couldn't help myself. I had to know.

"It was you," I said.

"Me?" Misty asked, confusion painting her features. "I didn't kill Charles."

"No, not that. You were in his room last night."

Misty's eyes widened, and she paled as realization dawned. "You were the one who chased me!" She gathered her bag and stood. "I've got to go."

I hurriedly rose and blocked her path. "Why were you in his room?" I demanded. "How did you get in?"

"Charles gave me a key. It was before I found out he was a lying cheat."

Which made sense. She *had* walked in on him in bed with someone else, and she could only have done that if she had a key to his room. I should have put it together the moment she'd mentioned it, but I hadn't been thinking about the break-in at the time.

"But why go into the room afterward?" I asked. "Were you looking for his coffee recipe?"

"What? No!" Misty looked past me to the door. People would start coming in soon for the next seminar, and I could tell she wanted to be long gone before they did. "If you must know, I'd left something of mine in there. I wanted it back."

"What was it?" I asked. I couldn't believe I'd been sitting there talking to the person who'd nearly run me to exhaustion the night before. She hardly looked affected, while I felt—and probably looked— like someone who'd barely slept.

"That," she said, "is none of your business. Suffice

it to say, it was something private, something I didn't want the police—or his wife—to find."

That could be just about anything, I realized. She could have left an article of clothing behind. Or perhaps she'd given him a love letter. Or maybe she was afraid someone would find a sheet of paper where he'd scrawled her phone number down and she didn't want anyone to make the connection.

"Why not tell anyone this?" I asked. "Why not tell the police, clear your name?"

"The police knew nothing of our relationship." The door opened and an old woman with a walker came in. She waved at us and then made her slow way across the room to a chair set off to the side.

"They'll find out, Misty," I said. "You need to find Detective Kimble and tell him everything you've told me. What do you think will happen if he finds out you were keeping secrets from him?"

She bit her lower lip, her eyes going worried.

"Trust me, you don't want to be caught lying. He's been asking questions, and someone has already mentioned you to him." I didn't want to tell her that someone was me. "He's looking for you, and it's only a matter of time before he finds you. It'll be better for everyone if you go to him and tell him everything."

More people started piling into the room. Misty looked like she might be sick, but she nodded. "I'll find him," she promised.

"Good."

She fingered her bag for a long moment and then strode out of the room.

I hoped she would go straight to Detective Kimble, because there was no way I was going to keep this to myself. I wanted to believe her innocent of killing Charles. Heck, I wanted to believe everyone innocent, at this rate, but I knew someone had to have done it.

But who? Was the killer one of Charles's women? Was it someone who was upset with him for his win at the tasting? Or was it someone I'd yet to talk to, someone who was keeping their connection to Charles a secret?

Chapter 22

Though I'd attended a few events, I realized I wasn't making much time to enjoy JavaCon. Sure, a murder did put a damper on things, but honestly, there was a lot to do, and I'd barely scratched the surface. Just because I was on the hunt for a killer didn't mean I couldn't have a little fun.

It was difficult to put what I'd learned from Misty out of my mind and focus on the con, but somehow, I managed it for a little while. I wandered from room to room, checking out smaller tables set up for demos and quick tutorials, including one on how to properly clean a coffeepot so that bacteria didn't build up in the machine.

After being thoroughly grossed out, I headed for the vendors' room. It was filled with people selling coffees, creamers, mugs, coffee makers, and other coffee-themed items. I paused at an espresso machine, but nixed it from my mind pretty quickly after seeing the price. Either I had underestimated how much those things cost or the guy was ripping people off.

Not wanting to leave empty-handed—or with an empty bank account—I decided to stock up on various coffees in the hope of finding one I liked. And even though I didn't often use creamer in my coffee, I picked up a few samples of those as well. If I didn't use them, I knew a few people who would.

I was about to leave when I spotted a travel mug with the JavaCon logo on it. I added it to my haul, and with purchases in hand, I left the room. Shopping had eased my mind considerably, and I was whistling under my breath as I returned to the main hall.

The admittedly out-of-key tune died on my lips the moment I saw who was sitting across the room.

Thomas was leaning forward, talking intently to Tara, who was shaking her head. They didn't look like they were fighting, but whatever they were talking about, it was obvious she wasn't happy about it.

It's probably my fault. I never should have put the idea into Thomas's head that Tara could have broken into Charles's room, but at the time, it had seemed like the right thing to do. He deserved to know if she had done so.

I thought about taking my purchases to my room and pretending I hadn't seen them, but I didn't. While Tara was still a suspect in Charles's murder, she wasn't a thief. I couldn't simply walk away and let things get out of hand, not when I could fix them with a simple word or two.

"Thomas," I said, as I approached the two of them. "Tara."

"Krissy." Thomas didn't smile when he looked up at me. From the look Tara gave me, I knew he'd confronted her about the break-in and had told her where he'd gotten his information.

Great. This is going to be fun.

They were sitting at a small table, nearly shoulder to shoulder. Two partially eaten bagels and a pair of mostly empty coffees sat in front of them. I set my bag aside and then took a seat across from them.

"I found out who broke into Charles's room," I said.

The vindicated look on Tara's face confirmed my suspicions that they were talking about the break-in. Thomas, who could easily have been angry with me for putting the idea in his head, looked relieved.

"Who was it?" Thomas asked.

"A woman named Misty Rodgers. She was the one who told Tara where to find Charles, the one who was upset with him."

Tara paled. "I remember her. Do you think she killed him and then sent me there to frame me?"

"I can't say for sure, but I don't think she did." I quickly relayed what she'd told me about that day to the both of them. "She went to Charles's room that night looking for a personal item of some sort. She didn't say what it was, or if she found it."

"It could have been evidence against her," Thomas said. "It sounds like she had a pretty good motive to kill him."

"Yeah." Which worried me. Had I let a killer walk away without making sure she went to Kimble? As far as I knew, she was already in her car and on the way to an airport. "I told her to talk to Detective Kimble." Speaking of whom, I pulled out my phone and checked. No return texts or calls.

"Do you think she will?" Thomas asked.

"I hope so. If she didn't kill Charles, it would be better if she told her story before it comes out some other way." My eyes drifted to Tara. I hated to do it, but I needed to ask her about Misty's suspicion. "She claims she walked in on Charles with someone else. Any idea who that might be?"

"Me?" she asked. "Why would I know?"

I wasn't sure how to answer that without accusing her of anything. While any number of women could have been in Charles's room when Misty walked in on him, there were only so many who'd shown a strong reaction to Charles's death.

Sure, her tears could be chalked up to the shock of finding him, but what if there was more to it? What if Misty was right and Tara knew him better than she was letting on? It was a stretch, but right then, it was all I had.

Thomas leaned forward in his chair, forcing me to take my eyes off of Tara and focus on him. "You can't seriously think . . ." He shook his head. "No. Impossible."

"A lot of women were mad at Charles yesterday," I said. "Tara was one of them."

"Wait." She sat forward. "You think *I* was sleeping with him? Are you out of your mind?"

"I'm not accusing you," I said, though I kind of was. "I'm just trying to make all the pieces fit together. That sometimes means asking uncomfortable questions of people I like." I tried on a smile, but she was having none of it.

"That's not just uncomfortable, it's downright rude," she said. "I can't believe you would think I could do that. With *him*, no less."

"Charles was with *someone*. And it had to be someone he knew, right?" I looked from face to face, hoping one of them would understand why I was asking.

"Not necessarily," Thomas said. "From what I knew of Charles, he didn't really care who he was with, just as long as it got him what he wanted. If I were to accuse anyone of sleeping with him, I'd pick one of the judges—maybe all of them. That would have been the best way to secure his win, right?"

"Charles?" Tara said. "Really?" She shuddered.

"Maybe," I allowed. "But I can't see Evaline or Dallas sleeping with Charles. I've talked to both." There was a moment when I almost spilled Evaline's secret about her relationship with Carmine, but I caught myself. No sense making things worse for everyone.

"There's hundreds of women here," Tara pointed out. "It could have been any one of them. I don't see why you'd even think I would consider it."

"And that Misty woman could be lying," Thomas put in. "She might not have caught him with anyone. She could have killed him and then made up the story about finding him with another woman to throw off the police."

"I suppose." I sighed. "But why make up a story that would make her seem guiltier than if she simply said she was having affair with him? Jealousy is a strong motive. And why not tell the police about it?"

"She could have . . ." Thomas frowned. "I don't know. I just know Tara wasn't with him."

"It was a long shot," I said. "And just because I didn't think it was true, it didn't mean it wasn't possible."

"That what? I was sleeping with him?" Tara asked. "Ew."

"Yeah, I know. It sounds stupid now that I said it. But what if Detective Kimble comes to the same conclusion? You found Charles's body and didn't report it. You were angry with him beforehand. And once Misty tells him that you were asking about Charles before he was found dead, he'll likely wonder why you were looking for him."

"I already told one of the cops I went in search of him," Tara said, though it came out sounding scared.

"I know. But did you explain why you were angry at the time? I have a feeling Misty won't hesitate to let them know."

Tara's eyes grew worried. When she spoke, it came out at a near whisper. "I wasn't with him."

"Do you have proof of that?" I asked. "Not for me; I believe you. But for when the detective comes asking. Anything you can give him will help."

Tara glanced at Thomas. He shook his head subtly.

But not subtly enough.

A rock fell from somewhere high above and crashed through my stomach. Things started to click into place, and boy, did I ever not want them to.

"You two were together at the time, weren't you?" I asked. It came out sounding flat, lifeless.

Thomas closed his eyes and fell back into his chair. Tara merely nodded and said, "We were."

"*Together* together?" I asked.

"It wasn't like that," Thomas said. "Well, I guess in some ways it was." He heaved a sigh and leaned toward me. "It just happened."

I nodded, unsure what to say.

"You and I hadn't really talked much," Thomas said. "Tara and I were working on our business plan—what we were going to do if one of us were to win the competition. It was late, we'd both had quite a bit to drink by then, and, well . . ."

I so didn't need to hear the details. "I understand," I said.

"It didn't mean anything."

I could tell by the way he said it that it wasn't entirely true. And then, looking at the hurt on Tara's face, I realized she didn't feel the same way either.

"No one knows, do they?" I asked. "Why keep it to yourselves?" What I was really asking was, "Why not tell me?"

"No one knows," Thomas answered. "No one but you."

"Wynona doesn't keep anything to herself," Tara said. There was a sadness to her voice. "If she found out about us, she would blab it to everyone at the con. Then people would talk and then start prying."

"Even if we were together for just that one night, they'd hold it against us," Thomas added.

I turned to him and gave him a smile, trying to make it appear as if I wasn't as hurt as I really felt. "You don't have to pretend," I said. "I can tell you like her."

"But . . ." He glanced at Tara, face reddening.

"It's clear you two have feelings for one another." I swallowed a lump that had grown in my throat. *This is for the best, Krissy.* It wasn't like anything could ever happen between Thomas and me. "You both deserve to be happy."

Thomas lowered his eyes and folded his hands on the table in front of him.

"I won't tell anyone," I said. "If you two want to keep it a secret, my lips are sealed." I looked to Tara. "But if you decide to go public, just know I approve. You two look great together."

Tara reached out a tentative hand and laid it on Thomas's own. "There's no reason to hide how I feel anymore," she said. "We didn't win. No one will care if we are working together or are, well, *together* now." She scooted to the edge of her seat so that they were nearly nose to nose. "And I do care about you. It was more than a one-night stand to me."

Thomas met Tara's eyes briefly, then he looked at me. I kept my smile in place as I nodded for him to go on; I was okay.

"It meant more to me too," Thomas said. "But what about our company? If we're together and something happens . . ."

"You can't think like that," I said, butting in. "Life is too short to play scared. If you want to be with her, then be with her." Something in the back of my mind raised its head in question.

I know, I told it. Considering my track record back home, I sounded like a hypocrite.

Thomas met Tara's eyes again. I could see the love between them. It had been there all along, yet I'd been too blind to see it for what it truly was. I think I'd felt it, though. Ever since I'd seen the two of them together, I'd known.

I gathered my bag and stood. "You two have a lot to talk about," I said. "I'll leave you to it."

I started to walk away, but Thomas stood and called out to me. "Krissy, wait."

My heart leapt into my throat as I turned. I was half-afraid he'd profess his love for me too and turn this entire thing into a mess of emotions on all sides.

Instead, he smiled. "Thank you."

I bowed my head to him and then left them to talk.

I needed to get away for a few minutes, so I took the elevator up to my room and deposited my bag of goodies next to the bed. Rita and Vicki were still down at the con, so I had the room to myself, which gave me a chance to think.

I'd done a good thing, yet I still felt sad. Nothing might have come of me and Thomas, but the romantic in me had hoped for one of those long goodbyes once the con ended.

Yeah, I know it was unlikely, but hey, a woman could dream.

Still, my advice to the two lovebirds stuck with me. I removed my phone, tapped it against my palm a few times, and then sent a quick text.

Thinking of you. Can't wait to get home.

It wasn't everything I wanted to say, but I thought that a man like Paul Dalton would be able to read between the lines.

I pocketed my phone, sucked in a cleansing breath, and then left the hotel room, determined to start putting everything in my life in order. For now, that started with finding Charles Maddox's killer.

Chapter 23

When I returned downstairs, the lobby and convention floor were mostly empty. Thomas and Tara were gone, and I hoped they'd gone off somewhere together to further discuss their future. If one good thing came out of JavaCon, I hoped their getting together would be it.

Checking my phone, I found I had a little more time until one of the big events of the con: an awards ceremony where the winner of the taste test was to be honored. I wanted to go to see what would happen since the victor, Charles Maddox, was dead. Would they give the prize to someone else? Would the killer be there? How would I know if they were?

The event was to be held in Ballroom C. The doors were closed, however, so they weren't seating quite yet. A few people were hanging around, waiting in the hope of getting a good seat when they did finally open.

Not wanting to miss out, I found an empty chair and sat down where I could watch the doors.

It didn't take long before a line began to form. The event was still twenty minutes away, yet people were anxious to get inside. Charles's death had put a damper on the festivities at first, but it appeared as if the mystery surrounding it had people interested again. I had a feeling I wasn't the only person who wanted to see what would happen when they talked about the winning coffee.

"It's time."

My ears perked up and I sat up straighter. I recognized that voice.

"It seems cruel."

I knew that one too. I glanced around and, after a few moments, saw Pierre and Dallas—the sources of the first two voices.

"I don't know . . ." This from Evaline Cobb, who looked extremely uncomfortable about the conversation. She glanced at the other woman with them, and I sucked in a shocked breath when I saw who it was.

"It's the right thing to do." Wynona Kepler stood tall and confident among the others. "We all know it."

"It's the only way we can save face," Pierre said. "If something isn't done, then we might as well give up now."

"I . . ." Wynona saw me looking at them and gave me the stink-eye. "We should continue this conversation inside." She took Evaline by the arm and led her toward the doors to Ballroom C.

Both Pierre and Dallas looked startled, but followed after obediently. They slipped into the room and were gone.

What was that all about? I wondered. It wasn't much of a stretch to think that it had to do with Charles's murder. But in what way? Were they going to strip Charles of the prize? Reveal his treachery, so to speak?

Or was it something else? Something regarding the con itself? After Carmine and Clint's fight, it wouldn't surprise me if it was.

Whatever it was, I had a feeling Wynona Kepler was the driving force behind it. She'd had a look about her that said she was in full control of the situation and planned to push things as far as she could in order to get her way.

"There you are!" Rita stomped toward me, shoulders slumped as if she was near collapse. "I've been looking all over for you! I swear, I was starting to wonder if you'd up and run off and left us here alone. I mean, the way you ran off like that, anything could have happened to you."

Considering I'd sent her chasing after Tara, not the other way around, I didn't think she had much room to talk. "I'm here, Rita," I said. "I talked to someone for a little while and then went up to the room for a few minutes."

"Well, I know that *now.*" She made it sound like I'd offended her by not telling her where I was going beforehand. "I was just about to burst, you know? Wait until you hear what I found out!"

I raised a hand to stop her from going on. "I already talked to Tara," I said. "I know about her and Thomas. I sent you on a fool's errand, and I apologize for that."

"About her and Thomas?" She gave me a questioning look before her eyes widened. "They're together?" I could almost see her brain filing the information away for later, though who she'd tell, I had no idea. "I saw you talking to them a little while ago, which was why I went for a drink. If I'd have known they were going to do that to you, I would have stuck around and given them a piece of my mind!"

"It's okay, Rita," I said, though I was touched she cared. "It's a good thing." When her eyebrows rose, I said, "Really. They're good together. It wouldn't have worked out between Thomas and me anyway."

"Well, if you say so." She crossed her arms and shook her head in a disapproving way.

I didn't want to get into it with Rita, especially since I wasn't completely over the fact that I'd played matchmaker for a pretty woman and a guy I kind of liked, so I asked, "What was it you heard?"

Her arms uncrossed and she leaned forward, eager to tell the tale.

"Well, as I said, when I saw you with Tara, I figured I had some time to take care of some business of my own. I needed a potty break—I didn't go when Tara did, for obvious reasons."

I nodded, though I really didn't need the details there.

"When I came back out, you were still there, so I decided to find myself something to drink. I was parched, let me tell you. Chasing after someone who doesn't seem to need a break is exhausting. If someone would have offered me water, I would have blessed the ground they walked on right then and there."

Applause came from a crowd of people near the doors. When I looked, the doors were still closed, and the applause died away with no indication as to what had caused the outburst.

"You'd be surprised at how many people are talking about this poor dead man like he deserved what happened to him," Rita went on, unfazed by the interruption. "It seemed like everyone was talking about it. It made it hard to discern what was important and what was just people flapping their lips to hear themselves speak."

This coming from someone who liked to spread rumors herself. "His death is a pretty big deal," I said. "I'd be surprised if no one was talking about it."

"Well, a lot of people believe what that woman said, that he cheated for his win somehow. There are quite a few calling into question whether or not the judges fixed it for him."

Which would hurt JavaCon's future. Was that what the others had been talking about before going into the ballroom? Could Dallas, Pierre, and Evaline be planning on coming clean at the ceremony? If that was the case, why was Wynona there? Was she the one who'd talked them into it?

Rita was still talking. I pushed my questions aside so I could pay closer attention.

"Some of the things people were saying would make your hair curl, let me tell you." She fanned herself with her program. "But it wasn't until I came across the dead man's wife that things started to get interesting."

I leaned forward. "You saw Tatiana?"

Rita nodded, a wide smile on her face. "She was talking to one of the judges, one of the ones who got into that fight earlier today. What was his name?" She frowned. "The one who looks like a rat." When I stared at her blankly, she added, "He's always tense, shoulders bunched." She patted her head. "He looks like he just came in from a snowstorm."

"Clint Sherman?" I asked.

"That's the one," Rita said with a snap of her fingers. "The woman never called him by name, and I keep getting them all mixed up."

Clint and Tatiana talking? Why did that surprise me so much? "What were they discussing?" I asked.

"At first, all she did was complain that no one was letting her take her husband's things." Which sounded just like Tatiana. The woman was practically a broken record. "That Clint fellow didn't seem too interested in hearing her out, because he kept telling her that she had no right to them."

"No right?" I wondered aloud.

Rita nodded. "The woman kept getting angrier and angrier the more he said it. It got to the point where someone asked them to keep it quiet or they'd have to leave. They lowered their voices then, but not so much that I couldn't still hear them."

A nearby woman erupted into laughter, causing me to jump. Her companion gave me an apologetic smile before the two walked away. The woman staggered slightly as she leaned on his shoulder, still giggling.

Rita didn't seem to hear them.

"So, there they are, fighting over a dead man's

things, when Clint finally seemed to have had enough. He slammed his hand down onto the table and said something to her at a near whisper."

"Did you hear what he said?" I asked when Rita didn't continue right away.

"Of course I did, dear. I was sitting right behind them."

I stared at her. She was grinning in a way that told me she was just dying for me to ask the question.

"What did he say?' I asked.

Rita beamed. She was just about rubbing her hands together in anticipation. "He said, 'You don't deserve a single thing, Tatiana. And if you keep pressing the issue, I'll tell everyone who you really are.' "

Rita riffled through her purse until she found lip balm. She ran it across her lips, capped it, and then went on. "Let me tell you, that really got under Tatiana's skin. She hissed at him like a snake, saying he'd better not, and then he called her Tatiana Copeland. When he said that, I thought she was going to rear off and slap him right across the face."

Tatiana Copeland? I ran the last name through my memory banks, but came up empty. "Is that her maiden name?" I asked.

"It could be," Rita said. "But I don't think it is. If you'd seen the look on her face, and the way she looked around the room like she was afraid someone might have overheard, you'd have thought he called her something far worse."

"What happened then?" I asked, mind racing. Why would Tatiana get so upset when Clint used her maiden name? The name meant nothing to me, but could it mean something to someone else? I had a feeling there was more to it than that. You didn't get angry at someone for using your name, not unless you were trying to hide something.

"They continued to argue, mostly about the same old stuff, before Clint rose and left her with one last warning to keep her mouth shut. I never did figure out what he was warning her from saying, but I'm sure it was a doozy. Those two really don't like one another one bit."

"Huh," I said. "I wonder why."

Rita shifted in her seat, finding a more comfortable position. She groaned audibly when she found it. "Well, I'd say that it's probably because Tatiana Copeland was never Tatiana Maddox."

"You heard them say that?" I asked.

"No, but it was pretty obvious to me. That woman doesn't seem very much like wife material, if you ask me. And with how she reacted to the name, I don't believe she wants anyone else to know it."

Now that Rita brought it up, I had to agree. Nothing in Tatiana's demeanor had ever screamed "mourning wife." I could definitely see her as someone who was trying to take advantage of a man's death, however.

But how did she know Clint Sherman? And why did she ever think coming here, claiming to be Charles's wife, would work? If they knew one another, he'd see right through the ploy.

Because she has something on Clint, that's why.

"Where did Tatiana go?" I asked, growing excited. If she had dirt on Clint, then she might have something on the other judges as well. She might even know who would have had a reason to kill Charles, assuming she hadn't done it herself.

"Last I knew, she was still sitting there, fuming," Rita said.

"Where?" I couldn't sit still any longer. While I wanted to attend the event in the ballroom, finding out exactly what was going on between Tatiana and Clint had jumped to priority number one.

"The hotel restaurant," Rita said, pointing. "Over there. Do you know they charge five dollars for a Coke? Five dollars!"

"Thanks, Rita," I said, ignoring her indignation. I wasn't about to jump down that rabbit hole. "You've been a big help."

Rita's "I know, dear; I know" followed me as I hurried toward the hotel restaurant, hoping to catch Tatiana Copeland before she vanished for good.

Chapter 24

The hotel restaurant was small. The seating was so cramped, customers had to be careful getting up, lest they bump into the person sitting behind them. A bar made up the far side of the room, with barely enough room behind it for the bartender to move without knocking over the bottles on the shelves behind him.

It was no wonder Rita had been able to eavesdrop without being noticed. Walking across the mostly empty room was more difficult than it should have been. Even pushed in beneath their tables, the chairs were in the way.

Tatiana was nursing a drink at the bar. She was alone, and looked like she wanted to be anywhere but at JavaCon. Her shoulders were slumped and her head lowered as she swirled her drink in slow circles with a thin red straw.

Light, barely audible music played overhead. It sounded like jazz, but I couldn't tell for sure, with it being so quiet. As far as I knew, it was some modern pop variant of the real thing.

Other than Tatiana, I didn't recognize anyone else from the con. There were four other people in the room, and they looked to me like businessmen on a work trip. They were dressed in suits and sat in a corner, talking among themselves, ties loose around their necks.

I slid onto the stool next to Tatiana. She glanced at me, but her face showed no reaction, let alone recognition.

"Seat's taken," she said before turning back to her drink. She wasn't quite slurring, but it was obvious she'd been drinking for a while now.

"I don't think Clint's coming back," I said.

Tatiana grunted, took a drink. "You watching me or something?"

"Just observant." The bartender wandered over, but I waved him away. "It doesn't appear as if you and Clint get along much. Has it always been that way?"

"Secrets." She shrugged. "You know how it is. I learn his, he learns mine. Fun ensues." She took another drink and waved the empty glass before setting it aside.

"Secrets, huh?" I waited as the bartender refilled her glass and then, feeling guilty for sitting there with nothing in front of me, I ordered a Coke for myself. I waited for the drinks to arrive before going on. "Secrets like how you aren't really Charles Maddox's widow?"

Tatiana's glass froze about halfway to her lips. She set it down slowly without taking a drink. "He's talking?" she asked. Her voice was hard, eyes blazing. "That jerk is actually talking?"

"No," I said. "But you two were talking louder than either of you realized. You're Tatiana Copeland, not Maddox. It wasn't hard to deduce that it meant you were likely faking your marriage to him."

"We were married," she said, though it came out sounding more petulant than forceful. "I didn't take his name."

"Come on, Tatiana. We both know that's not true. You all but admitted it a second ago. There's no use denying it; you and Charles were never married."

This time, she drained her glass in one go. When it hit the bar, it came down hard enough that I thought it might shatter. She shoved the glass away and turned on her stool to stare at me.

"Who do you think you are?" she asked. The heat in her voice had me leaning away, afraid she might take a swing at me. "Why does any of this matter to you?"

"I'm no one," I said. "But it will matter when it comes out. You know you can't hide something like that forever, not with the police asking questions."

Her jaw worked as she looked me up and down with bloodshot eyes. "I suppose it matters little now," she said with a resigned sigh. "Hardly anyone believed me to begin with, and those who did refused to give in to my demands." She sucked in a breath and let it out in a huff. "No, I wasn't married to Charles Maddox. He was never my husband, and we never dated. Happy?"

"Honestly? Not really," I said. "Why lie? You had to

know someone would figure it out eventually. What did you think would happen when they did?"

"I just wanted his coffee recipe," she said. "The stupid thing won the competition, which meant it had value. I figured if I managed to get hold of it, I could make a dollar or two off it. Or at least make a knockoff of it or whatever."

She spoke like the café mocha was one of the most valuable items in the world. Sure, it won the tasting, but how much could that really be worth? JavaCon was new. Once the event was over, there was a good chance no one would be talking about Charles's coffee outside those who'd attended.

Yet look at how many people were interested in the recipe. Tatiana, obviously. But so was Wynona Kepler. And I had a feeling there was more to Misty's story than that she had been looking for a personal item when she'd ransacked his room. She might have gone in looking for something of hers, but if she'd found the exact blend he'd used to win the tasting lying around, I was sure she'd have been tempted to nick it.

"I saw you talking to Charles before he died," I said. "Were you trying to get it from him then?" The timing put it after his win, but before his death. I didn't recall seeing her with him before then, but it was always possible they'd snuck away together somewhere private earlier.

She sucked on her teeth a moment before opening her purse. She removed a tin of mints, opened it, and popped three into her mouth. She didn't suck on them, but rather chewed them with a grimace of distaste.

"Why does it matter?" she asked. "He's dead. The recipe is who knows where. I've wasted my time, and burned a few bridges in doing so. I'm ready to go home and forget I ever met Charles Maddox. This was a big mistake."

"It matters because he *is* dead," I said. "We've both met the detective on the case, right?" Tatiana grimaced as she nodded. "He's smart. He'll figure out you're not who you say you are and he'll come calling. When that happens, it's going to be awfully hard to explain yourself without looking guilty of something. Now's your chance to tell your story to someone who won't immediately jump to the conclusion that you killed a man. I can *help* you, if you let me."

She stared at me as she weighed my words. I could see the calculation behind her eyes and hoped she'd come to the right decision. There was a chance she might implicate herself in Charles's murder no matter what she said, and I was sure she knew that.

But sitting silent wouldn't do her any favors either. Detective Kimble wouldn't look kindly on her whether she told the truth or not. I hoped she'd realize that not fessing up would only make matters worse for her in the long run.

Tatiana sighed. "I heard about how Charles was, how if you showed the least bit of interest in him, he'd jump all over you. I thought I could seduce him, and then when he took me to his room, I'd find the recipe lying around somewhere, or, at least, could get him to talk about it. You know how men like to brag." Her smile was bitter. "That's all there was to our relationship."

"Did you succeed in seducing him?" I asked. If so,

that would complicate things further. Could she have been the woman Misty had caught him with in bed? The timing didn't quite work since he'd had yet to win the tasting, but I supposed it was possible Tatiana had known about Charles's blackmail attempts long before the tasting and had known he'd win. Just because I didn't see her with him before the competition didn't mean they hadn't hooked up the night before.

"Not even close," she said. "He saw right through me the moment I opened my mouth. He said he saw the resemblance and that was that."

"Resemblance?" I asked. I studied her features, her red hair, her bright blue eyes. There were tired lines around her eyes, a strain that made her look older, yet she was still pretty. With Charles's reputation, I was surprised he'd turned her down.

Tatiana bore my scrutiny for a few moments before she turned her head slightly and scowled.

The light hit her just right, accentuating her nose, the way it bent ever so slightly upward at the tip. It showed the lines of her mouth, the deep grooves that weren't simply age lines, but were genetic.

I gasped. I knew those features.

"You're related to Wynona Kepler!"

Tatiana nodded, turning back to me. "We're half sisters. Our father had a penchant for sleeping around before he settled down with some floozy in New Mexico. Wynona and I are only two weeks apart, if you can believe it."

My head spun. "Does she know?"

"Of course she does," Tatiana said. "She was in on the whole plan from the start."

I rocked back in my stool, nearly falling off since there was no back. "She *knew*?" I couldn't wrap my mind around it. Wynona had been doing everything she could to sabotage Charles. How did that fit in with what Tatiana was trying to do?

Tatiana's smile was grim. "She tried her hand with Charles first, but they knew each other too well. He figured she was after something other than him and shot her down the moment she tried to come on to him. It was a blow to her ego, let me tell you."

"She said he came on to her at a con a few months ago, not the other way around."

"She would." Tatiana actually rolled her eyes. "I'm sure that by now, she believes it. Truth is, she tried to snag him and struck out. She knew all about what he was planning to do here at JavaCon even back then. I'm not sure how, but she knew he would win, and she tried to plan accordingly."

"Wow." If she had known about his plan to black-mail the judges months ago, then why hadn't she done something about it beforehand?

Because she was going to take advantage of it, that's why.

If Wynona had realized she wouldn't win a competition on her own, then why not tie herself to someone she knew would?

"Charles knew nothing about me," Tatiana went on. "I'd never gone to one of these things before, so hardly anyone did. We thought it might work if I tried my hand at seducing him in her stead. He saw through it, of course. But we had other plans set in place, just in case. No one knew much about his private life. All we needed was to get into his room for five minutes and we'd have what we needed. Who cared what happened afterward?"

"But Wynona was trying to sabotage him," I said, still trying to make sense of it. "When Charles won, she was angry—accused him of cheating—which I understand, but why keep at it afterward if she was wanting to . . ." To what? Make a profit? I was still having a hard time seeing how a coffee blend could be worth so much trouble.

"It was all a ploy," Tatiana said. "We'd hoped it would distract Charles long enough that he wouldn't see through our facade, and by the time he realized what was going on, we'd have the recipe and could re-create his café mocha on our own. We could then 'produce' the recipe and claim he stole it from us."

Then it clicked. "He never did steal it, did he?" I asked.

"No, the blend was of his own make."

It was an underhanded thing for them to do, yet I could see how it could work. Charles would've claimed he'd come up with it himself, yet they'd have been able to show their work. I'm sure they would have doctored it somehow, created a fake digital footprint, and then capitalized on it.

It would be easy for someone good with computer skills to prove they'd faked it, but who would care enough to investigate?

"But then he died," I said, thinking out loud. "It must have put a kink in your plans."

"We planned for nearly everything," Tatiana said. "He won, just like expected, and we even had a plan as to how to get into his room if I failed to win him over. And then some idiot comes along and murders the bastard. We had to come up with something quick, or else all that hard work would be for naught."

"When he died, Wynona continued to claim he cheated," I said, working it out. "This allowed you to become the distraught widow. You hoped people would feel for you so much, they wouldn't look into your credentials until it was too late."

"It should have worked," Tatiana said. "But because he was murdered and it wasn't an accident, the police were far more careful with his things than we liked. Nothing I did or said seemed to work. I tried to carry on and hope that someone would feel bad for me and let me slip into the room for a few minutes, but that detective had the staff afraid to so much as talk to me."

I could see that. Kimble could be intimidating. "And now?" I asked. JavaCon was almost over. Since she was telling me all of this, it was clear she wasn't going to pretend to be the grieving widow any longer.

"And now, nothing." Tatiana handed a credit card to the bartender, who cashed her out. "We had everything planned out and it blew up in our faces. We might have been willing to cheat Charles Maddox of his winnings, but neither of us killed him. His death ruined everything."

I wondered how much of that was true. She'd admitted that their plan hadn't worked. Charles wasn't going to give up the recipe, and without that, it would've been hard to "prove" he'd stolen it from them.

So could one of them have killed him for it? Tatiana might have tried to seduce him again, but when he rejected her a second time, she could have struck him with a carafe of his own coffee. Or had Wynona confronted him and then attacked him in a fit of rage? Charles had done his research, that was obvious, so perhaps he had something on the sisters, something bad enough to kill for.

The bartender returned, handing Tatiana her card back. She stood, then tottered a moment before righting herself. "If you'll excuse me, I think I need to find a dark, quiet corner to sleep this off." She walked away without waiting for me to respond.

I let her go, figuring she wasn't going to go far. Detective Kimble needed to hear the story, but I figured he could find her easily enough. She wasn't hard to miss, not with that hair.

I produced a couple of bills and tossed them onto the counter to pay for my Coke—which, as Rita had said it would, cost me a cool five bucks.

As I made for the exit, I removed my phone from my pocket, thinking I'd text Detective Kimble again to let him know I had something more for him. The little green light was blinking, telling me I had a message. I hoped that Kimble was finally responding to my earlier text.

The message wasn't from the detective.

Hope they're good thoughts. Get home safely.

Paul Dalton had replied. I very nearly squealed in delight.

I shot him a smiley face emoji and then, regretfully, moved on to business. I double-checked Kimble's number to make sure I had it right and then sent him three rapid-fire texts, briefly telling him what I'd learned. They were light on details, which was intentional. I needed to talk to him face-to-face, lest I forget something important. It's hard to convey everything in a handful of texts.

I paused just outside the restaurant doors to wait to see if he'd reply. A few patrons walked in while I waited but left without ordering anything. Glancing at the menu that was plastered to the wall outside the restaurant, I could see why—nearly twenty dollars for a burger and fries. No thank you.

My phone pinged. I don't know what I was expecting him to say, but I thought it would be more than the simple *Meet me in the lobby* I got.

But it would do. With a decided spring in my step, I headed for the hotel lobby and my meeting with Detective Kimble.

Chapter 25

The hotel lobby was bustling with activity when I arrived. The awards ceremony had finished a lot quicker than I'd anticipated, and most everyone was milling around the room talking about it. I didn't see Detective Kimble right away, so I moved to stand near the big glass windows to get a better view. There was excitement bubbling throughout the room, though the noise made it hard to pinpoint exactly what everyone was so excited about.

"Krissy!" I turned to find Vicki hurrying my way with two overstuffed bags in hand. "Have you seen Rita? I haven't seen her all day, and there's something I want to show her."

"She's around here somewhere," I said, hoping that she was keeping out of trouble. I might have sent her after Tara, but I didn't want her getting too involved with the murder. Knowing her, she was probably neck-deep in it by now. *As if I'm one to talk.*

"I'm sorry I haven't been around much today either. It's been crazy."

"Tell me about it." Vicki raised both her bags so I could get a better look at them. One was filled with coffee bags of various brands. I couldn't see what was in the other, thanks to a big bow on the handle. "I found a room with a ton of people giving stuff away." She indicated the bag with all the coffee in it. "I also managed to win a raffle." She jiggled the other bag. "It's one of those high-end coffee makers that does just about everything. I'm really excited to try it."

"Wow," I said, jealous. I'd always wanted something that brewed more than just a plain cup of coffee, but had never wanted to spend the money on one. "You'll have to make me something when we get home."

"Plan on it. Mason's going to be thrilled." She glanced toward the elevator. "I'm going to run these up to the room. Are you going to the seminar later?"

"I'll be there," I said. We'd planned on going to one together, and I wasn't going to miss it. "If I don't see you beforehand, make sure to save me a seat."

"Will do." She perked up. "Ah, there's Rita." I followed her gaze. Rita was getting onto the elevator, hands full of a couple of bags of her own. "You coming up?"

"In a bit," I said. "I'm supposed to meet someone here." Glancing around the room, I still didn't see Detective Kimble. "I'll be up afterward."

"Good luck," Vicki said. "It's crowded in here." Even as she said it, someone bumped into her as they hurried toward the elevator, which was being held open by a man gesturing toward a woman I took to be his wife. She looked content to continue her conversation with the group of older ladies she was with.

"I'll see you later," Vicki said, gathering her bags and making for the elevator. She rushed across the room, reaching the doors just as the man keeping them open gave up and stepped off to join his wife. An animated Rita promptly started talking Vicki's ear off, bags and arms flailing about wildly. As the doors closed, I saw a man behind her scowl as one of the bags thumped into his thigh.

Shaking my head in amusement, I turned away and scoured the room until I finally spotted Detective Kimble near the front desk. He was looking right at me, and as soon as my eyes landed on him, he motioned me over. He didn't look happy.

I felt like a kid going to the principal's office as I weaved my way through the crowd to join him.

"Explain yourself." Kimble crossed his arms and glared at me hard enough that I cringed.

"What do you mean?" I asked, already pretty sure I knew what he was going to say.

"I've received a half dozen texts from you today, all of which seem to reference my investigation. You know the one. The murder. The one you aren't supposed to be interfering in."

"I'm not interfering," I said.

He only glared.

"I'm not! Not really." I couldn't meet his eye. "I was merely passing on information that happened to come my way. I can't help it that people are willing to talk to me. It's not like I did it on purpose."

His glare turned into a glower.

"Did you talk to Misty?" I asked, hoping to divert his anger away from me and toward something more constructive. Something like solving the case. "I told her to find you. She had some interesting things to say."

"I did," Kimble said. He left it at that, giving me no clue as to whether or not Misty had told him the whole story or if she'd changed it to make it appear as if she had less of a motive for murder.

"Do you know who the other woman might be?" I asked, hoping for the former. "The one Charles was in bed with when Misty walked in on them?"

He stared at me, seemed to weigh whether or not to tell me anything, before he relented. "I currently have no leads in that regard."

"What about Wynona Kepler or Tatiana Copeland? You got my texts about those two, right?"

"I did," he said. "And I still don't understand why you were talking to Mrs. Maddox"—he scowled—"Ms. Copeland about any of this."

"We were sitting at the bar, talking," I said. "It came up."

"She just up and admitted to lying? To you. A stranger."

I shrugged. "Maybe she felt guilty."

"I highly doubt that."

I did too, but I wasn't going to say it out loud. "Do you think one of them could have been the other woman?" I pressed. "Just because Tatiana claims she failed in seducing Charles doesn't mean she was being honest with me. The same goes for Wynona. Maybe she slept with him without telling her sister, and it somehow led to his murder."

"It's hard to say. Your texts weren't very clear on the exact details," Kimble said. "Run everything by me again. Leave nothing out."

I decided to start with my conversation with Evaline, even though I'd already talked to him about it. This time, however, I told him about her affair with Carmine, figuring it best to do as he said and tell him everything. From there, I moved on to my chat with Misty, then ended with my conversation with Tatiana.

After laying it all out like that, I realized how convoluted these people's relationships were.

Not that mine was much better, mind you.

"It appears I'm going to need to talk to Ms. Copeland again," Kimble said with a weary sigh. He seemed less than thrilled by the prospect. I didn't blame him; Tatiana wasn't the easiest person to talk to.

"I don't think she was actually trying to hurt anyone," I said. "Other than Charles's reputation, I guess." Though with how he'd apparently been sleeping around, he'd been doing a good enough job of that on his own already.

"Do you have any reason to suspect one of them as being the other woman?" Kimble asked. "It sounds to me like Mr. Maddox rejected Ms. Copeland's advances, and from what I've been able to piece together, I doubt he'd been inclined to spend any more time with Ms. Kepler than need be."

"No, not really," I admitted. "But who else could it be?"

I tried to come up with a name that made sense. Misty had caught him with the woman, so it wasn't her. According to Tatiana, both she and Wynona had struck out with him, so they were unlikely. Who did that leave? Tara? She had been with Thomas at the time. Evaline? Dallas? I couldn't see either of them with him, especially since Dallas hadn't given in to his blackmail demands and Evaline had already been having an affair with Carmine.

So then, who?

There were hundreds of women at the con. Any number of them could have been drawn to Charles for one reason or another. Sometimes, people get lonely. They hook up. There's nothing sinister in that.

Detective Kimble seemed to be thinking along the same lines. I could see the calculation behind his eyes as he scanned the thinning room. Any woman here could have been with Charles at any time before his death.

"Aren't there cameras in the hotel?" I asked. "Like, in the elevators, and maybe in the halls outside the rooms? Maybe one of them caught whoever Charles was sleeping with leaving his room."

Kimble's expression grew hard. "There are cameras, but I'm told they are currently down. Apparently, they still haven't hooked everything back up after recent renovations. The cameras are there, but they aren't recording anything."

"Isn't that a violation of some kind?" While I wasn't a fan of Big Brother always watching, it's sometimes comforting to know that there *is* someone out there keeping us safe.

He shrugged. "Not my jurisdiction. It's inconvenient, but I can't fine them for it. They're promising that they'll have them up and running by the end of next week."

"That isn't going to help us much now," I said.

"No, it's not," Kimble said. "And anyway, Mr. Maddox was murdered in one of the ballrooms. Hotel cameras wouldn't help there. Just because someone was seen leaving his room doesn't make them a killer."

"It might give you a good suspect, though."

"It would," he agreed.

Across the room, an older woman clutched at a young man half her age. They hugged briefly before parting. She gathered her luggage and then, alone, walked out the hotel doors.

"What are you going to do?" I asked Kimble, heart sinking. "The con ends tomorrow. Everyone's going to go home."

"I know that." He seemed angry at the reminder. "For now, I'm going to find Ms. Copeland and Ms. Kepler and see what they have to say for themselves." He leveled a finger at me. "And *you* are going to stay out of the way and keep to yourself. I don't want to get any more texts claiming you happened by new information. Do you understand me?"

"I'll do my best," I said. When his eyes narrowed, I shrugged. "I can't help it if I bump into these people and they tell me things. People like talking to me."

He rolled his eyes, hiked up his belt, and then walked away, muttering under his breath.

Despite his glowers and warnings, I knew Detective Kimble appreciated my help. He'd never admit it, of course. But without me, he never would have gotten some of his leads. That had to count for something, didn't it?

I was about to head to the elevator when I noticed

Thomas and Tara across the room, near where the woman and man had recently embraced. They were holding hands as they talked to two other people I didn't know. My chest tightened briefly before a feeling of calm washed over me. It wasn't just the detective I was helping. I was glad the two of them had finally admitted they had feelings for one another and were willing to show it. Suppressing those feelings did no one any good. I should know.

Thomas saw me looking and waved. I returned the gesture before shooting him a thumbs-up. He grinned and winked, and then he turned back to the conversation.

"Stop, Clint!"

I spun and leapt out of the way as Clint Sherman stormed past. Carmine Wright and Evaline Cobb were hot on his heels. All three of them looked upset, though Clint looked the angriest, with his red face and scowl. I was worried I was about to witness yet another scuffle between the organizers of Java-Con.

"I don't see why I should," Clint said, spinning around. "They've made it abundantly clear we aren't wanted."

"Do you blame them?" Evaline asked. "We've made a mockery of this entire endeavor by our actions."

"*Our* actions?" Clint spat. "I did nothing to deserve this. I've worked hard for this, and they are going to oust us, just like that? It's unfair, and unwarranted. They made the decision to cancel the awards ceremony without us, Carmine. And then to stand there, in front of everyone, and say they're taking over control of the con? What did they think they were doing?"

Carmine reached out as if to take Clint by the arm, but Clint jerked away. "We'll work something out," he said. "Dallas and Pierre will reconsider. Everyone is emotional right now."

"I don't understand why you defend them." Clint aimed the comment at Carmine. "JavaCon is supposed to be your baby. They're going to rip it right out from under you, and you're just going to let them? And for what? Because they don't like how we handled things."

"Mishandled, you mean," Evaline said.

"You stay out of it." Clint jabbed a finger into her face before turning to Carmine. "They're working with that Kepler woman, I know it."

"You don't know that for sure," Carmine said.

"She was *there*. I saw the look on her face." Clint clenched his fists. "She knew it was coming—and to do it right in front of everyone! They all stared at us, Carmine. They stared and judged us without knowing anything about what was going on."

"Do you blame them?" Evaline asked.

Clint spun on her, and for a moment, I was afraid he might strike her.

"And *you*. You went along with it," he hissed. "Whose side are you really on, Evaline?"

Carmine stepped in, putting himself between Clint and Evaline in a protective way. "Leave her alone," he said. "We should all calm down and take a few minutes to breathe. Just because Dallas and Pierre wish to take JavaCon from us doesn't mean they can."

"Really?" Clint said. "I didn't see you fighting back when they confronted you. Am I the only one who cares about anything around here?"

And with that, he spun on his heel and marched toward the elevator, which currently had a line of people in front of it. Most of them appeared torn between watching the exchange and heading to their rooms.

Carmine and Evaline shared a long look with one another before walking off in different directions. They both appeared defeated, shoulders slumped, steps dragging.

I stared after them. It sounded like Dallas Edmonds and Pierre Longview had laid claim to Java-Con, but I wasn't sure how that would work. Carmine had funded the thing. And, as Clint had said, it was Carmine's baby. He wouldn't give it up so easily, not unless there was something else going on that would make him back off.

I needed to know more on the off chance it had something to do with Charles's murder. I joined Clint in line. His arms were crossed and it was clear he didn't want to talk to anyone. Before I could test his resolve in that regard, the elevator doors opened and he pushed his way past a small group of people who were waiting in front of him. He entered the car without paying their complaints any mind.

"Sorry," I said, pushing my way forward to join Clint. "I'm with him."

The group glared as they got on with us, but no one tried to stop us either. Clint and I were crammed next to one another, near the back of the car, with about seven other people pressed against one another in front of us. He wouldn't be able to escape me easily.

"That was a pretty big fight," I said, keeping my voice down and my tone light. "Is something going on between you, Carmine, and Evaline?"

Clint glared at me and then pointedly looked away.

"Did it have anything to do with Charles?" I asked in a whisper. I figured everyone in the car could hear me, but if I at least pretended our conversation was private, then perhaps he might as well.

Clint continued to stare angrily forward. The doors opened and three people stepped out, giving us breathing room.

"If you think Dallas and Pierre are doing something illegal, you could always take it to Detective Kimble," I continued to press, hoping he'd eventually break. "He's the one looking into Charles's murder. I'm sure he knows a thing or two about the law."

Clint showed no reaction other than a tightening of his jaw. If I wasn't careful, there was a chance he might rear off and punch me, as was evidenced by his earlier fight with Carmine. I settled back, not wanting to push him that far.

We reached the tenth floor and the doors opened. Clint shoved his way forward and stepped off the elevator, not bothering to look back at me, let alone acknowledge anything I'd said.

Wait.

My brain sputtered, revving into high gear.

This was the tenth floor. Every time I'd seen Clint, he'd gotten on or off the elevator here.

Every time but one.

A light bulb burst to life in my head as the pieces clicked into place.

I knew who had killed Charles Maddox, and thanks to that one sighting on the fifteenth floor, I was pretty sure I knew why.

Chapter 26

My arm shot out just as the elevator doors were about to close.

"Sorry," I told the other passengers as I slid past them and stepped off onto the tenth floor. "Forgot where I was going."

Someone grumbled at me as the doors closed and the elevator zipped away, leaving me alone in the hall with a man I now suspected was a murderer.

"Clint!" I called after him. He was hurrying away and didn't bother looking back when I called his name. "Clint, we need to talk."

"Leave me alone," he shouted over his shoulder. He reached the end of the hall, then turned the corner without even a glance my way.

I increased my pace to a near run. My mind was working twice as fast, going over everything I'd seen and heard since I'd arrived at JavaCon—all the interactions, all the rumors. It seemed like everyone was accusing everyone else of doing something wrong, mostly in regard to the actual con itself. It was all noise that had masked what was really going on.

"Clint!" I shouted, rounding the corner. "Wait!"

He was at a door halfway down the hall. He glanced at me as he held his keycard over the reader. The door clicked, and he reached for the handle. In seconds, he would be gone, and I would miss my chance.

I knew I'd said I'd avoid putting myself in situations like this—to Paul, to Detective Kimble, and to myself—but I couldn't help it; this was who I was.

As Clint's fingers brushed the metal handle, I said the first thing that came to mind.

"You killed him, didn't you?"

The door opened a sliver before his entire posture went stiff. His head turned toward me slowly, a shocked expression on his face. "What did you just say to me?"

I closed the distance between us, taking my time so that I could arrange my thoughts in my head. Pieces were still clicking into place, albeit slowly, and not always with a perfect fit. I knew if I said the wrong thing, Clint would laugh me off, and it would end up being my word against his.

But if I hit the right note, managed to somehow force him into talking, I thought I might finally make things right.

"Charles Maddox," I said. "His murder. You were involved."

"That's preposterous." I noted Clint didn't push the door open the rest of the way, but he did keep his hand on the door handle in anticipation of going in.

I think he was waiting to see what kind of proof I had before deciding whether he should ignore me or not.

"Is it?" I asked. I spoke loudly in the hope that someone was in one of the other rooms and would call the hotel staff—or, better yet, Detective Kimble—once they figured out the topic of our conversation. "Because I'm having a hard time putting your movements on the day of his death together without coming to that conclusion."

"My movements?" he asked with a bark of a laugh. It sounded half-crazed, telling me I was onto something. "I'm a very busy man. Even *I* struggle to keep track of where I'm going and where I've been half the time. Running a con isn't easy, so if you'll excuse me . . ." He started to push the door open.

"I'm sure it's not," I said, taking a quick step toward him. "There's a lot of stress involved. I own my own business, and even with others helping me, it's overwhelming sometimes. It isn't much of a stretch to think that the pressure got to you and you snapped."

"I didn't kill anyone," Clint said. "I really do need to make some calls. In case you haven't heard, my partners are trying to force me out of the board, and I'd rather not make it easy for them."

"Do they know?" I asked, taking another quick step forward when Clint moved as if he might enter his room. We were inches apart now. "The others? Do they know about you and Charles?"

"What about me and Charles?" Clint asked. "The man died at my con. I knew him. That's all there was to it."

"You see, I don't quite buy that," I said, glancing down the hall. I should have tried to text Detective Kimble while I was chasing after Clint. Here I was, confronting someone who might be a murderer without backup. Again. When would I ever learn?

Clint followed my gaze before he pushed the door open the rest of the way with a muttered "I don't have time for this."

The door started to swing closed, but I put myself just inside, holding the door open with my foot. "Where were you that first night?" I asked. "Or, more specifically, where were you the following morning before you went down to the con?"

"Here, in my room. Where else would I be?"

"Were you?" I asked. "Because I distinctly remember seeing you on the fifteenth floor that morning." I hadn't put it together until back at the elevator. "I left my room about the same time Charles did. You came down the hall from that direction a few moments later."

"I had something I needed to take care of before heading to the con," he said. "As you pointed out, there is a lot of pressure on me. I wanted everything to go off without a hitch, so I paid him a quick visit. That's what I was doing." He crossed his arms and glared. "Now, would you please get out of my room? If you won't, I'll be forced to call security and have you escorted out."

"Go ahead," I said, standing my ground, though I did keep my foot against the door so it wouldn't close on me. "I'm sure they'd love to hear what I have to say."

Clint continued to glare, but he started chewing

on his lower lip at the same time. He was trying to determine what I actually knew and what I was only guessing at. There was a pretty large gap between speculation and knowledge, and what filled that gap went a long way in being able to prove someone guilty of murder.

So, in order to make him think I knew far more than I really did, I said, "She saw you."

Clint sucked in a breath, eyes going wide briefly, but he regained his composure quickly. "Close the door," he said.

It was my turn to debate. If I let the door close behind me, then I'd be trapped in a possible murderer's room. Sure, I could still make a run for it, but opening the door would slow me down. There wasn't a whole lot of space between the far wall and the door. If he were to come at me, it was likely he'd catch me before I could get out into the hall.

But if I didn't do as he said, he'd never talk. Sure, I could walk away, call Detective Kimble, and let him deal with it, but Clint might be gone by then. The time might also allow him to come up with a better excuse for what happened, a story the detective might believe.

Going against my better judgment, I stepped fully into the room. The door swung closed behind me with a click that sounded ominous in the quiet space.

"What did she say?" Clint asked. His voice was a lot calmer than I'd have expected out of someone who'd just been accused of killing another man. Could I be wrong about him? A part of me was kind of hoping I was.

"She walked in on the two of you together," I said,

not using Misty's name, just in case Clint didn't know it. I didn't need him looking her up and silencing her later. "You were with Charles that night, and into the morning. She walked in and saw you."

He shook his head. "Impossible."

"No, not impossible," I said. "She didn't want to say anything, since she was embarrassed, but she told me after I put some pressure on her. I'm sure she's telling Detective Kimble everything she knows right now. They were together the last time I saw them." Which wasn't quite true, but I hoped it would make Clint think twice about attacking me.

Clint's face drained of color. His eyes darted around the room, never landing on any one thing for more than a second. "Okay, fine, I was there. But she didn't see anything, because there was nothing to see. Nothing happened. There's no reason for anything to come out."

"Nothing happened?" I asked. "Are you saying you weren't sleeping with Charles?"

"I'm married." Clint said it as if the fact made it impossible for him to have cheated on his wife. "I would never do such a thing. I'm nothing like *Carmine.*" He spat the other man's name like a curse.

Another piece clicked into place then. "No, you're not," I said. "Not exactly anyway."

Clint's eyes narrowed. "And what's that supposed to mean?"

I took a moment to think it through before I spoke. There were so many connections, so many people doing private things with people they shouldn't be, it was hard to keep everything straight.

"Your wife isn't here, is she?" I asked.

"She's not," he said. "She is in poor health and can't attend events like this."

Which, in my mind, only made what he'd done worse. To cheat on someone you are supposed to love is bad enough; to do it while they are ill is far worse.

"When I saw you that first day, you were talking to Charles. I bet he was trying to get to you then, wasn't he?" Clint showed no reaction, so I went on. "Somehow, he convinced you to come to his room, and you two ended up in bed together."

Clint took a step back like I'd shoved him. I could see in his eyes that I was on the right track, so I kept talking.

"He used that one night to blackmail you, didn't he?" I asked. When he still didn't answer, I pressed. "He threatened to tell everyone what you did. He had a witness, thanks to the two of you getting caught. If he told, then everyone would know you're an adulterer. Your wife would eventually find out. Your reputation would be ruined, your marriage destroyed. You'd lose everything."

"He used my weakness against me," Clint whispered, and I knew I had him.

"What did he want?" I asked. "For you to vote for his coffee? There's quite a lot of talk that he'd blackmailed the judges into giving him the win."

"It wasn't too much to ask," Clint said, taking another step back, putting him beside the desk in the corner of the room. He rested a hand on it as if he needed its support to keep him upright. "We give him the win, he goes away. So a few of us conspired to give it to him. That's all that happened."

I paused. Clint *had* given Charles what he wanted, hadn't he? Carmine and Evaline had caved, thanks to their own secret. Even with Dallas and Pierre holding out, their three votes were just enough to give Charles the crown for best coffee.

So why kill him? Charles's death put everyone in the spotlight. It would only be a matter of time before someone figured out what had happened. Detective Kimble seemed like a smart man. Just because I figured this part of the puzzle out before him didn't mean he wouldn't discover the rest on his own. He was probably already way ahead of me in other areas.

Dallas and Pierre. They both viewed Charles's victory as a travesty. They knew the other judges were bought, knew how it would hurt the con's reputation if and when it came out. They had a motive to do something about it.

But how would killing Charles help anything? It would only make things worse for the both of them.

I spun it over in my mind. Clint watched me, still using the desk for support.

And then, another memory surfaced.

"He wasn't keeping silent," I said.

Clint didn't so much as twitch. *He already knew.*

"I remember seeing him talking to someone," I said, once again not wanting to bring up the person's name, just in case Clint didn't know it. "I didn't hear what they were saying, but they were talking about you, weren't they?"

But I did remember how both Charles and Tatiana had looked at Clint, how Charles had pointed him out, and how Clint had reacted when he saw them looking.

"He promised me," Clint said, voice barely above a whisper. "He swore to me that he'd keep his mouth shut."

"But he didn't."

Clint squeezed his eyes shut. "He wasn't doing it to the others, just me. Why? Why did I deserve to be the butt of his jokes? I let him use my weakness—my need to be close to someone—against me, and then he continued to bludgeon me with it, over and over again."

His voice rose as he spoke, his entire body going tense.

"He had no right," Clint said. "He should have kept his mouth shut, and everything would have been okay. He'd be alive. Life, and the con, could have gone on like nothing had ever happened."

"You killed him," I said, reiterating what I'd said in the hall. We'd come full circle, but this time, it was more than mere speculation.

I knew the truth.

Clint's eyes met mine. His jaw was clenched, and his entire body was tense and thrumming with anger.

Ever so subtly, his hand—the one I'd thought he'd been using to support himself on the desk—moved to the drawer. With an abrupt jerk, he opened it, and before I could react, he drew a gun and leveled it at me.

"I did," Clint said. His voice was cold, emotionless. "And, I'm sorry to say, it looks like you're going to be next."

Chapter 27

"Move away from the door."
Clint's aim shook as he pointed the gun at me. He didn't *look* like he wanted to shoot me, but going by what he'd just said, I was pretty sure he was planning to do it anyway.

"We could always talk about this," I said, not budging from my spot. If I moved farther into the room, he wouldn't need to shoot me. He was bigger than me, and even though he was older, I was betting he was stronger too. "There's no need for this to get violent."

"I think we're past the negotiations," he said. "Move away from the door." This time, he motioned with the gun.

I raised my hands, but still refused to move. "Come on, Clint," I said. "If you shoot me, there's no way you'll walk away. The cops will know who did it. We're in your room, for goodness' sake. And if you kill me, it'll make it that much easier to tie you to Charles's death."

"I'll think of something." A bead of sweat ran down his brow, into his right eye. He winced, hand and gun jerking erratically as he tried to wipe it with his shoulder.

I flinched, expecting the gun to go off, but he was keeping his finger off the trigger.

For now.

One eye was still on me as he blinked the other rapidly. He was sweating profusely now, which was a feat, considering how chilly his room was. The air had to be set in the low sixties.

Then again, I was sweating too. Having a gun pointed at you has a tendency to do that to a person.

I kept my hands up, eyes on Clint, as I leaned ever so slightly back on my heel. All I needed was a few good seconds, for him to look away or close his eyes, and I could be gone.

Another droplet of sweat ran down his face. This one fell into his left eye.

Clint raised his gun arm and wiped it across his face and eyes in an effort to clear them.

It was all the time I needed.

I spun, hand flying toward the door handle. I misjudged and cracked my wrist hard on the door, but managed to grab hold of the handle on the recoil. I yanked the door open, just as Clint shouted, "Hey! Stop!"

Needless to say, I didn't do as he said.

I expected him to shoot, so I ducked my head between my shoulders as I ran out the door. Fumbling into my back pocket, I removed my phone. Even as the door behind me swung closed, I was swiping the screen and hitting the call button.

Clint's shouts could still be heard, and they were getting closer. He was giving chase, which meant I only had a few seconds before he caught up to me.

I dialed.

No service.

"What? No!" I dialed again, thinking it was somehow a mistake. "Come on, come on, come on."

No service.

The door behind me opened.

I spun and flung my phone at Clint. My aim was surprisingly good, and it struck him on the cheek before bouncing into his room.

"Gah!" Clint jerked back for an instant before he realized he wasn't actually hurt. I used that moment to make a run for it.

"Stop!" Clint called behind me. I kept praying a door would open and I could dive inside and slam it closed behind me. But if anyone was in their room listening to our shouts, they were laying low.

I couldn't say I blamed them. With Clint screaming, waving a gun wildly around in the hall, and me bouncing off the walls, flailing my arms like a reckless pinball, it was no wonder no one wanted to risk a peek outside. I know I wouldn't.

Clint's pounding footsteps neared. The elevator—and the stairwell—were around the corner, but were too far away for me to reach before Clint caught up to me. He was faster and had a weapon that could put an end to my escape in the blink of an eye.

Since he hadn't fired yet, I hoped he was reluctant to risk hurting an innocent bystander—not that any were within view. I reached the corner, but instead of rushing around it like I knew he'd expect me to do, I spun back toward him, lowered my shoulder, and rammed into him like a linebacker might a running back.

Clint grunted as my shoulder struck him in the lower chest. The hand holding the gun struck the wall, which in turn caused him to lose his grip on the weapon. It clattered to the floor, thankfully without going off.

The force of my charge propelled Clint straight to the floor as well. I struck my head in a glancing blow on the carpeted surface, which dazed me for a heartbeat, but I quickly regained my senses. Clint, who was now on his back with me atop him rammed both his palms into my shoulders in an effort to dislodge me. I managed to hold my ground, though I did grunt with the impact. That was definitely going to leave a pair of hand-shaped bruises.

"Get off me," Clint growled, punching me with his palms again.

For a man who'd pulled a gun on a woman and who'd murdered another man in cold blood, he didn't seem very willing to hurt me.

Gritting my teeth against the blows, I adjusted my weight so I had a better center of gravity. I needed to figure out what to do now. I couldn't sit astride Clint all day. There was no telling when someone would happen down the hall. My phone was now lying useless in Clint's room, so I couldn't call Kimble for help.

My eyes fell on the gun a few feet away.

I am not a gun person. I've never been big on anything that's sole purpose is to kill. I've had them pulled on me, and can say I didn't like the feeling of staring down the dark barrel very much. I've never in my life thought I'd do the same to someone else.

But this was starting to feel like a life-or-death situation, and sometimes, you have to do things you don't like just to survive.

Clint's body tensed as he prepared to lash out at me once more. I waited until he struck before I rolled off him, angling myself toward the gun as I fell.

Clint's swing missed and he ended up nearly rolling over from the momentum of it. He grunted and cursed under his breath.

I snatched the gun off the floor as I came to my feet, a little less gracefully than I'd intended, but I made it without falling on my face. I reoriented the gun and aimed it at Clint, who was slowly standing.

"Stay right there," I said. Clint's hand had trembled when he'd held the gun on me, but it was nothing compared to the shake of my own. "I don't want to hurt you."

Clint wiped his mouth with the back of his hand. It came away bloody. I didn't recall striking him when I'd rolled off him, but I supposed it was possible. The adrenaline was pumping so hard by now, I wouldn't feel much of anything, even if someone smacked me in the back with a baseball bat.

"Clint," I warned when he took a step toward me. "Stay where you are."

He paused, spat on the carpet. "This has gotten

out of hand," he said. "I never wanted any of this to happen. If Charles would have kept his mouth shut, we'd all be enjoying the con right now."

Or if you'd kept it in your pants, I thought. Why was it that so many men had to go and get themselves into trouble by climbing into bed with someone they shouldn't? I had a feeling there'd be a lot less murder if people would think about the consequences of their actions a little more often.

"We can't change what's happened," I said. "We can only move forward and face whatever consequences lay before us. No one else needs to get hurt over this. Too many have been harmed already."

Clint shook his head. "You know that's not true. If I let you go, you'll go straight to the police. *That* will hurt me. My life is already in shambles. I won't let you take it away from me completely, especially not for *him.*"

He took a step toward me.

It seemed as if the entire world had slowed to a crawl. I had the gun, and it was aimed in Clint's general direction. With the way my hand shook, I could easily miss, but with him being so close, I doubted it.

But if I shot him, what did that make me? Sure, it would be self-defense. No one would fault me for it. No one would think of me as a killer.

No one, that was, but me.

Life was far too valuable to throw away so easily, even for a man who'd admitted to murder.

"Clint," I warned, but there was no force to it.

As casually as you'd like, he walked right up to me and plucked the gun from my hand. He turned it over twice before looking at me, smirking, and then he raised the gun level with my face.

"I think we should head back to my room now, don't you?"

I most definitely did not. I was so not going to get gunned down in hotel room.

Clint was only standing a foot away from me, which was far too close for him to avoid what came next.

Ducking my head, I swung my arm up wildly at his own, connecting solidly with his wrist. He cried out as the gun spun from his hand. It once more clattered to the floor without going off. Either we were extremely lucky, or the safety was on. Either way, it meant no one was accidentally shot, which was a blessing in my book.

I could have leapt for the weapon again, but this time, I'd have to fight Clint for it. He was closer to it than I was, and as he'd already proven, he was quicker.

There was no real question as to who would win if it came down to a physical fight.

Spinning on my heel, I did the only thing I could. I made a run for it.

Clint cursed and I heard him scramble for the gun. He shouted a warning, saying he'd shoot, but I didn't hesitate. I reached the end of the hall and hammered on the down button for the elevator.

"Come on," I said, glancing up at the numbers above the four elevator doors: *15, 3, 2,* and *14.*

There was no way any of them were going to reach me in time.

Clint shouted again. I spun and noted he'd turned

the corner and was coming right for me, so I darted the short distance to the door to the stairwell, shoulders hunched against the possibility Clint would give up and finally shoot me. I jerked open the door and practically dove headfirst inside.

Freedom lay a mere nine floors below me.

I pounded down the stairs, knowing my life depended on it. I'd reached the landing to the ninth floor as the door above me opened and Clint rushed inside. He continued to shout, his voice echoing off the walls, propelling me even faster.

My heart felt like it would burst as I rounded landing after landing. I kept expecting Clint to catch me, but every time I rounded a corner, I could hear him still on the stairs above me.

More than once, I considered opening a door and hoping Clint wouldn't notice I wasn't still descending. Nine floors don't seem like a lot, but when you're running for your life, they feel endless.

But if I got off on a floor void of guests, Clint would catch me. I'd have nowhere to go, nowhere I could hide. I had to keep going.

The number four was painted on the wall as I rounded the next corner and rushed down the stairs. My chest was tight, my breath coming in pained gasps. A stitch in my side made every step hurt.

I honestly thought I was going to make it, that I'd burst out into the lobby and would be saved by some kind soul who would see Clint chasing after me and would stop him from hurting anyone ever again. I rounded the second-floor landing, turned to descend farther.

That's when Clint leapt from the stairwell above and crashed into me.

We slammed into the wall with bone-crunching force. Something clattered to the stairs. I assumed it was the gun, but at that point, I was too exhausted, and too hurt, to care.

Both Clint and I collapsed onto the stairwell. His face was an alarming shade of red, which was accentuated by the whiteness of his hair. His mouth was moving, opening and closing, as if he couldn't get enough air.

"Give up," I gasped, hardly able to breathe myself. "This can't go on."

"I can't," he gasped in return. "My life. Over."

I struggled to sit upright. My feet were splayed in front of me, gun resting between them. The mere thought of leaning forward to pick it up was enough to make me sick. When I'd hit the wall, it had felt like every organ in my body had swapped places.

Clint didn't look inclined to move for the gun either. He was sitting next to me, blood tricking down his chin from a split lip. Something stirred in me. I was surprised to find it was pity.

"I understand why you did it," I said. My voice came out as a dry rasp. "Others will too."

"I'll lose everything."

"It's going to happen anyway," I said. "But you can take it standing up." I found the comment slightly ironic, considering neither of us had the energy to sit upright without the wall for support, let alone stand. "Confess. Explain what happened. The judge might

take it easy on you." Though I doubted it. Murder
was murder.

Clint's eyes moved to the gun. His face wasn't as
red as it was before. He was covered in sweat, and I
was afraid a man his age might end up having a heart
attack after the run he'd just had. Heck, *I* might suf-
fer one if I were forced to make another run for it.

He shifted as if prepping to lunge for the weapon.
I tensed, ready to do something if he did, though
what, I had no idea.

Below us, a door opened. Footsteps started up the
stairs. Much to my relief, they were moving at a run.

All the fight went out of Clint then. He collapsed
back against the wall and closed his eyes.

"Ms. Hancock?" Detective Kimble said as he
rounded the corner and came to a stop. His eyes
found the gun and he rested a hand on the butt of
his own weapon.

"I got him," I said with a weak smile, gesturing to
Clint, who didn't so much as twitch. "He's all yours
now."

Detective Kimble stared at me for a long moment
before asking, "He killed Mr. Maddox?"

"Admitted it and everything," I said.

Kimble regarded Clint a moment before he
snatched up the gun from between my feet, produced
a set of handcuffs, and with some effort, got an exhausted Clint to his feet. He started back down the
stairs with his killer in tow, but paused halfway down.
He glanced back at me, an expectant look on his
face.

"Are you coming?" he asked. When I shook my

head, he asked, "Do you need me to send someone? A paramedic?"

"No," I said, leaning my head against the wall. "I'll be okay. I'll be here when you get back."

He started to walk away.

"Wait!" I called.

Kimble stopped and glanced back at me.

"Bring me a water when you're done with him, okay?"

Detective Kimble's dark face brightened and he actually laughed. "I'll do that," he said. "Anything else?"

"No." I slumped and closed my eyes. "I'm good."

The stairwell was silent a few seconds more, and then with one more chuckle, Detective Kimble led Clint Sherman away, their footfalls echoing on the blessedly cool walls.

Chapter 28

I dropped my bags to floor of the elevator with a groan. Everything hurt. My shoulders, my arms. Even my toes were thumping. I sagged against the mirrored wall and closed my eyes.

"Are you sure you're going to be okay?" Vicki asked. "I could always come back for your stuff if you want me to carry it. It's no trouble."

"No, I'm good." The elevator stopped midway down, and four more people piled in, making the space feel overly claustrophobic.

"If you're sure?" Vicki asked, eyeing me.

"I'm sure."

Rita tittered. She was anxious to continue to talk about my unlikely unveiling of yet another murder suspect, but I made her promise she wouldn't talk about it until after we were home. Merely thinking about it reminded me of my aches and pains. I wasn't sure a part of me *didn't* hurt.

Rita had reluctantly agreed to my request, but I

could tell she was having a hard time holding it in. I'd already caught her on the phone once, whispering to her gossip buddy, Andi Caldwell, about it. The story would be all over Pine Hills long before I got there.

Some variant of it would, anyway. I had a feeling I'd be doing damage control for the next few weeks.

The elevator stopped twice more on the way down, but no one else got on, choosing to wait for the next car instead of trying to cram themselves inside. It was a good thing too. I didn't think I could handle another one or two people pressed up against me.

JavaCon was over. Somehow, despite the odds, it had run until its official end. I think Pierre's and Dallas's determination kept it running. Clint's arrest helped. Guests no longer had to worry about getting murdered in the middle of a session, and it gave them something to gossip about. In a way, the murder had brought a lot of people closer together.

Still, I thought it unlikely the con would continue the next year, at least in its current state. Things would have to change so something like this could never happen again. I was sure the remaining organizers were already coming up with new rules that would prevent it.

We reached the lobby, and everyone piled out of the elevator. I picked up my bags with yet another groan and followed after Rita and Vicki. The hotel didn't have a parking garage, but rather, a parking lot at the side of the building. There was a loading and unloading lane out front, which was currently full.

"Let me get the car," Vicki said. "You two stay here."

"I'll come with," Rita said. "I could use the fresh air."

I narrowed my eyes at her, but then put it out of my mind. I knew she was going to call her other friend, Georgina McCully, the moment she was out of my sight. Her phone was already in her hand.

I waved them off with an "I'll wait in here."

As long as Rita gossiped out of my hearing, I was okay with it. Let her have her fun.

I sank down into a cushy lobby chair, thankful to be off my feet, as the two of them carried their bags out the door. My backside hurt, and I wondered when I'd managed to bruise that too. The car ride was going to be uncomfortable, but the thought of sleeping in my own bed was enough to make me willing to power through the aches and pains for a little while longer.

My phone rang. I dug it out of my purse and answered with a tired "Hello?"

"Hi, Krissy, it's Beth."

I sat up straighter. Well, as much straighter as I could manage. "Beth, I'm so glad you called. Mason told me what happened. How are you doing?"

"I'm good. Honestly, I should have expected it. He caught me by surprise, and it hit me a lot harder than it should have. I'm over it now."

"Are you sure? If you need a few days off, we can manage it. I'll be home later today."

"No, I'm fine. I want to work. I just wanted to call to let you know that there's nothing to worry about."

"If you're sure . . ."

"I am." I could hear the smile in her voice, yet she still sounded upset. I had a feeling that this wouldn't be the last time we'd have to deal with Raymond Lawyer's beef with Beth.

But, for now, I was willing to let it go.

We said our goodbyes and I tucked my phone away. Vicki could talk to Mason some more once we were back home and perhaps together they'd be able to talk some sense into Raymond. There was no reason for him to treat Beth like that, especially now that she no longer worked for him.

"Ms. Hancock." I looked up to find Detective Kimble approaching. "Good to see you've moved from where I last left you."

"It took some doing, but I managed," I said with a smile. He hadn't made it back to retrieve me from the stairwell, but I *had* seen him after I'd finally dragged myself from it. I'd given him my statement then. "Is there anything else I need to do for you?"

"No, we're all set. This isn't business, thankfully. I happened to see you sitting here and thought I'd stop by and see how you were doing."

"I hurt," I admitted, "but otherwise, I'm okay."

"Good to hear." A smile played at the corners of his mouth. "You'll be glad to know you were in no danger of being shot yesterday."

"No danger?" I asked. "He pulled a gun on me! You saw it."

"I did. I also saw the writing on the barrel. The company does make some pretty convincing toys, don't they?"

"Wait, what?" I asked sitting up. I quickly eased back down when my back barked at me. "It wasn't a real gun?"

"It looked like one, but yes, it was only a toy. Mr.

Sherman admitted as much when I interviewed him. I think he was hoping that telling us you were in no real danger would make us go easy on him."

"A toy?" I repeated, still unable to believe it. "Why would he carry a toy gun with him?" And keep it in a drawer in his hotel room, of all places.

"Protection, he says." Kimble chuckled. "He was robbed a few months ago, so he started carrying it with him, thinking that if something like that happened again, he could pull it and scare the perpetrator off. He kept it in his room because the convention center doesn't allow weapons and he was afraid he'd get into trouble for carrying the fake one around."

"Wow," I said. If I'd known it was a toy, I probably could have saved myself from a lot of bruises. "Does that mean Clint confessed?"

"He did." Kimble shoved his thumbs into his belt loops. "He seems pretty remorseful of the whole thing too. Maybe the judge will take some pity on him, but I doubt it."

Clint was likely looking at a very long vacation in a jail cell. At least the bars would keep his wife from ripping into him once she found out about his infidelity. I know from experience that having someone cheat on you wasn't a pleasant feeling. "Will I need to testify?"

"You shouldn't need to," Kimble said. "Between your statement and the others I've gathered, combined with his confession, it shouldn't be necessary. If that changes, I have your information and will give you a call."

I nodded. I hoped that I'd never receive that call.

I liked Kimble well enough, but I was anxious to put the whole ordeal behind me.

"I'd better get going," Kimble said. "I've got a few more loose ends to tie up before I can close this case for good."

"Thanks for being a stairs kind of guy," I said as he started to walk away. Kimble hadn't been racing to save me when he'd entered the stairwell. He'd merely been running to his room for something and had happened across us.

"Don't mention it. Stay out of trouble." He winked and walked away with a laugh.

Across the room, I saw Pierre, Dallas, Evaline, and Carmine talking. Wynona Kepler was nearby, watching them, but this time, she wasn't throwing accusations around. Next to her, Tatiana stood with her shoulders slumped. She looked miserable. I wondered if their elaborate plan to cheat Charles out of his coffee had cost them a chance to work with the others on the next JavaCon—*if* there was a next Java-Con.

Carmine said something to Pierre, who held out his hand. Both men shook before Dallas hugged Carmine. He looked to Evaline. Something passed between them, something unspoken, and then Carmine Wright walked away.

I got the feeling that whatever there was between the two of them, it was over. It also felt like he was walking away from the con for good.

At least it appeared he was leaving on good terms. It was more than either Charles or Clint had gotten.

A car left the loading lane. Vicki's car pulled into

the vacated spot, and Vicki got out. I rose from my seat and gathered my bags. She met me just inside.

"Let me," she said. "You've been through enough."

I let her take the bags with a "Thanks" that was more of a grunt than an actual word. I might want to prove to everyone I was okay, but I was really sore and really tired. I could let someone carry some of the load, at least for a little while.

Vicki took the bags to the car. I was about to follow her when I was stopped by two people I was glad to run into before I left: Thomas and Tara.

"I heard about what happened," Thomas said, looking me over. "Are you all right?"

"I'm fine." I straightened my back, despite how it hurt. I noticed how close Tara was standing to Thomas and smiled. "Everything working out between the two of you?"

"It is," Thomas said. He put his arm around Tara. She snuggled in close. "We're going to see where this takes us. Maybe down the line, our company will become a family-run business." Their eyes met, and by the glimmer I saw there, I had a feeling it very well might.

"That's good to hear," I said. "I'm glad something positive came out of this."

"We have you to thank," Tara said. "If you wouldn't have forced us to confront our feelings . . ."

I waved off the comment, though admittedly, it felt good to have done something to help that didn't involve me getting beaten to a pulp. "You would have figured it out eventually. I only hurried things along."

Vicki had the bags in the car. She waved to me and

got into the driver's seat. I could just barely make Rita out in the back, jabbering away on her phone.

"I'd better go," I said. "We've got a long drive ahead of us."

"It was good meeting you, Krissy Hancock," Thomas said, extending a hand.

I took it. "I'm glad we met, Thomas Cole." I turned to Tara. "You too, Tara."

She smiled, snuggled in even closer to Thomas.

I started to walk away, heart just about bursting from joy. I wasn't even jealous anymore. Those two deserved to be happy, and I was thrilled I could be a part of that happiness.

"Krissy, wait." I turned as Thomas jogged over to me. He produced a card and handed it to me. "Call us if you ever need anything; coffee, or whatever. Or just to talk. I'd like it if we remained friends."

"I'd like that too," I said, pocketing the card and then patting it for good measure.

I left Thomas and Tara at the door. I got into the car and promptly tuned out Rita, who was in the middle of her tale. Apparently, I'd thrown Clint down the stairs and had held him down until the police arrived. Not quite the truth, but I didn't correct her. It sounded far more heroic than what had really happened. I could always set the record straight when I got back home.

Maybe. It felt good to be the hero.

"Everything all right?" Vicki asked, glancing toward where Thomas and Tara stood, arm in arm, watching us.

"Perfect," I said. Thomas might be nice to look at, and could turn into a good friend, but there was someone even better waiting for me back in Pine Hills. I was anxious to get back home to see him.

In the back seat, Rita said, "She's so purple, she looks like an eggplant!"

Shaking my head, I couldn't help but smile. She wasn't wrong.

"Ready?" Vicki asked.

"Ready," I said, settling back into my seat with only the slightest of winces. "Let's go home."

Vicki put the car into gear, and then we were on our way.